# Smith's
## MONTHLY

*Every Month Original Novels, Stories, and Articles*

*USA Today Bestselling Writer*
*Dean Wesley Smith*

I0550650

# TABLE OF CONTENTS

# Smith's Monthly Issue #4

The Writings and Opinions of

# Dean Wesley Smith

*Introduction*

# Happy New Year

**A BRAND NEW YEAR.**

What great fun. The promise of things to come fills the air with everyone doing new and wonderful resolutions. Lose weight, be nicer, find a new job, and so on and so on.

And writers always resolve to write more. I never do that, since I just sort of write along at my own pace all year long, as those following my blog online have seen.

Still, I do tend to enjoy the fresh feeling of the New Year. Sort of like I enjoy the first snowstorm of the year falling in big white flakes. It's beautiful until it turns to dirty slush and gets my feet wet as the reality sets in.

Even though I am writing this near the first of December, this issue to me is a symbol of this magazine actually making it. The magazine has more support, more subscribers than I thought possible when I started this idea. And the issues sell through everyone's favorite bookseller stores better than I had hoped.

Of course, this magazine could not exist without the new world of publishing. And for that I am thankful.

So now, with this fourth issue, the first issue in a full new year, I feel that *Smith's Monthly* is just starting to hit its stride. I want to thank you all for the support. It means more to me than you can ever imagine.

So, what's coming in this New Year? Well, to be blunt, all sorts of fun stuff.

Since this is my magazine, with only my stuff in it, and the fine people at WMG Publishing Inc. have given me the freedom to do what I want, I have some great surprises in store.

And honestly, a bunch of ideas, stories, and novels I haven't thought of yet.

---

# Thanks for the Support

---

## Dean Wesley Smith

Here are some of the topics of fiction I hope to bring to you in this New Year.

—At least one, if not two, new Poker Boy novels and more Poker Boy short stories.

—Jukebox stories origin novel. Duster and Bonnie Kendal built the time-traveling jukebox that I have used in a dozen short stories over the decades. I hope to have more jukebox stories here this year.

—More Bonnie and Duster short stories and novels.

—More "I Killed…" short stories.

—More "Cold Poker Gang" short stories. Maybe even the first novel.

—A finish of both serial novels, plus continuing the series onward with second books.

—More "Seeder Universe" novels and stories.

—More Captain Brian Saber stories and possibly a novel.

And a bunch of fiction I haven't even thought about yet.

You get the idea.

This year will bring twelve issues of around 90,000 words of fiction each. Over one million words of fiction headed your way. Some of it you might like, some you might hate. But I'll do my best to keep you entertained no matter what you think of the story.

And that's my New Year's resolution: To keep being an entertainer. That's what writers are, after all.

So stick with me for this New Year. I'll make the journey interesting, if nothing else.

*Dean Wesley Smith*
*December 8, 2013*
*Lincoln City, Oregon*

# Now Available
## from all your favorite booksellers in trade paper and electronic editions.

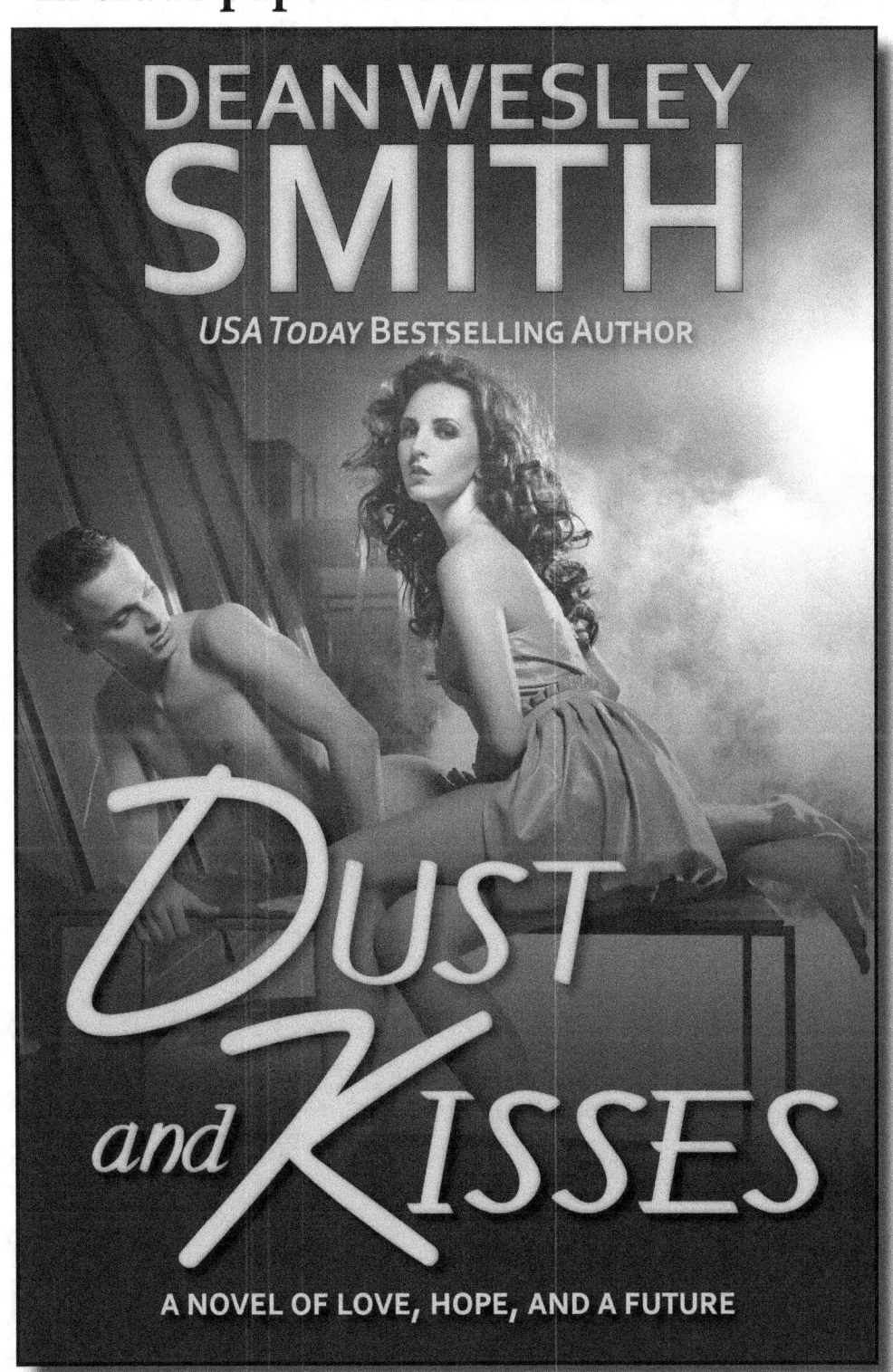

DEAN WESLEY
SMITH
*USA Today* BESTSELLING AUTHOR

*Dust* and *Kisses*

A NOVEL OF LOVE, HOPE, AND A FUTURE

USA *Today* Bestselling Writer

# DEAN WESLEY SMITH

A
**Poker Boy
Story**

THE
MATCH

*Poker Boy awakes one morning in his own past, before he became a superhero in the gambling universe, before he met the love of his life, before Stan, the God of Poker, even knew Poker Boy existed.*

*One problem: Poker Boy remembers the next fifteen years. He belongs in 2014, not 1999.*

*So who broke all rules against time travel and transported him into his own past? The fate of the world rested once again on finding answers. And sometimes those answers can only be found in a poker game.*

# THE MATCH
## A POKER BOY STORY

## ONE

**I HAD A HUNCH** that something was very, very wrong when I woke up in my own bed, in my doublewide trailer in the Oregon Coast Mountains. I know it sounds weird to say I knew something was wrong because I woke up in my own bed. Where else was I supposed to wake up, after all?

Problem being, I hadn't slept in that bed in years. Every night I normally slept with Patty Ledgerwood, aka Front Desk Girl, my girlfriend and sidekick. And she didn't much like (read that hated) my old doublewide, so we always stayed in her apartment in Las Vegas.

I didn't remember us having a fight.

And my sheets didn't smell musty from lack of use for years.

So something was very wrong.

Outside a slight rain and wind was rattling the windows and drumming on the flat roof.

In five or six months, Patty and I would have a big new mansion built on land I owned up in the mountains near here that we had designed together. But until that was finished, we stayed in her wonderful apartment in Las Vegas.

I remembered going to bed last night with her.

She had already been asleep, since I had gotten in late from a tournament at the Bellagio. I remember clearly she cuddled with me for a moment, still asleep, then rolled over.

As always, she had smelled wonderful and I remember rolling over as well, thinking I was the luckiest man alive.

Which, I had to admit, I was.

So how did I get here?

Was I sleep-teleporting or something?

I put on my clothes, which were Levis, tennis shoes, a plain dress shirt, black Fedora-like hat and black leather coat that was my uniform. I got my power from casinos, and it felt that when I had that coat and hat on I could channel the power better.

Then I jumped back to Patty's apartment.

Only I didn't jump.

I didn't go anywhere.

I just stood there in the middle of the doublewide's living room with a face that looked like I might take a crap on the green shag carpet at any moment.

Normally I just thought about where I wanted to go, concentrated, and then went there.

I tried again.

Nothing.

My old couch with a tan blanket covering it still sat there, a half-eaten tv dinner filled the center of the fake-wood coffee table, and the rain still drummed on the roof.

For some reason, my ability to teleport was shut off.

I felt a slight twisting of worry in my stomach, but there were a thousand reasons for this happening, not the least of which was a practical joke by one of the gods.

I did another quick check of the living room of my big doublewide to see if I could see anything at all different. The big box television was on as I normally left it on when here. Sort of background sounds.

I moved over into the kitchen area and checked my fridge. It was stocked, something I hadn't done in a couple years, and there were a few dirty dishes in the sink that didn't even look that crusty yet.

Whoever had done this to me had gotten the details right.

There was a carton of unopened milk in the fridge. I always kept milk there, and I went to open it for a drink to try to calm my twisting stomach. That was when I noticed the sell-by date.

June 18, 1999.

Only the milk inside was very fresh.

That date was almost a year before I was first approached by Stan to be a superhero.

I put the milk back without drinking any of it.

My stomach was now twisting a lot harder than it had a moment before. Had something happened that shifted me back in time? I had learned that time travel was possible, but very protected by the gods and not allowed. In fact, from my understanding, there were very few gods who could even do it.

Had I been sleepwalking through time? Not likely. Which left only one conclusion.

Someone had sent me back here.

But who would send me back to this date and why?

Actually I didn't know the exact date.

I went over to the television and flipped around a few channels until I hit one with a running banner.

It said the day was June 7th, 1999. It was 10:07 in the morning Pacific Daylight Time.

I dropped onto the couch and tried to remember for a moment what I was doing on this day in 1999. All I knew that in general I was a professional poker player and winning my share. Even though I lived like a broke gambler in an old doublewide trailer with furnishings decades out of date, I was already pretty rich by the early summer of 1999.

Actually very, very rich.

And I was still years from meeting Patty.

But what I had done on June 7th, 1999 was beyond me.

Finally, I had had enough. I glanced up at the ceiling and shouted "Stan, a little help?"

I have no idea why I shouted at the ceiling for my boss, Stan, the God of Poker. But I always did.

He didn't appear.

"Hey, Stan, funny joke. Now tell me what's happening?"

No Stan.

And without Stan, that meant I had no team either to help me solve this.

I stood and headed for the front door. I needed to get to a casino and the closest one was my home casino, Spirit Winds, about a mile away.

I opened the door not knowing what to expect.

The old black Thunderbird that I had sold in 2010 was sitting out front in the gravel driveway where I always used to park. The doublewide was tucked in under some tall pine and the rain was dripping through the trees.

I took the keys off the hook beside the front door where I always left them and went out.

The Thunderbird started right up. I let it warm up a little and checked my wallet. I had just under five hundred, which was a pretty normal amount for me to carry at that point in time. Even my 1999 driver's license was current.

As I approached the big casino, I could see that the new additions had not yet been added.

I really was in 1999.

And totally alone once again.

# TWO

**MY STOMACH WAS TWISTING** like a bad pretzel under a carnival vender's heat lamp. I was going to need some food and time to think. And some power from the casino.

I parked in my normal spot around to the side of the big building and headed inside, letting the power of the casino fill me. I flat loved walking into casinos. They felt like my home and I could always feel the power they gave me, even before I had become a superhero.

The casino power calmed me as I strode toward the buffet in its old location across from the front door.

Then suddenly it dawned on me that maybe the reason I couldn't teleport to Patty's apartment was because it wasn't there yet. It didn't get built until 2004 and her apartment was on the fourteenth floor.

Damn this time travel stuff could give a guy a headache.

I quickly turned and went into the men's restroom. No one was in there.

Then I thought of the front room of my trailer and jumped there.

It worked.

Worked fine, actually.

I clicked off the television I had left on when I left a few minutes earlier, feeling very, very relieved that I still had my powers.

I wasn't losing my mind completely.

I jumped back to the casino's men's room and resumed my journey to the buffet for breakfast. Somehow I needed to figure out why I was here, who had sent me here, and how to get back to 2014.

And without my team, I had no idea how to even start doing that.

What worried me even more was that someone had done this to get me out of the way. If I disappeared into the past, out of contact, my team might not be able to stop what danger might be happening in 2014.

I paid for breakfast and asked for a table against the wall. As the woman seated me and took my orange juice order, I glanced around at the few people eating in the buffet. I didn't know a one of them. Or at least I didn't remember any of them.

And none of them seemed to be giving me any strange looks.

I filled my plate with some ham, scrambled eggs, and a piece of toast and sat down with my back to the wall. No one said hello or even gave me a second glance.

I took myself out of time, freezing everyone around me. It felt like I stopped time, but I really didn't. I just stepped into a bubble between instants of time.

The sounds from the kitchen and the casino floor vanished, leaving me in complete silence.

The stepping between instants of time power was one of my most favorite powers. Right up there next to teleportation.

I took a bite of the eggs, then the ham, letting any of the gods who might be paying attention figure out there was a time bubble here that no one knew about.

I knew these things were fairly easy to see for most gods.

After a full minute, I once again said, "Stan! Calling Stan, the God of Poker."

I imagined him clearly.

He appeared in front of me, frowning, not something I normally saw on my boss's face. The guy had the best poker face of anyone I had ever met. He was dressed as he always did, in tan slacks, a tan shirt, a plain button-down sweater and loafers. His short hair made him the plainest person I had ever met.

He glanced around at the time bubble, then back at me.

"How did you do this? And who are you?"

"My name is Poker Boy," I said. "And you recruit me out of this casino to be a superhero in about a year. You taught me how to do this a few years later."

He opened his mouth and shut it.

"I somehow got pulled here from 2014. I have no idea how or why."

"Time travel is not allowed," he said.

"I know," I said. "You want to tell the person who did this to me?"

He opened his mouth, then shut it again without saying a word. I knew how he was feeling. Time travel was a scary thing and even my telling him as much as I had might change history. But I had to take that chance.

I indicated that he sit down and he did in the chair across from me.

"I am figuring that in the future someone needed me out of the way," I said. "So who, among the gods, could do this? Trap me back here? More than likely Laverne, but she wouldn't do this, so who else?"

He started to answer, but I stopped him. "I don't want to know. We need to be careful. I just need you and Laverne to figure this out and then tell me how I get back to 2014 without going through the last, or next, as the case might be, 15 years."

He nodded and vanished.

I moved myself back into the flow of time and the sounds came crashing back around me. Then I went to work on my breakfast again. When I got back to my own time, I'd ask Stan about this one. I had a hunch he was going to remember more about this day than I did at this moment.

I didn't want to think about where the real me was at this moment.

At least I hadn't woken up this morning next to myself. That might have been a tough thing to explain.

But my car had been in front of my trailer. So if I hadn't been home, exactly where was the other me?

Then I had the worst thought of the morning.

Maybe the old me had switched places with me in the future.

"Oh, I'm sorry, Patty," I said out loud, shaking my head and smiling at that idea.

"You should be," a voice said beside me.

Suddenly I was back out of time, the noise of the casino and buffet gone, and Stan was sitting across from me, smiling.

And Patty was sitting beside me, giving me her pretend angry look.

She kissed me before I had time to even say anything.

And let me say, after thinking I was alone, stuck in the past, that kiss felt wonderful, even better than normal, which was going some with kissing Patty.

# THREE

**STAN CLEARED HIS THROAT.** "Sorry to break this up," he said, "but I'll be back in about one minute and we have to be very careful this is not seen."

"The past you?" I asked.

Stan nodded.

"And you have the other me in a time bubble waiting somewhere for this to finish up?"

"Got it," Stan said.

"You were cute," Patty said, smiling at me.

"Am I going to need counseling after waking up with an older woman?" I asked her, smiling.

She whacked me and laughed. "You might."

I turned to Stan, my Stan from the future. "So what do I do?"

"I can't tell you a thing," Stan said. "At least not at this point. It has to play out. And it concerns this time."

"Isn't this part of it playing out?" I asked.

"All we can say at the moment," Stan said, shaking his head.

"Watch yourself there as well," I said. "This might be to get me out of the way."

"Good thinking," Stan said.

But I could tell he didn't give it a second thought. So this had nothing to do with a threat in 2014. It was completely about something here in 1999.

"See you in about fifteen years," Patty said, kissing me again.

"Be nice to the other me," I said.

She winked. "Oh, I will."

Then they were both gone and the time bubble was gone. The sounds of the buffet came crashing back in.

I sipped on the last of my orange juice, thinking about her last joke. I sure couldn't be jealous of my girlfriend spending time with me, even though it wasn't really me. At least not the me of now.

I was pretty sure, from my memory, which seemed oddly blank for this time period, I hadn't been allowed to remember what had happened.

A moment later another time bubble formed around me, plunging me back into silence and the young Stan appeared. Actually, he looked exactly like the Stan in fifteen years. I even think he was dressed in the same sweater and slacks.

"The other you is in your time in the future," Stan said, sitting down.

Around us everyone remained frozen, some in stride, others with a mouthful of food.

"I know," I said and he looked surprised, again losing his normal poker face.

He started to ask a question, but I waved him off.

"Only thing that could happen. I can't think of one reason I would be brought back in time."

"To play poker," Stan said.

Now it was my turn to be surprised. "Not something you could handle. You are as good as I am, if not better."

"I am told I am not," Stan said.

Again I was surprised.

"Laverne switched you out last night," Stan said. "The window was so tight for the transfer that she did not have time to warn you. She sends her apologies."

"Window?" I asked, getting more confused by the moment.

Stan nodded. "The entity who is setting this up needs to think you are not a superhero yet. When Laverne learned of

what was to happen, she only had a few seconds to act."

"I'm to play this entity?" I'd done that a few times, the most memorable being an alien who looked like a snake. Actually, it was the same snake alien who messed up the Garden of Eden.

"No," Stan said. "You are to play another professional poker player."

Now I was getting very, very worried. And not about playing another professional poker player, but about the stakes. This was a lot of trouble to go through to set up a friendly game. And clearly Laverne was worried about it as well.

"So what kind of alien invasion is this going to stop if I win?"

Stan actually laughed. "Don't I wish?"

Now I was beyond worried.

"If I lose the world ends?" I asked.

Again Stan just laughed and shook his head. "Wow, you develop a wild ego, don't you? I hope your poker is as good as the ego."

"Better," I said. "So what am I playing for?"

"My job," Stan said.

I kind of opened and then closed my mouth.

"So you are actually playing for your job as well," Stan said, half laughing. "Since I hire you."

All I could do was sit there and think over all of the times my team and I rescued the entire planet. I really was playing for everything. The survival of the entire world. But Stan, this Stan, would have no way of knowing that.

And I didn't dare tell him.

No wonder Laverne had sent me back here.

"So Bernice, the God of Keno, is the entity that set this up?" I asked.

It was Stan's turn to open his mouth, then shut it. He nodded.

"And a lot of betting is going on among gods right now. Correct?"

Again Stan nodded.

"Bernice makes a run at me a few years after you hire me to get your job that way. She tried using all her 'charms' on me and failed."

"Wow, you turned down those looks?" Stan said.

Model looks, a soft voice, and huge breasts didn't much do it for me. And her laugh sounded more like a baying donkey anyway. She was the best-looking of all the gods in classical beauty, and I didn't blame her for wanting to get out of the dead-end world of Keno. Only problem was, she had the brains of a Keno player.

As poker players like to joke, a Keno player is a gambler who has lost the will to live.

Why she kept making runs at Stan's job was beyond me. But if she got it this time, she would never hire me and the world would end at any number of different points in the next fifteen years when me and my team were not together to save it.

I was going to have to win this.

One way or another.

# FOUR

**"SO I HAVE TO PRETEND** I have no powers and don't understand what is happening? Right?"

Stan nodded.

"And no one has seen this time bubble?"

"Laverne's been blocking this," he said. "She feels it's critical that you win this."

Now I was puzzled again. "Isn't she the boss? Can't she just kill this entire idea?"

"I could," Laverne said, appearing next to the table in the time bubble. In the future, Laverne, known as Lady Luck, was always in my floating office over Las Vegas and was treated like one of the gang.

She had on her standard black business suit and her dark hair was pulled back, making her face seem all business.

1999 Stan scooted back and stood. He clearly didn't spend much, if any, time around one of the most powerful gods and his boss at this point in time.

Laverne dropped into a chair and faced me. "If I have to, I'll pull rank on this. But it will damage my power base at this point in time."

"Bernice has been sleeping with a number of gods who would like a little more power, huh?" I asked.

"She may be as dumb as this fork," Laverne said, nodding, "but she can manipulate men. And she's dangerous."

"Does she have any idea what she's risking with this?" I asked.

Laverne glanced at the stunned look on Stan's face, then shook her head. "No, she would have no way of knowing. No one at her level in this time period would know. Just win this match."

"Can I use my powers?"

"Just the ones you had at this point in time," Laverne said. "Safer. A lot of gods will be watching."

I nodded. "I'll win it. But you already know that."

"Honestly, I don't," she said. "This entire thing is a side timeline on the normal timeline and I'm working to figure out who's doing this. And how and why. This did not originally happen in 1999 to you."

"No wonder I have no memory of any of this."

She nodded and said nothing.

"I'll still win it," I said, doing my best to keep my stomach from twisting right out of my side with sudden fear.

"Thanks," she said, and vanished.

I took a deep breath and glanced at the shocked look on Stan's face.

"So where and when?"

"You need to get to Vegas in two days," he said. "Special room set up at Binion's Horseshoe."

"Who am I playing?" I asked.

"Doc Hill," he said.

And my stomach twisted one more twist tighter which, up until that point, I didn't think it could.

Doc Hill was the best No Limit Hold'em player in the world. Even in 2014 I didn't often play against him, since he was mostly a tournament player. But in 1999 he was coming off of two years as Card Player Magazine Player of the Year and he had won more World Series of Poker bracelets than any person alive.

My future just looked a lot dimmer. And my promise to Lady Luck sounded like bluster instead of fact. Doc Hill was going to be damn hard to beat.

I hoped Lady Luck and my team in the future could figure who was doing this and why before I had to sit down across from Doc.

# FIVE

**I HADN'T BEEN** on an airline since I had learned how to teleport. And after the two hours in the airport and the four-hour flight to Vegas, I didn't miss airports and the lines and the waiting. Not in the slightest. And I swore they had put the seats closer together. Even in first class.

I took a cab to Binion's Horseshoe Casino and Hotel in the downtown area. At this point in time, Fremont Street had been covered with the light show but a lot of the remodeling wasn't done and the area had a feel of being rundown.

Binion's hadn't seemed to change. There were low ceilings and far too much smoke in the air. I felt the power from the casino fill me as I walked in, but then a moment later I coughed. My lungs were just not used to all the smoke. It was amazing how much that one detail had changed in fifteen years.

I headed through the clouds of smoke and past the small poker area toward the hotel front desk.

And there, standing behind the desk, was my future girlfriend, Patty Ledgerwood.

I damn near fell flat on my face. In 2002, after I had been a superhero for a number of years, I would come here for the last time the World Series of Poker was held in this casino. And I would meet Patty at the front desk, just like this.

And she would become my sidekick and my girlfriend.

She was dressed in the Binion's Hotel uniform of the time. Brown dress slacks, a white blouse, and a light brown vest with a nametag on the vest.

Somehow, I was going to have to talk with her. I was going to have to be very, very careful.

And not trip over the ropes that blocked off the front like I did the first time I met her.

As I approached the desk, she looked up and winked at me. "Enjoy the flight?"

I was stunned. I leaned in over the counter and whispered, "Patty?"

She smiled and I knew it was my Patty from the future. "Laverne has the entire team back here," she whispered, "trying to figure out who's doing this."

Then she said in a normal voice, "Would you like to check in, sir?"

"I would," I said, and gave her my real-world name.

"Flying sucks," I whispered and she laughed that wonderful high laugh of hers as she checked her computer.

"We have you in a suite," she said, sliding me the paperwork I needed to sign. "Laverne has it blocked," she whispered, "so we'll all see you there later with an update."

"Wonderful," I said in my normal voice.

She handed me my key card and I took it. "Thanks for the great service."

"Oh, that comes later," she whispered without moving her lips.

It was everything I could do to not laugh and not trip over the ropes on the way out of the front desk area.

I couldn't begin to say how relieved I was that the team was here.

And how much I was in love with that girl behind the front desk.

# SIX

**PATTY, STAN, SCREAMER, AND BEN** all appeared in my suite about an hour after I had settled into the place. You could tell the suite had seen better days, but I knew that in a few years the entire hotel would be remodeled and would turn out wonderful.

Patty was still in her Binion's uniform, Stan looked the same in both timelines, Screamer had on his standard jeans, sweater, and tennis shoes, and Ben was dressed like an old librarian, only without the tie.

It felt fantastic to see them again. Not only were we all a team, but they were my closest friends.

On the long flight down, I had come up with a few conclusions and I wanted to run them past the team. I had no idea where the Stan of this time was. Or where any of the 1999 members of the team were. Not sure I wanted to know.

Patty hugged me, then kissed me, then we all gathered in the suite's living room area.

I looked at Ben, who was the oldest member of the team and was now a god in the book and reading area. He had a memory of every fact about the gods known or not known.

"Who is the God of Time?" I asked Ben as we settled in.

"Chronos," Ben said.

I nodded. I sort of had known that.

"Does he have a younger son he's training?"

"He does," Ben said, nodding, but looking puzzled. "Two of them, actually."

"You don't think Tick or Tock have anything to do with this?" Stan asked, his face very serious.

"Tick? Tock?" I asked, trying my best not to laugh. Never a good idea to laugh at the gods. "Nicknames I hope?"

I glanced around, but not one of my team seemed to think those names odd or funny in any way.

"No," Ben said, also very serious.

I took a deep breath to calm myself to keep from laughing, then asked the next question. "Which one has an outsized interest in women? Or reputation as a woman chaser?"

"Tock," Stan said. "It's gotten him in trouble more than once over the centuries.

But I don't see why you think he might have something to do with this. It was Laverne that brought you back from the future."

"I know," I said, nodding. "But how did any of the gods of this time even know who I was?"

Stan started to open his mouth to answer, then shut it.

"You don't recruit me for almost a year," I said. "At this point in time I'm just a good local grinder. So only someone with the ability to see through time would know about me," I said.

"But Doc Hill could beat just about anyone of this time," Patty said. "If Bernice is behind this, why pick a player that might actually have a shot at beating Doc?"

"Because she and her boyfriend don't really know me," I said. "But his dad would be able to see the problem if Bernice became the God of Poker."

"And he would pick the player," Stan said.

"And give Laverne enough time to switch me out," I said, nodding. "And put this entire thing off in a side loop in time without anyone knowing."

"You being here is finally starting to make sense," Stan said and everyone was nodding.

"Only one more question," I said, "that I can't figure out."

Everyone looked at me, waiting.

"Why did Doc Hill agree to this match?"

Silence from my team.

"He wouldn't," I said. "He's richer than I am and that's going some, so money isn't a factor. And I'm an unknown at this point in time, so there's no fun in playing an unknown player heads-up. He would never agree unless…"

"Tock and Bernice are holding something over him," Screamer said.

I nodded. "I know this much about Doc Hill. At this point in time, he doesn't care about his father. But he and his mother and his grandfather are very close. And his best friend is his lawyer. Any of them in danger would force him to agree to this."

"I wonder if Tock's father knows about this?"

"I doubt it," I said.

Stan nodded and looked at me. "Well, he's going to. Stay put. The match is scheduled to start on the second floor in three hours. We have work to do."

They were suddenly all gone.

I looked around. Since Stan didn't want me leaving, that meant I couldn't go to the great steak restaurant on the upper floor. But I could go for room service.

If I ended up having to play Doc Hill, I wanted to at least go into it on a full stomach.

# SEVEN

**I HAD JUST FINISHED** with my steak and fries and was sitting back watching 1999 news, which seemed both fresh and strange at the same time, when Stan, Patty, Laverne, and Doc Hill appeared in my room.

They were all smiling, except Doc, who just looked stunned.

"All wrapped up?" I asked as I clicked off the television.

Laverne nodded.

I was surprised that they had brought Doc. More than likely his memory would be erased. He had no powers and no real reason to know about any of this sort of thing.

He was looking around, clearly having troubles getting grounded. He was a tall man and clearly young. If I remembered right, he had only left college a few years ago just short of a doctorate in something, which is why they called him Doc. He had long, sun-streaked brown hair and a deep tan. He rafted summers in the Idaho wilderness and seemed to be naturally good at anything he did.

"I am pretty sure I don't want to know how you did that," Doc said, looking around at the room before looking at Stan.

Stan nodded. "You don't."

"Great seeing you again, Doc," I said, moving to shake his hand, then realized he looked even more confused. "Great meeting you, at least."

"And who are you?" Doc asked.

"I'll become known as Poker Boy," I said. "I was the one you were supposed to play. Have you met the others?"

He shook his head. "Patty Ledgerwood," I said, introducing Patty. When she shook his hand I could see him visibly calm down. I loved that power of hers to do that.

I pointed to Stan. "He's the God of Poker and that's Laverne, Lady Luck herself."

He started to say something, then stopped. "If I hadn't just been teleported here, I would be laughing."

"Don't blame you," I said.

I glanced at Laverne. "I assume he's not going to remember any of this?"

"This side timeline will vanish when we return," Laverne said. "And Doc, we would like to apologize for the worry. Your mother will be fine and not remember any of this either."

"And that's why I had no memory of it," I said.

"We'll remember it now," Stan said. "It happened in our timeline in 2014."

"Now that makes sense," I said. "But why bring Doc here?"

"We have a lot of the gods interested in this match between you two," Laverne said.

I laughed. "Of course they are. But no nasty problems over the outcome?"

"Nothing," Laverne said. "But there are a lot of bets among gods."

"Which way are the odds?" I asked.

Laverne laughed. "Since they have discovered it's actually you, Poker Boy, playing the match, the odds have tightened up. They are now two-to-one."

"That I win?" I asked.

Laverne shook her head. "That Doc kicks your ass."

Now it was my turn to feel stunned and Patty and Stan both laughed. Even Doc smiled.

I looked at him. "You up for a match?'

He smiled and shrugged. "Why not? No limit hold'em, heads-up, best of five matches. No superpowers or whatever you have."

"No powers beyond normal poker player powers," I said.

He nodded and I shook his hand, agreeing to the match. "You ready?"

"Any time," he said.

Laverne smiled and jumped us to a private room on the second floor of Binion's Horseshoe Casino.

I was in heaven. I got to play the best poker player in the world heads-up. It didn't get any better than this, even if I had to travel back in time 15 years to do it.

Now the key was to not make a fool of myself.

# EIGHT

**THE ROOM WE WERE IN** had high ceilings and was mostly used by the casino as a banquet room I was sure, with the red felt wallpaper of old casinos and polished wood pillars. The poker table we were to play at was square in the middle of the room under a bright light. On three sides were grandstands ten seats high, making the table feel like it was in the bottom of a pit.

A male dealer with a Binion's uniform sat at the table, the cards spread out in front of him as was standard. There were no chips in his tray, but two stacks of chips were in positions facing each other down the length of the table.

Patty kissed me, then she and Stan and Lady Luck moved over to the stands and sat down near the middle. The rest of the stands were empty at the moment.

"So that really is Lady Luck?" Doc asked, standing there beside me next to the table, clearly trying to get his footing.

I was amazed he wasn't just sitting in a chair with his head in his hands. Clearly the guy was as good as dealing with pressure and unusual circumstances as people said he was. It didn't come any more unusual than this.

"It is," I said.

"Is she going to help you then?"

I laughed. "Even if she could, she wouldn't. Luck is a natural force in the world. She's the god of that force. She'll just let it run its natural course and make sure, at the same time, no one else interferes."

Doc nodded. Then he turned to face me. "How about a side bet?"

I looked at him and shook my head. "Lady Luck won't let you remember any of this."

He waved his hand. "Trust me, I don't want to."

"So what kind of bet are you thinking of."

He looked at me with those intense brown eyes and suntanned face. "You look a little pale. I assume I'm still running the rivers in Idaho in 2014."

"You are," I said.

"If I win," Doc said, "since you'll remember this, you and your girlfriend book a raft trip with me."

Even though I hated the very idea, I had to act brave. I motioned for Patty to come over and told her the idea.

She just laughed and said she would make sure I held up my end of the deal if I lost. She would love to go on a raft trip into the Idaho Primitive Area.

I, on the other hand, was more scared of that idea than facing the alien snake that had screwed up the Garden of Eden.

"And if I win," I asked.

Doc Hill just smiled. "You'll always know you beat the best tournament player in the world at his own game."

Patty laughed. "And I thought Poker Boy had an ego when it came to cards. Does that come with being a poker player?"

Both Doc and I said at the same time, "It does."

# NINE

**ROUND ONE:**

The rules were pretty simple in heads-up No-Limit Hold'em. We both started with the same amount of chips, in this case $500,000. The chips were in denominations of one thousand, five thousand, and twenty-five thousand.

When one person had the full million and the other player had no chips, the round was over.

Winner of the best of five rounds won the match.

The blinds were one thousand for the small blind and two thousand for the large blind.

In Hold'em, there was a dealer's button, which was the position that always got to bet last after the first round. In heads-up, the dealer button was under the small blind and before the flop (first three cards) the small blind had to act first.

After the flop the other player had to act first.

Position from that button was critical in all Hold'em poker, even more so in heads-up play.

So I shook Doc's hand, tried to clear out the idea of going into the Idaho Primitive area, and we sat down facing each other.

Again, the young poker player in me came screaming back in, all happy and excited. I was actually facing the best poker player on the planet in a private match. It didn't get any better than this.

Doc drew the button first and I tossed out my big blind of two thousand and he put a one thousand dollar chip on top of the button. A half million might seem like a lot of money, but in this game it wouldn't last long.

The dealer, a middle-aged man who clearly worked for the gods somewhere, shuffled the cards, tapped the table and asked, "Ready, gentleman?"

We both said we were

As he shuffled, the grandstands around us filled.

I saw some gods I knew and a few hundred I didn't. An older guy with a long white beard was now sitting next to Laverne. I guessed that was Chronos.

On the other side of him was a younger guy I assumed was his son, Tock. Beside him was Bernice, dressed to kill and with larger breasts than I remembered. But she had a very sour look on her classically-beautiful face and kept brushing Tock's hand off her leg.

That was going to be a very short-lived relationship.

I looked at Doc, who had his mouth open and was just staring.

"Better to not ask and just forget," I said.

He swallowed hard and looked back at me, nodding.

He had to call the bet first. He glanced at his two cards and folded.

We exchanged blinds for the next few hands and I could sense that Doc Hill was slowly starting to get his feet under him.

On his third big blind I raised him and he folded.

He called with his next small blind, I raised him, and he folded again.

I wasn't even really looking at my cards. I just needed to build up a little cushion while he was off balance. But I had no doubt that advantage wouldn't last long.

I took two more of his hands before he finally decided to fight back with a medium-sized raise of twenty-five thousand.

I happened to have two eights in my hand, a fantastic hand in heads-up, so I re-raised him four times his bet, shoving out one-hundred thousand.

He cold called.

The flop showed another eight. Plus an ace and a deuce, all colors.

I checked my set, hoping to trap him. What I really hoped was that he had an ace in his hand.

He bet one-hundred thousand.

I raised, pushing my entire stack in.

He had no choice, since I assumed he had hit his ace. He would be crippled if he lost that hand.

He shook his head, knowing what happened as he called. My three eights stood up against his pair of aces.

First round to me.

And around us the gods applauded.

# TEN

**ROUND TWO:**

As I had been afraid would happen, Doc Hill finally got his feet under him and ignored the strange people sitting all around us.

He came after me at the start of the second round like a mother trying to protect her child and I was the attacker.

He raised every hand to ten thousand. That was a small raise, but still effective at chewing up a stack of chips.

My chips.

And when I raised him on the third hand, he just re-raised back, forcing me to fold like a bad cliché about wet paper.

I flat called two of his raises in the first ten hands and had to fold into his betting pressure because the flop had missed my cards entirely.

In No-Limit Hold'em, aggressive action tended to win more than it lost. I could be aggressive with the best of them, but after those first ten hands of Round Two, I felt I had been pushed through a buzz saw and cut down to size. He handled me like I handled a low-level player.

And I hated that feeling.

Once the momentum of aggression was set, it was damn hard to shut it off. I knew that from experience.

I had about three hundred thousand left, not in panic mode, but close.

So I folded to his raises three more hands, then suddenly re-raised him one hundred thousand, letting him think I had a decent hand for the first time.

I actually had a jack-nine off-suit. Not horrible, but not bad for this kind of game.

He didn't even blink. He re-raised me by shoving all in.

If I folded, my two-hundred thousand against his eight-hundred thousand would be like throwing chum in a tank full of sharks. He would chew it up in a matter of minutes.

My best bet right now was to ride the hand with my jack-nine. If it won, I was back in the round.

I called and he flipped over queen-six off-suit.

His hand was slightly better statistically.

But not by that much.

And then on the flop he hit his second queen and Round Two went to him with the Gods again applauding.

# ELEVEN

**ROUND THREE:**

Doc came out aggressive again in the third round and this time I fired right back, matching aggressive move with aggressive move.

On the fourth hand I finally got him to lay a hand down with a two-hundred thousand raise.

As the dealer shuffled, Doc smiled at me and nodded. "Tough to stop a steamroller, isn't it? Well done."

"And to you as well," I said. "And thanks again for doing this."

"Are you kidding?" he asked. "Getting to play against a player at your level is something I don't get to do very often."

"This is fun, isn't it?" I asked as the dealer dealt out our cards.

"As fun as having you and Patty in whitewater rapids with me."

He smiled at me.

I shuddered.

From the nearby stands I heard Patty laugh.

And then Doc raised before I had time to even get my mind out of the terror of an Idaho Wilderness trip.

Four hands later, we were still about even in chips. Doc glanced at his cards and flat called my big blind.

I looked down at my two hole cards. I had an Ace-King of hearts, nicknamed "A Big Slick." That was one of the most powerful hands in all of poker, especially heads-up. It wasn't a made hand, but it was powerful.

So hoping to get Doc betting and trap him, I just checked and we went to the flop.

The flop came ace, ten, four. The four was a heart.

I had a pair of aces. In heads-up it didn't come any more powerful.

Doc would expect me to bet into that flop since we were playing aggressive poker, so I did, making the bet fifty thousand. I wanted him to think I was over-betting it to take the blinds.

He thought for a moment and called.

I had no idea why he called. Maybe he had a small pair, maybe he just figured I had nothing.

Or maybe he had an ace as well.

The next card came a six of hearts.

I checked. My check forced him into betting to get me out of the pot. He bet a smooth one-hundred thousand.

I called and he looked up at me, trying to get a read on me.

I could read nothing from him.

Nothing.

The next card came ten of hearts. So I had the best flush possible.

I bet out exactly the size of his last bet. One-hundred thousand.

He pushed all in.

I called.

He rolled over a pair of aces for aces full over tens.

I didn't show him my flush.

Round three to Doc.

The audience of Gods applauded.

I was down two rounds to one against the best poker player on the planet. This was not looking good for me staying off a raft in the middle of a river.

# TWELVE

**ROUND FOUR:**

For almost a half hour, Doc and I exchanged raises and folds at the start of the new round, ending up pretty close to where we started.

That's a very long time for no one to make a move in no-limit heads-up poker.

I just couldn't find a weakness anywhere in his game. And he seemed to be in my head more than I was in his.

The way he trapped me with those aces in the last round was masterful. So while I thought I was trapping him, he had me already at a huge disadvantage.

So after thirty minutes, I figured that the best way to play him in this fourth round was just to do what he did to me in the second round.

I just stared raising everything, and re-raising him on his raises.

I could see he knew what I was doing and was just waiting to be dealt some decent cards to make me pay.

If I had a chance at all, I needed to get him doubting he had a read on me.

So as my chips passed six hundred thousand, he raised. If I followed my pattern, I would re-raise him.

Instead I just tossed the cards in the muck.

He looked up at me, surprised.

He had a hand and was about to teach me a lesson. My folding gave him pause.

He leaned forward slightly as the dealer shuffled. "Bring a suit for swimming in the river and a heavy coat for the nights around the campfire."

He sat back, smiling at me.

Again I heard Patty laugh.

There were a lot of weapons in poker and Doc Hill was showing me how to blatantly use them all. Time for me to play that same game a little.

"I will," I said, smiling back. "I'm just glad we're not playing to save the entire world as we were planning to do."

He tried to keep the smile on his face.

Again the wonderful laugh of my girlfriend got to my ears.

After a moment Doc glanced at the audience, then back at his cards.

I raised and he folded, muttering something about "Well-played."

I went back to being aggressive, slowly chipping away at his chips.

Then he cold-called one of my raises.

I had king-ten off-suit. The flop missed me completely.

I raised fifty thousand.

He again flat called like a beginner would do against a raise.

The turn card missed me as well.

I checked.

He checked.

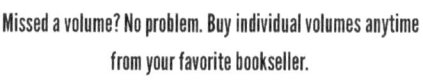

Again a beginner play. But I knew for a fact I didn't have him that rattled.

The river card also missed my two cards. I had King high.

I checked.

He checked.

I rolled over my king.

He rolled over an ace and took the pot.

And suddenly we were back to almost even.

Doc Hill turned back into a buzz saw, raising and re-raising everything.

I had to fold just about everything for six hands as he took the chip lead.

Then as he raised, I glanced down and saw a pair of tens. Great hand in heads-up.

I re-raised him with one hundred thousand.

He re-raised me all in.

I called.

He had more chips than I did, so my entire tournament life was on the line.

I rolled over my tens.

Doc nodded and rolled over ace-jack.

This was called "A Race" because the statistical odds were pretty even going into the flop, especially when you take into account the straight possibilities.

Everyone in the audience knew it might be over and they were all standing.

Doc stayed seated.

I stayed seated.

There was an ace on the flop.

The odds of my surviving went to very small. I could only win if one of the other two tens came out of the deck.

They did not.

I lost the fourth round.

And the match.

All the Gods applauded and then vanished as I stood to shake Doc's hand.

The entire thing had taken just under two hours.

And even though I had lost, I had enjoyed those two hours more than I wanted to admit.

"That was great fun," Doc said, shaking my hand.

"It really was," I said. "Thanks for taking part."

"My pleasure," Doc said, "even though I'm not going to remember it. See you on the river in about fifteen years."

"We'll be there," Patty said, coming over and taking my arm.

With that Doc vanished.

Right behind him the room faded.

And then 1999 vanished.

# THIRTEEN

**I WOKE UP IN 2014** next to Patty in her apartment. She rolled over against me and sighed, still mostly asleep. She smelled wonderful, like soft roses and faint earth.

Around the edges of the sun-blocking drapes, the Las Vegas day looked bright and dry, not at all like the rain in Oregon.

That had been one very strange dream.

I lay there on my back, holding the love of my life, staring at the ceiling, thinking back over the dream of going back to 1999 and playing Doc Hill.

It had felt so real.

It had to have been real. But yet I remember clearly coming home late last night from the Bellagio tournament and crawling in with Patty.

After a moment, Patty stirred, and opened one eye. When she saw I was awake, she laughed softly. "Stewing about Doc beating you?"

So it hadn't been a dream.

Then I remembered Laverne had said it had been a loop in the normal timeline, so of course we had returned to the moment the loop started to end it.

"Not stewing," I said, hugging her. "I gave him a good fight."

"It was a lot of fun to watch," she said, snuggling against me and closing her eyes. "You did better than Doc expected. You even won the first of the four matches, remember?"

"Before he got a read on me," I said. "Thank heavens there was no life on the line."

"Or world destruction," Patty said.

"Yeah, that too," I said.

"Just a wonderful trip into the Idaho Wilderness."

I tried not to shudder. The Oregon Mountains where my doublewide trailer was were wild enough for me.

She leaned up on one elbow and looked me right in the eyes. "Is he that good or did you let him win?"

I laughed. "He's that good. And no real poker player ever lets another win for any reason."

She smiled and kissed me. "You're still my superhero."

I kissed her back and pressed against her. After a moment we came up for air and she looked at me again, her wonderful brown eyes twinkling. "We might have to change your superhero name, though."

"To what?" I asked, holding her fantastic body tight against me.

"Well, it sure can't be "River Man," she said.

I laughed.

"I'm thinking right now," she said, "about something like "Man of Steel.""

She kissed me and I kissed her back, doing my best to live up to my new superhero name.

~

## Poems by DEAN WESLEY SMITH

# Starting Fresh and Bloodied

I love January 1st
like a father loves a newborn child.
I hold the day like a bundle of promises
and stare into the future like I can time travel.

I start fresh every January 1st
like a baby just emerging into the world,
the past nothing more than food and nutrients
dripped down a short cord.

I stare into the truth on January 1st,
a newborn in a new year,
slapped around by somebody I don't know,
covered in the blood of someone who loves me.

I dread January 1st,
for I am no longer in the comfort of the known
as I slip forward into the arms of a strange day,
crying my eyes out.

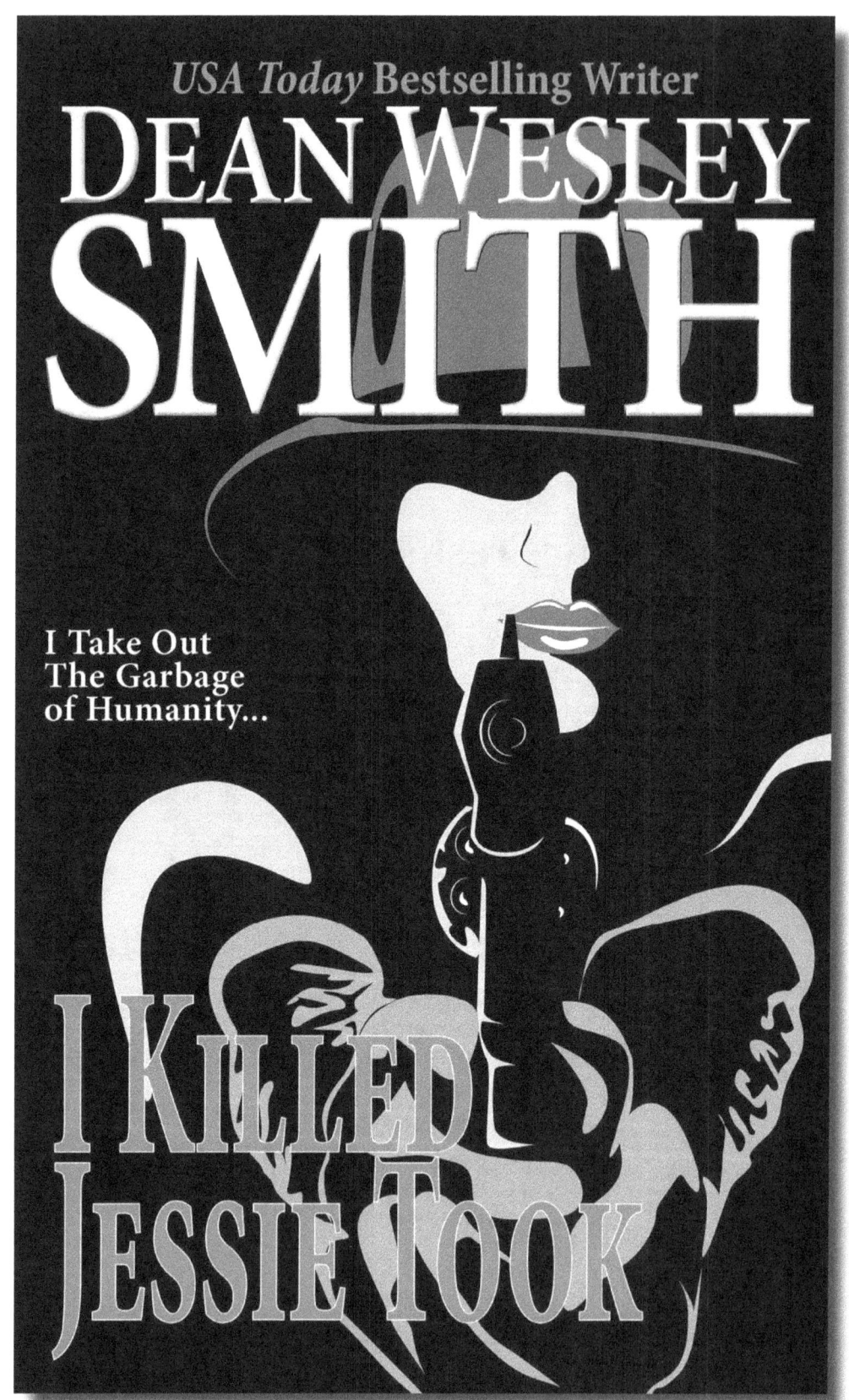

*USA Today bestselling writer, Dean Wesley Smith, returns to the world of his human garbage collector. A man without a real name who prides himself in his ability to take out the garbage of society.*

*After going freelance, his former employer wants to take him to the curb as well. Not only must the garbage collector finish what he started, but play the killers coming after him as well.*

*A twisted mystery in this second installment in the "I Killed..." series.*

# I Killed Jessie Took

## ONE

**I TAKE OUT HUMAN GARBAGE.** It's what I do.

Since my former employer decided that I needed to be taken out as garbage as well, I have gone freelance. It was never difficult for me to go freelance, since I had saved almost every penny of all the millions I had earned from all my garbage runs for them. My former employer never really ever knew who I was or where I was or where I was based.

I had always made sure of that.

My real name is long lost in the past. As are my real looks.

I only had contact with my former employer from a distance when getting an assignment and when reporting in that the garbage was removed. I was always paid through accounts that only existed for each job and then vanished and could not be traced back to me or any business associated with me.

My former employer didn't even know what I looked like exactly. I had made sure of that with changing looks for every assignment.

I could do little about my six-foot height, but I changed hair color, facial features, walk, and other features with simple disguises and a vast amount of training.

I am also an expert in the modern computer age. I can make an identity appear and disappear at will. I can change identities easily, and study my targets carefully.

Before being a freelance human garbage collector, I never felt any need to record my job. It was just a job, after all.

But now, as a freelancer, I have decided to record these events in a case-by-case nature.

And since my first official case on my own had actually been my last for my former employer, I have recorded it under the case title "I Killed Adam Chaser."

Granted, my former employer did transfer my standard four-point-one million to my accounts after the initial job was finished, but I considered that a freelance fee in killing the agent they sent to kill me. Seemed only a fair trade.

I unofficially call my little business "I Killed…" I could think of no name that suited "Garbage Man for Human Waste" that I liked. So simply "I Killed…" But no one would ever be able to track it under that name or any other name.

I am that good.

This, my first job after becoming a freelance human garbage man, taking out the human waste of society, I will call "I Killed Jessie Took."

The reason for that, I decided, was to track easily what each case is about. The target's original name is Jessie Took, but he went by Joe Harley in Portland, Oregon.

And I know for a fact that this case will also involve my former employer. It must.

It is the nature of my former employee, to leave nothing unfinished. I am a very unfinished business they cannot leave open.

I must be killed. I must be taken to the curb.

I welcome their involvement.

And they have presented me this Jessie Took, my first freelance case, like it's tied up in a bow, a bow they know I will not resist.

They believe that sometimes garbage men must be taken to the curb as well.

I've killed other garbage men in the past; I can do it again if they force my hand.

Which, of course, they will do.

# TWO

**UNLIKE WHEN I WORKED** for my former employer, I am fed no information on which garbage needs to be taken out. So over the last year, since the Adam Chaser case, I developed a method of searching for unsolved crimes, of criminals going free for various reasons, of simple "talk" about a person.

One series of unsolved teenage girl disappearances came to light, seeming to string across the country from Michigan to Oregon. They did not seem to be related and each remained active cases in their local areas.

But since I was looking at patterns as my former employer knew I would, the cases came together for me fairly clearly. Each girl was sixteen, each brunette, each had slight problems in school, often with minor drugs and boys.

And each had brown eyes.

Seven missing teenage girls in seven years. A trail leading to Portland, Oregon, like a neon arrow as far as I was concerned.

Right back to the same town of my first freelance case, my last working assignment that became "I Killed Adam Chaser."

That seemed to tell me that more than likely my former employer had set this up, made it clear, to attract me like a bee to a flower.

It would not matter. They could keep sending agents and I would keep helping them remove that agent from their workforce.

But before I could have that looked-forward-to meeting with another garbage man or woman, I needed to find who was taking the girls and why. I was sure my former employer already knew.

So for each girl's disappearance, I searched for the one common denominator that held that trail together. That took me almost four months of searching from my Las Vegas home near the University of Nevada.

Of course, my research could not be traced in any fashion.

I spotted a few attempts to backtrack on my traces, but they were blocked easily.

What became the clear connection in all the disappearances was a yard maintenance man who went under a different name in every town. He seemed about twenty-five, had short brown hair, a slight moustache, and dark eyes that seemed to see everything. And they looked hungry.

I could find no picture of him in any fashion where he was smiling. Even in security camera footage, stoplight security cameras, and so on.

He never smiled.

He worked for different yard maintenance firms in every city, always under different names, and always quit early in the fall to move on. Always a month before a girl disappeared.

He had been born and raised under the name Jessie Ben Took in Lansing, Michigan. Right out of high school he had started working yard maintenance and he had left two months before a popular girl from his former high school had gone missing. The reports of her disappearance never mentioned his name

in any way since he was already out of town and living outside of Madison, Wisconsin.

Every fall he moved on. A month or so later a girl went missing from his former town.

It was a trail I could not miss.

And my former employers would know that if I remained freelance, I would not miss it.

So I went back to Portland, Oregon, changing identities as I traveled and setting up escape routes.

The day I finally settled into Portland was a warm early-summer day, the leaves green, and the air smelling of open restaurants baking bread. The apartment I found was in the Northwest section of Portland with a slight view down the street of the river and one of the many bridges.

The apartment had large windows and too much light. It was on the second floor of an old Victorian that had been divided into four apartments, plus a manager's apartment on the main floor.

I went in under the name Nick Benson, an engineer from Idaho brought in to work on a new building down on the riverfront. I told the woman with large sixties' gray hair who was the landlord that I would be in and out of town a great deal and not to worry. I paid her four months in advance, which she liked.

The apartment was directly across the tree-shaded street from Jessie's apartment in a small ten-apartment complex that had been built in the mid 1960s out of cinder blocks and concrete stairs.

I bugged his small two-bedroom apartment one afternoon when he was at work, filled his walls with tiny cameras that looked like fly specks so there was no place in the apartment I couldn't see.

Then I put a few cameras in my apartment as well and rented another house a quick train-ride and identity change away. The second apartment was in a complex similar to Jessie's and the apartment had a very clear method of entry that required me to climb a flight of stairs.

The cameras in Jessie's walls any agent from my former employer would recognize. They would know I was here.

The ones in my apartment in the old Victorian were far better hidden and the signals could not be traced in any fashion. I wanted to know when my former employer's agent came snooping around my apartment.

But I knew they were already here. This had been a set-up, of that there was no doubt. They were well-trained in situational death, otherwise one of them would have attempted to kill me the first moment they realized who I was.

But as I said, they would work to cover their tracks. It was the nature of the business they worked for.

I doubted my employer had yet to realize I no longer needed to follow those same rules.

In my second apartment, as one more level of protection, I rented under a corporation name the empty apartment under my second apartment. That had a number of varied exits through a back door and a couple windows. I cut a hidden escape hatch through the closet floor of my second apartment to the third apartment's closet.

Then, protected with a number of back-up plans, I went about the business of making sure that Jessie Ben Took, maintenance man from Lansing, Michigan, really was responsible for all of the disappearances of the girls.

It became clear in very short order that he was human garbage that really, really needed to be taken out. He had a notebook hidden in his apartment of pictures of all the girls. All of them were nude and he was posing with all of them.

Typical of sick humans like him, he kept trophies.

All of them were the old Kodak-style prints. And I found an old camera in his apartment as well.

I captured each of the images, then spent the next day checking that none of them had been faked, that the locations and times were accurate. I did not put it past my former employer to set up an innocent man.

But with very little research, it became clear that Jessie was far from innocent. He spent a night a week poring over that notebook and reliving sexual acts he must have performed on each girl.

So I was the major target in this game and he was just a bonus.

So I spent the next few days tracing back through his employment in a new town, searching for where the girl's body would be buried. It made sense that since he worked yard maintenance and landscape work, he would bury the girl when he was finished with her in one of his projects.

He clearly had no young girl in his apartment across from my Victorian apartment, so I started tracing him. His last victim had been a girl from Boise. I doubted she would still be alive since it had been six months since she had been taken, but there might be a chance.

I found in a quick search, under his mother's maiden name, a storage locker that had been rented outside of Portland off of I-84.

I watched the rental for a few days to make sure it was not a trap by my former employers. They were not there and he did not visit the unit at all.

So after two days I moved in so that no security camera could see me and I opened the storage unit.

She was there.

In a large wooden crate inside the unit, with high levels of soundproofing covering the inside. She wasn't dead, but she might as well have been. She would be in another day at most. He had left her tied up and gagged to starve to death.

Now I was very, very angry at my former employee. They were willing to let this young girl die just to get me.

This had to end, and end now.

# THREE

**I LEFT,** locked everything back up, and made sure I was not seen when leaving.

Then, from a secure phone, I called the police and told them where they would find the poor young girl from Boise and who she was. She would survive.

That left me only a few hours at most. Jessie wasn't good at covering his tracks and clearly would be identified and quickly arrested. So I needed to move fast and take care of my former employer's agents.

I went back to my Victorian apartment and made sure no one had been in. I knew no one would be, but better to be safe. My former employer had sat this trap up a long time in advance.

I had to admit, it was a well-done trap. And if I hadn't been expecting it, I would have walked right into it.

I set the signal to self-destruct all my cameras in Jessie's apartment and the Victorian apartment.

On the way out, carrying a suitcase with everything I would need to make my escape clean, I knocked on my landlord's door and told her that I would be gone for a few weeks on a trip to Boise.

To any other agent, that would be the signal that I was leaving and she had to act and act fast.

"I've got a package that came for you today," she said, turning away from me.

She should have been ready for me. Sloppy work.

I put a bullet in the back of her head.

Actually, she should have shot me the first moment she saw me. But my former employer had taught all its agents, including me, to play out the scene and cover tracks. She had lived, and now died, by that rule.

I glanced around. No one had seen.

My sound-suppresser was good and the shot had not been heard.

I quickly pushed her body back inside and closed the door. Her computer had cameras all over the building next door. And as I had suspected, the young guy in the apartment next to Jessie's apartment was the second agent on this job.

He was asleep in his apartment.

I sent a coded message from her computer to my former employer that said simply, "The garbage has been taken out."

That was a signal that she should be paid.

That I was dead.

I gave them an account number as was standard.

I made sure that the ten million and change she was paid was moved out of that account quickly and shuttled around so that it couldn't be traced. It would eventually land in accounts I controlled, but could not be traced back to me in Las Vegas.

She would have instantly moved the money as well if she had been a good agent.

She had been far higher paid than I had ever been. That meant she was in charge of this entire hunt for me. And that meant that more than likely there was more than just a second agent. Otherwise her pay would not have been so high.

I hadn't expected to make any money on this job, but a few extra million would make up for the extra mess I was being forced to cause.

Then I triggered her computer to self-destruct and destroy all her cameras in both buildings.

As I turned to leave, I could see that the mask over her face had been blown partially off her face by my shot. She had been far more beautiful than her disguise had played.

And far younger.

The local police were going to have a field day with this one. I wonder what happened to the actual landlady of this building.

I walked across the street and up to the location of Jessie's apartment. I knew for a fact the other agent was asleep. The two agents slept in shifts as they had been trained.

Just to be sure, I planted a few small explosive charges along the staircase. Blinding charges. In case I missed a third agent, I didn't want to be surprised and caught without a defense in this hallway.

I entered the second agent's small apartment very silently and put two bullets in him before he could even roll over.

Then I went to his computer and sent the same coded message to my former employer.

"The garbage had been taken out."

I moved another four million that was his payment to my accounts, then set his computer to self-destruct, along with all the cameras he had set up.

Two down, one to go. This was a lot of trips to the curb.

A lot of human garbage to haul.

As I stepped into the hallway, I saw Jessie coming up the stairs.

And my little voice rang out clearly.

My former employee had already killed Jessie and had replaced him with a disguised agent as bait.

Of course.

This Jessie was smiling. The original Jessie never smiled.

And this agent was pulling out a gun as he saw me.

The tiny button in my left hand instantly triggered the string explosives across the stairs and I dropped to the concrete entrance floor.

The small, but bright and violent, explosion sent the agent back as he fired and tried to catch his balance at the same time.

His shots went over me and into the old wood siding behind me. I put two in his chest and another between his eyes before he could get off a third shot.

He was dead before he hit the bottom of the stairs.

My small explosions were also designed to start a heavy-smoke fire.

I went down the stairs quickly, moving through the smoke and out into the street, my gun now hidden in my suit-coat pocket, but my hand on it.

The day was warming up by the moment and the heat on the street was more than I had noticed the first time across.

I pretended to cough and stagger to the far side of the street and the mowed lawns there, keeping my head down as neighbors came running.

"Fire," I said, pointing at the smoke now pouring out of the staircase of the building while keeping my head down and then again pretending to cough.

I had to be really, really careful in case there was a fourth agent close by.

Around me a dozen people were on their cell phones and two men were running at the building while another man was banging on apartment doors on the ground floor.

The fire I had set wouldn't spread, but they didn't know that.

"You all right, mister?" a woman asked.

I didn't want to look up, but I had to.

I stood and nodded, taking a deep breath of the warm Portland afternoon air.

The woman had a cell phone against her ear and as I looked at her and nodded, I saw a flicker of recognition cross her eyes.

She was young and I had surprised her. She did not expect to be talking with me.

Her hand went for her jacket pocket and I put one shot through my jacket pocket into her forehead.

She slumped and I caught her, pulling her over toward the shade of a nearby tree, talking to her as if she had just grown faint from the heat.

The wound in her forehead wasn't bleeding much, so I pulled her medium length hair from her wig down over her forehead and sat her down on a bus stop bench and posed her with her head between her knees, talking with her all the time as if I was trying to calm her.

I quickly slipped her gun from her pocket and put it in mine.

*She would have instantly moved the money as well if she had been a good agent.*

Then I pointed to a young guy about twenty feet away standing watching the fire, holding his bike that he clearly had been riding.

"She fainted," I shouted. "She's going to be all right. I'm going to get her meds for her. Watch her, would you?"

The guy nodded, looking at her as I turned and went toward the Victorian house with my apartment in it.

Walking quickly and still carrying my case, as if I was in a hurry to get her meds, I went inside and then through and into a back corridor. There I lost the coat and the brown hair and the slacks, switching them out for a pair of jeans and a light Levi jacket.

When I ambled out the back door I had long blonde hair flowing out of the back of a Oregon Ducks baseball cap. Any sign of Nick Benson, the former engineer from Boise, was gone.

I unlocked a used Jeep I had bought and parked a dozen blocks away as the sounds of police and fire sirens filled the afternoon air. I drove it to a Mongolian restaurant in Tigard, Oregon, about five miles outside of Portland.

I parked the Jeep down the street from the restaurant near some suburban homes and behind a new Dodge minivan that I had bought as well under yet a different name.

Then in the bathroom of the restaurant, I lost the Levi jacket and the long blonde hair and replaced it with gray hair pulled back under a plain gray baseball cap, different color contacts for my eyes, and padded shoulders in a sports jacket over the jeans.

I collapsed the small suitcase I had been carrying and put it inside a brown backpack.

I sat and ate, then paid with the credit card of my new name, Dan Curtis. After an amazingly good meal, I climbed into the mini-van and headed for Salt Lake City, going through Bend, Oregon, and across the desert.

Salt Lake was where the identity of Dan Curtis was from.

Two days later, Dan vanished there, never to be seen or heard of again.

Driving my three-year-old Cadillac, I headed back to Las Vegas and my teaching job at the university. I was a tenured professor in prelaw and law enforcement.

And I was a garbage man on the side, between semesters.

I took out the human garbage.

And sometimes that included other garbage men.

~

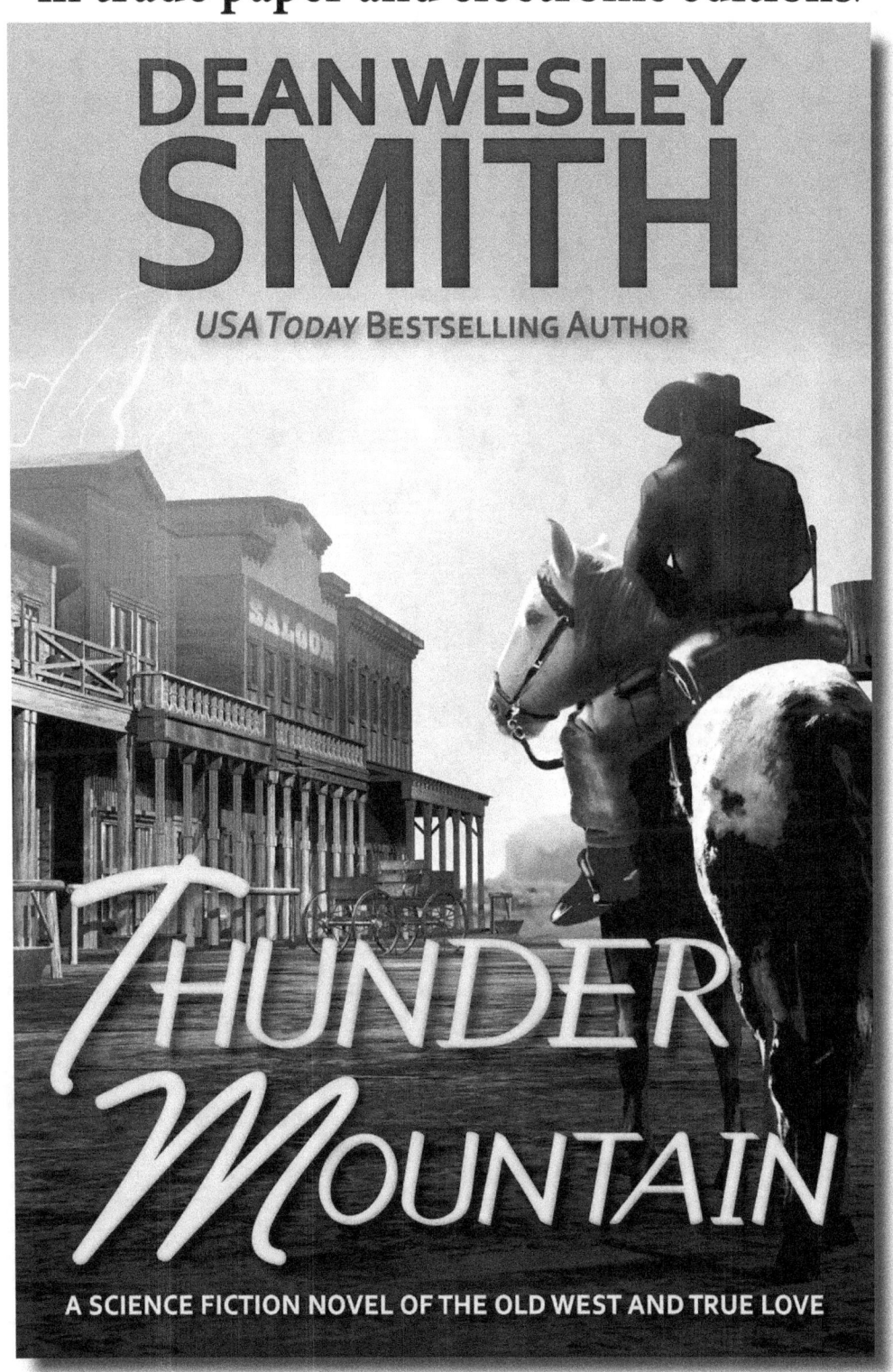

# DEAN WESLEY SMITH

# THE LIFE AND TIMES OF BUFFALO JIMMY

## Chapters 10-12

## What Came Before…

NINETEEN-YEAR-OLD BOSTON NATIVE *Jimmy Gray had been traveling with his parents and older brother, Luke, headed west to find a new home and new riches.*

*Before even reaching Independence, they were attacked and robbed by Jake Benson and his gang. Jimmy's parents were killed, his brother wounded.*

*In one of the wildest towns in all of American history, Jimmy Gray, a sheltered, educated son of a banker from Boston, suddenly finds himself very, very much alone.*

*But then through some luck, he finds other young men about his age and down on their luck who might be able to help him.*

*Together, the five of them head west after Benson.*

# THE LIFE AND TIMES OF BUFFALO JIMMY

*Part Seven*
## HEADED WEST AGAIN

**JIMMY FINALLY GOT HIS WISH** to see a buffalo ten days out of Independence. It was May 7th.

It had taken two days for the five of them to sell the wagon and equipment and buy three more horses. During the first days on the trail, Long had pointed out some plants that were poison, and others that were good to eat. It seemed to Jimmy that there was a lot to learn about Long. And he had a lot to teach them about survival in the west.

Before they left, Jimmy had paid for three months in advance for Luke's hotel room and food, and gave Doc Davis another payment for his services. Then he gave some money to Luke, enough for Luke to pay for a year in the hotel and supplies to get west next spring.

Jimmy had left a few of the family's most personal things with Luke in the hotel room, and had given his father's rifle to Zach. He seemed to be the only one of them who wanted to touch it. Jimmy said it would come in handy for hunting. Everything else, Jimmy sold to buy camping gear and supplies that they packed on the extra horses and in their own saddlebags.

After all that, he didn't have much money left, but he didn't tell anyone but Zach.

The goodbye with Luke had been hard for Jimmy, but after a few days on the trail, Jimmy's mood had lightened and he had started looking forward to the adventure ahead.

On Long's suggestion, they didn't push the horses, but instead just walked them along at a steady pace, often between wagons in the long trains. Jimmy had figured that Benson was only five or six days ahead by the time they left Independence. Considering the eighteen different legs of the trip that lay between Independence and Sacramento, and how far they all had to travel, that wasn't very far.

Zach had said that since Benson and his men didn't have any money when they were chased out of town, more than likely they would join onto a train to find food and rob some unsuspecting family.

So each night, they camped near a different train camp, not only for protection, but to get to know those in the train to make sure Benson wasn't among them. The last thing they wanted to do was pass him without knowing it.

For the first leg, which was about a hundred miles from Independence to the Kansas River ferry, the trail was packed with wagons and people walking. At times, the trail seemed more like a busy city street than the main wagon road west.

But on the second leg, a two hundred mile stretch northwest across grasslands to the Platte River, the wagons seemed to spread out some, even inside the same train. It usually took a wagon about two weeks to make that leg, but they made it in six days, traveling at a steady pace, passing wagon after wagon, all with

friendly faces waving at them as they went by.

Jimmy was starting to get a better idea of the vastness of the country. As far as the eye could see, it was green grasslands and low hills. The air was clean and fresh, especially after a rain. The only real excitement they encountered during the first days out of Independence was getting across a couple of swollen streams. It was clear that wagons had been lost in those streambeds, from the looks of the ruined equipment scattered downstream. Some family's dreams hadn't lasted very long.

When they reached the South Fork of the Platte River, the trail turned back westward and followed the south bank. The river was wide and brown and seemed to flow slowly and gently along. By this third leg of the trip, the wagons were really starting to spread out more and more, and sometimes it was impossible to tell where one company ended and another started. And there were more and more travelers in groups of two or three wagons, easy pickings for a man like Benson.

At one point, C. J. asked Long about Indians in this area. Long had pointed to the north. "Pawnee territory. To the south is Cheyenne. We're moving between them, so no problems."

Jimmy was glad to hear that, and glad even more that Long was with them. Not only did he know where the Indian territories were, but he had found some great roots that Truitt had used in some wonderful tasting stews.

The next morning, Long pointed at a dried brown pile to one side of the trail. "Fuel for a fire," he said. "Buffalo chips."

That had gotten them all excited and searching along the rolling hills around the river for any signs of actual buffalo. But they didn't see any that day. However,

Long was correct about the dried chips being great fuel for the campfire.

Finally, on the tenth day out of Independence, a man from one of the wagon trains they were slowly passing came riding hard and fast back toward his wagon from a ridge to the south. "Buffalo!" he shouted when he got close enough.

The cry went up and down the wagon train like a brush fire.

"Looks like we might be eating meat tonight," Truitt had said, smiling at Jimmy.

Jimmy was so excited, he could hardly keep his heart from beating right out of his chest,

"Can a rifle like this stop one?" Zach asked Long, pointing to Jimmy's father's rifle tied to his saddle bag.

"In the heart, right behind the front legs," Long said. "Two or three shots, maybe. But don't shoot a bull. The meat is too tough. A small cow is the best."

Zach nodded.

Then Long turned to Jimmy. "I will camp below that rock ledge with the pack horses until you return."

"Not interested in seeing a buffalo?" C. J. asked.

"I have seen far too many of them," Long said, then took the pack horses and moved slowly off toward the rocks.

"Let's go find some buffalo," Jimmy said, smiling at his friends.

With that, they headed at full ride toward the hill where the man had come from. Two other men were right ahead of them, and Jimmy had no doubt many others from the train would be following.

As they crested over the rise, at first Jimmy couldn't see anything different. Then it dawned on him that part of the shallow valley to his right was covered in brown instead of waving green grass.

Buffalo!

What looked to be thousands of them. The stories were right. It did look like a sea of buffalo.

"Oh, my," Truitt said, awe in his voice.

Jimmy just stared. The buffalo were majestic creatures. Jimmy could see a number of larger bulls, and hundreds of smaller calves, grazing near their mothers. Even from a distance, he could tell they were bigger than any cattle he had ever seen. The bulls looked to be almost as big as their horses, not as tall but much wider.

A half dozen men rode past the Wild Boys, heading for the buffalo, rifles out and ready.

Jimmy glanced over at Zach. "Think you might be able to down one of those?"

Zach looked stunned, but then he smiled and nodded. "My dad said I was the best shot he had ever seen. I just have to get close enough."

"Let's go," Jimmy said. "C.J., Truitt, we'll try to cut out a small cow from the herd, let Zach get a clean shot."

"Right with you," C. J. said.

With that, Jimmy spurred his horse into motion down the hill toward the herd, following the men from the train. His heart was racing and he was having trouble catching his breath. Never, in all his life in Boston, did he think he would ever be doing something like this. What

*The cry went up and down the wagon train like a brush fire.*

would his friends back there think if they could see him?

What would Luke think?

The buffalo were spooked by the men riding at them, and turned to run, in mass. The sound was almost deafening, louder than a train pulling into a station. And even on the horse, Jimmy could feel the ground shaking from that many large animals running at once.

Jimmy led them to the right, while the other men went to the left side of the herd. He had his eye on one medium-sized cow that was on the edge of the herd. He pointed at it and beside him Truitt shouted, "Got it, boss!"

Then C.J., seemingly completely fearless, did something that Jimmy would have never thought of doing. He took his horse into the herd, running with it, trying to cut the cow farther away from the herd.

It seemed to be working until suddenly shots echoed through the air from the other side of the herd.

The buffalo got even more frantic, running faster and harder.

And the entire herd turned toward them.

Jimmy found himself and his horse surrounded by buffalo, all running at top speed. He and his horse had no choice but to run with the herd.

He didn't dare stop.

He tried to ease his horse sideways, but there was no place to go. He was completely penned in by stampeding buffalo that smashed against his legs and his horse.

It was like riding while the ground around him was moving at the same time.

To his left, C. J. was stuck as well, a look of total concentration on his face as he tried to keep his horse on its feet.

Jimmy couldn't see either Truitt or Zach, and hoped they were out of the herd and behind them.

"Ease back!" Jimmy shouted at C. J., pulling his horse back just enough to slow him, but not turn him. He didn't dare try to stop fast or turn. In the thundering of the herd, he could barely hear his own yell.

As he slowed just a little, the buffalo started moving around him, running forward, opening up spaces as the herd started to pass him.

C. J. glanced over and saw what Jimmy was doing, then started to do the same thing.

It seemed to take forever for the herd to pass Jimmy completely, but actually it must have only been a few seconds. As he made it into the open behind the herd, he let out the breath he must have been holding. He was sweating and his heart was beating so hard, it felt like it might explode.

If his horse had gone down in that herd, he would have died a horrible death.

He glanced around. Zach and Truitt were following a distance back, looks of worry on both of their faces.

The herd passed C. J. and the four of them stopped and tried to catch their breaths.

"I thought you two were dead for sure," Truitt said, shaking his head and laughing.

"I thought we were too," Jimmy said. He held his hands on his pants legs so that the others wouldn't see them shaking.

"Let's not do that again," C. J. said, sweat pouring down off his face. He took off his glasses and tried to clean them, but his hands were shaking too much, so he gave up. "I think next time, I'll just stay with Long and the horses."

"Great buffalo hunters we are, huh?" Zach said, then he laughed. After a moment, all four of them were laughing.

Jimmy was just glad that all four of them were still alive so that they could laugh.

## Part Eleven
# A REAL HUNT

**SINCE THEIR FIRST EXPERIENCE** with buffalo, they had seen a half dozen other herds before reaching the South Fork crossing. Some of the herds were smaller, some closer to the trail. But Jimmy' great desire to see them had now worn off completely. He now had a huge respect for the big creatures.

After spotting the third herd, Long had finally agreed, after much pushing from Zach and Truitt, to help them to get some meat for dinner. As far as C. J. was concerned, he never wanted to see a buffalo again and he said he would be glad to watch the horses.

Long showed Zach a rock to sit behind with the rifle just down a shallow valley from the herd. "Shoot a small cow or large calf as it runs past. That will be more meat than we can carry."

Zach had nodded and looked worried when Long took his horse away, walking it slowly back to let C. J. hold it.

Then Long told Jimmy to go to the left of the herd, Truitt to the right, and he said he would stay directly behind them. "We move up to them slowly," Long said, "then when I give the signal, wave your hat and shout."

"We'll drive them directly at Zach," Jimmy said, glancing down the valley ahead of the herd where Zach crouched behind a rock.

"The beasts will turn slightly left, following the valley, and will pass beside Zach's position," Long said. "They are lazy creatures by nature and will not run up a hill unless they are forced to."

Jimmy just hoped, for Zach's sake, Long was right about that.

A few minutes later, they were all in position and Long gave the signal. This time, Jimmy had no plan on getting too close to the herd, and he noticed that Truitt stayed a safe distance away as well.

The herd of large beasts rumbled into motion, moving toward Zach. Again, Jimmy couldn't believe the noise and how much the ground shook.

For a moment, Jimmy thought Long was going to be wrong and Zach was going to have to depend on hiding behind a rock to save his life. But then, as Long had said they would, the herd turned left, giving Zach a clear and close shot at the nearest creatures.

Zach leveled the rifle on one small cow and fired twice.

The cow went nose down, tumbled once, and then lay there, not moving.

Long motioned for C. J. to bring Zach's horse and the pack horses, and all of them moved toward the dead buffalo.

Jimmy was amazed at how ugly the creature was up close. And Long had been right, they were very smelly beasts, like a rancid stew left out in the sun for too many days. Their hair was patchy and bugs crawled all over them.

Long gave Jimmy, Truitt, and Zach step-by-step instructions on how to get the meat out of the beast, how to pack it, and so on. By the time they were finished, all three of them had to take a swim in the cold brown water of the river just to get the smell off.

But that night, the buffalo steaks that Truitt cooked were wonderful. Jimmy figured it was almost worth it.

Almost.

## *Part Twelve*
# A BIG STORM

**THE NEXT AFTERNOON** they reached the South Fork Crossing.

All Jimmy could think about was that it wasn't possible to cross that wide a river. It had to be at least a half-mile across. It looked more like a lake than a river. He could swim, but not that good.

"We're going across that?" Truitt asked.

"All of them are," Jimmy said, pointing at the two hundred wagons that were camped along the banks of the river. "We can make it."

"I'm not much of a swimmer," Truitt said, clearly not happy with the idea.

"Neither am I," C.J. said.

"Your horse can swim," Long said. "Just stay in the saddle."

Truitt looked at Long. "Oh, sure, easy for you to say."

As the five of them sat and stared at the ford from the high bank, at least twenty wagons were in the water at one point or another in the crossing. And more were camped on the other side.

From what Jimmy could tell, none of the wagons seemed to be in too far over their beds, and none of the horses seemed to be swimming. That, at least, was a good sign.

They spent the rest of that day camped with the wagons, making sure Benson wasn't among those waiting to cross, then the next morning, they went into the water.

As Jimmy pushed his horse gently into the slowly moving river, he wasn't sure what was more frightening, riding in a herd of buffalo or crossing a river a half-mile wide. At that moment, he almost wished he was back with the buffalo.

But the river turned out to be shallow all the way across, and he didn't even get his boots wet. That afternoon, after checking the wagons camped on the other side for any sign of Benson, they headed away from the river into the fourth leg of the long trip.

From what C. J. told them, it was just over one hundred and eighty miles from the crossing to Fort Laramie. More than likely, that would be where they would catch up to Benson.

The trail from the crossing cut across a shallow range of hills and started up the North Fork of the Platte River.

The hills around them now were rocky and higher, and the brush thinner. And by this point, the wagons were really spread out. Sometimes they would ride for a few hours before catching up to a stopped band of wagons.

"We're in Sioux territory," Long said on the third day. "We should camp at night with a wagon company for safety."

Jimmy had no argument with that.

Jimmy wanted to ask Long many questions about his mother's people, but figured now wouldn't be the time. Maybe later in the trip. Right now, Long looked very serious and focused on the rocks and hills around them and Jimmy let him concentrate.

On the third evening as they were moving along the river, it seemed as if the sky around them and above the mountains just suddenly turned a pitch black. It had rained off and on for the entire trip, but no storm before had looked this bad.

Zach pointed at the coming clouds. "I think we need to take cover."

"I agree," Long said. "That will have some strong winds and lightening with those clouds."

"How about up that canyon there?" Truitt pointed to a rock-lined canyon "We should be able to anchor our tents pretty well there."

"It's not with a wagon company," Jimmy said. He didn't much like the looks of the coming clouds either, but he also didn't like the idea of camping alone in Sioux territory without a lot of people around them. And at the moment, there was no wagon company within sight along the trail.

"The Sioux will take cover as well," Long said. "They consider a storm like this one bad medicine."

"Can't argue with them there," Truitt said as a rumbling of thunder echoed out over the river.

With one more look at the clouds, Jimmy shouted over the growing storm winds, "Let's move before we get soaked."

At a full gallop, they turned away from the trail and headed up the rocky canyon, following a shallow stream. There were numbers of side canyons off the main one, but Long led them to what seemed like an alcove water had cut into the rock. The walls of the canyon would shelter them both from most of the wind and the lightening.

They secured the horses, then madly worked to pitch and secure their tents. Jimmy had just finished and crawled inside when the first gust of wind really rocked his tent and a moment later the rains started.

Chances are, it was going to be a very long night.

He must have dozed because the next thing he realized, lighting and thunder were shaking the ground around him, and water was pouring into his tent.

He grabbed his saddlebags and got out into the storm quickly. In one flash of lighting, he saw that the small stream they had camped beside was quickly rising.

"Water!" he shouted. "Everybody up and out!"

Another very close strike of lightning spooked the horses and he barely got to them in time to hold them from trying to break away.

"We need to get out of this canyon!" Long shouted over the thundering of the storm.

"And fast!" Jimmy shouted.

He could only see the others through the pitch black pouring rain when lightning lit up the canyon. But from what he could see, the others were scrambling to gather up their gear and get to the horses.

The water around them was coming up faster than Jimmy could have imagined possible. He decided to leave his tent and bedroll. He doubted he could get to them in the rising water anyway.

He managed to get a saddle on his horse while the others worked frantically in the pouring rain beside him. By the time he got the gear on one of the packhorses and got mounted, the water had risen so fast, it was up to his waist.

Somehow, he got his horse and the packhorse headed downstream, but now both horses seemed to be swimming in the strong current and it was everything Jimmy could do to just hang on.

A lightning strike showed a side canyon ahead that looked mostly dry. He tried to turn his horse in that direction, and somehow the horse got footing and pulled out of the water, the packhorse following.

Lightning strikes, one right after another, gave him just enough light in the rain to work his way up the canyon to a high, wide shelf area that would be above any flooding.

There he dismounted and tried to hold the horses as tight as he could against the shelter of the rock wall.

The rain pounded on him as he knelt down. He was so cold, he was shivering and his fingers were numb.

Around him, the storm raged, as if the Earth itself was mad at him.

He stayed pressed against the rocks, trying to hold the horses from bolting with every close lightning strike and thunderous clap.

None of the others had made it into this side canyon.

More than likely, they had been swept downstream and into the big river and were dead. Even if they could swim, no one could survive that swirling torrent in the rock canyon for very long.

It was going to be a very long night.

He had lost his friends.

Mother Nature and the west had clearly won this battle.

And again, he was completely alone.

*To be continued next issue…*

---

# Coming Next Issue in Smith's Monthly
A little sex in your science fiction
never hurt anyone.

USA *Today* Bestselling Writer

# DEAN WESLEY SMITH

# SLEEPING WITH THE GODDESS

*USA Today bestselling writer, Dean Wesley Smith, remembers clearly the early days of dating. The fear, the dreams, and the vivid imagination.*

*"Sleeping with the Goddess" takes a glance inside one special date when reality sometimes gets mixed up in a guy's mind. Especially when things on the date seem great and all girls represent a goddess.*

# SLEEPING WITH THE GODDESS

**OKAY, BAST HAD LEGS** that touched the ground and extended all the way up into heaven. I knew the ground part of the equation because her heels clicked when she walked on the sidewalk beside me as we headed into the movie.

Click. Click. Click. Click. Proof the goddess walked on the earth.

The heaven part I hoped to visit later in the evening. It was a faith issue, and I wanted to be the converted.

The date had started off well, the conversation light but strained as I walked with her from her parents' suburban house down the driveway to my car. I even held the passenger door of my Bug open for her to get in.

She liked that, said she liked the car, and gave me a beaming smile with perfect white teeth.

I liked what the seat belt did to her chest, but I didn't say that of course.

Bast had been named after an Egyptian goddess, so I figured the best way to find my way into her stone chamber was to treat her like a goddess. Tonight, I would be on my best behavior. So far, so good.

She was wearing a bright blue blouse with short sleeves, a matching blue short skirt, and heels that made her almost as tall as I am.

She had pulled back her long blonde hair like she did when she was wearing her cheerleader uniform and leading the school to shout and yell for the football players.

With her hair pulled back tight like that, her face seemed to stretch and she actually had a cat-like look that could melt any guy in the school.

Kind of creepy when you consider her name, Bast, was the name of the Egyptian cat goddess.

I know because I had looked it up after the second day of sitting beside her. I loved the part about Bast that she was the pleasure-loving goddess in whose honor wild parties were thrown.

However, I sure didn't look like any goddess consort. I had on my normal jeans, sweatshirt, and Reeboks. I wasn't one of the football or basketball jocks cheerleaders normally went for. My only sport was snowboarding and I did it well. In fact, with luck, I hoped to have a shot at the regional tryouts for the Olympics next spring.

We had ended up sitting next to each other in a second period English literature class. It had taken me a week just to get up the nerve to nod at her before class, and after the first nod I just sat there and sweated the entire hour.

It took me another week to say hi.

And another week to actually ask her a question.

I think my first question was where she was thinking about going to college the following year. I'm not sure if I stammered or not.

I hope not.

Stanford was the answer. Prelaw major.

She asked me in return and when I told her Columbia, if things worked out, she had given me my first smile.

I remember sort of melting into the chair after that smile. It had taken another two days for me to get up the nerve to talk to her again.

After that we sort of talked every day, sometimes just a hi, sometimes a few sentences. I looked forward to every word, to be honest.

Then the big day came when she even asked me my name after one class in which I had answered correctly a fairly hard Shakespeare question.

There is nothing like a beautiful girl wanting to know the name of a boy in her class. The simple question can send a boy into masturbation heaven. I was no exception to the rule.

Then when the school newspaper did the article on me trying for the Olympics, she got real friendly and we talked before and after every class, even walking twice to our next classes together. I guess having a goal beyond making the next touchdown was a little interesting to her.

A week later I finally got up the nerve to ask her out.

Or she asked me out.

I'm not really sure how the date happened, but it sort of did.

Luckily, a film we both wanted to see was opening on Friday night, so we decided that would be perfect.

And unlike what I had feared might happen, the date went very, very well.

She looked like a goddess. I looked like a snowboarder.

I made no gaffes in the car as we talked about why she wanted to go to Stanford, and managed to keep my gaze on her beautiful blue eyes instead of her beautiful blue blouse.

I bought the tickets to the show. She insisted on buying the popcorn and Diet Coke.

The movie was good. We both laughed a lot, which broke even more of the first-date tension.

After the show we went for pizza, discovering both of us liked Canadian bacon and tomatoes. Having the same taste in pizza is important.

I asked her about her family, which I found out consisted of one brother and her mother who worked. Her dad lived across town and was a college professor of ancient history, thus her name. I discovered she wanted to be a lawyer and help people.

She asked about my Olympic hopes, about me going to New York to go to college, which was a long way from a snowboard hill, and my family, which consisted of one younger sister and parents who should be divorced but didn't know it yet.

We talked for hours, working at the pizza and drinking Diet Coke, having a blast, to be honest. By the end of the conversation, my single-minded thoughts of finding goddess heaven had faded back to actually enjoying Bast's company.

I took her back to her house, parked the Bug on the street, and turned to her, suddenly realizing the tension was high again between us.

Sexual tension?

First kiss tension?

How to end a really perfect evening tension?

All of the above more than likely.

"Now this was fun," I said after we stared into each other's eyes for a few moments.

"It sure was," she said, giving me that melting smile and a wonderful laugh. "Want to do it again?"

"Sure do," I said. "Different movie though. I hate seeing the same movie twice."

Again she laughed, which was nice of her for such a lame joke.

USA Today *bestselling writer Dean Wesley Smith returns with a second novel to the world of* Dust and Kisses *from the first issue of* Smith's Monthly.

*Together, Callie and Fisher work to discover the secrets of a galaxy that have been hidden in plain sight, even from the powerful humans who had rescued millions. And in the process, they just might change everything.*

## Coming in February
**from all your favorite booksellers in trade paper and electronic editions.**

"Deal," she said.

She started to reach for the door handle, hesitated, glancing back at me.

The moment seemed to take a lifetime. Then she turned to me, leaned toward me, used one hand to grab my sweatshirt, and pulled me into a kiss.

Now understand, I have kissed my share of girls before. Being around ski lodges certainly gives a guy like me lots of chances for meeting and finding private places to end up with girls. I hadn't lost my virginity yet, but kissing I was downright good at.

She was better.

She kissed like a goddess.

I melted and lost my mind, all at the same moment.

From that kiss on I have no idea what actually happened.

Granted, I have a memory of the events that followed, but no belief in those events.

I think what happened is that she pulled away from the kiss and said, "Let's go inside."

I asked about her mother and what would she say.

"She is not a problem," she had said, getting out and motioning for me to follow.

I don't remember my feet touching the driveway. I don't remember closing my car door. I don't remember opening her front door.

I do remember staring at her wonderful body and thinking of the smooth skin and wonderful feel of her lips.

That I remember.

We went inside, her holding my hand and pulling my stumbling body along.

I do remember stopping just inside the front door as she closed it behind me, staring. And I remember being stunned.

The inside of the house wasn't a three bedroom standard American. It looked like an Egyptian King's bedroom, with silk hanging from impossibly high ceilings, and dozens of people bowing to Bast.

As we entered her clothes seemed to change from the short skirt and blue blouse to blue Egyptian silk that shimmered around her as she walked, showing off the smooth skin of her legs, her shoulders, her neck.

Two large men came forward and bowed to her, two others fanned her with reed fans.

I remember thinking they should be fanning me instead, because I was the one that was having the heat stroke.

She directed still another two men to take me, strip me, and put me in the hot baths.

They were big guys, and I don't remember fighting them as they helped me undress.

Then after I was in the water, she slowly let the silk slide off her shoulders into a pile beside the pools.

I swear trumpets rang out somewhere in the distance.

She had the most perfect body I could have ever imagined, and as an eighteen-year-old boy, I had done some pretty good imagining. Her body was even better than anything in the men's magazines. She came down the steps into the water very, very slowly, smiling at me and clearly enjoying my stare.

I remember that we kissed again.

Then we washed each other, we kissed some more, did more washing.

Kiss on, wash off. Kiss on, wash off. I explored her body.

Finally, I think I remember that she took me by the hand and led me to the biggest bed I had ever seen, where we made love for hours, and I truly became a believer.

The first real sexual experience with anyone would do that for any boy my age, but with a goddess, it was special, real special.

We slept for hours after that. Then she had two of her slaves help me dress and send me out to my car in the driveway of the very ordinary looking suburban house, while she stood and waved at me from the front step, dressed again in her movie attire.

I was surprised it was still dark.

Now I think all that happened.

But I'm convinced it couldn't have.

More than likely she just kissed me, got out of the car, and I came to after the kiss about the point she reached the front step and turned to wave.

I turned on the car engine as she stepped inside and closed the door.

I managed to get the car out into the street and headed home, wondering about the weird power-dream one kiss could bring on.

Then I noticed it was a lot later than I had thought it was. All the way home I questioned myself if the dream had been real or not.

I still, even the next day, don't know for sure, because I'm not really sure of the power of a true goddess. And I'm sure not going to ask her between classes.

But I do know that when I got home, I had my underwear on backwards.

And I smelled like rose petals.

# DEAN WESLEY SMITH

# THE ADVENTURES OF HAWK

## Chapters 10-12

# What came before in…

*Nineteen-year-old Danny Hawk, his uncle, and his best friend Craig, were in Cairo to look for his missing father. Danny had witnessed the death of his only contact in Cairo, Professor Davis, because the professor had Danny's father's journals.*

*Danny knows that the men who had killed the professor were now after him and the journals. Danny finds the journals and gets his uncle and friend to safety in an airport hotel where he tells them what happened. They decide to keep searching for Danny's father and try to rescue him.*

*Along the way, Danny and Craig find some help from a street kid named Bud and twins from South Africa who had worked with Danny's father.*

# THE ADVENTURES OF HAWK

## CHAPTER TEN

*August 19, 1970*
*Gizera Hotel, Cairo, Egypt*

**THE SUN WAS DROPPING** over the desert to the west when they finally left the twins' apartment. The bazaar had wound down in the heat of the day, and now the street looked almost deserted.

Waves of shimmering heat came off the pavement and Danny, this time with Bud's help, bought them all bottles of Coke again. Bud paid less than a quarter of an LE for the five bottles, and seemed upset that he hadn't gotten a better deal.

The five took two cabs to the hotel where Danny and Craig were staying. The twins and Bud took a cab to the hotel first, to scout out the area to make sure no one was waiting for Craig and Danny, who followed in a second cab a few minutes later.

There was no one, Bud swore to that, but Danny was convinced that their luck wouldn't last. He and Craig had to move to a safer place near the bazaar that couldn't be traced. Bud said he knew the best place, but he wouldn't be able to get it for them until tomorrow morning. So they decided to risk one more night in the hotel and all read Danny's father's journals while there.

Danny brought them all food after getting the notebooks from the hiding place in the ceiling tile. The twins were well into the notebooks, writing like crazy. They had brought second spiral notebooks, and were going to copy by hand every word Danny's father had said.

And put it all in English.

"Your father is an amazing man," Ernie said as he ate and read at the same time. "He put together clues from diverse sources that no other archeologist would have thought of doing."

"Yeah," Danny said, "but he wasn't much of a father."

"Never home?" Ed asked.

Danny nodded.

Bud shrugged. "Never knew my father. Or my mother for that matter."

Danny glanced at Bud. He had said it so matter-of-factly, it seemed like he actually didn't care. But Danny had a hunch that under that tough shell, Bud actually did care.

"Our father was killed in prison for speaking out against the South African white government," Ed said.

"Our mother never recovered," Ernie said. "She was also killed for the same cause."

Bud glanced up at them, surprised. Clearly they were not runaways as he had suspected, except maybe running away from their country.

"My father drinks, can't hold a job, and gets mean," Craig said. "I try not to be around him much, but I still like the old guy."

Danny looked at his new friends, suddenly understanding just how lucky he had been to have the father he had. His mother had never complained, and neither had Uncle Steve. They had just accepted Professor Kenneth Hawk for what he was, a driven scientist in search of something mythical.

Danny had been the only one angry at him for not being home more. And now it was up to Danny to save his father.

After they finished eating, all five boys went back to reading, with Bud going out to check the surrounding area around the hotel every fifteen minutes.

Craig dosed off around one, and Danny finally fell asleep at two.

When he woke to the sun streaming in through the window, the two twins were still writing as fast as they could, and Bud was napping in a chair near the door.

"We almost have it finished," Ernie said without slowing down.

"Another fifteen minutes at most," Ed said.

"But I can tell you this much," Ernie said. "We're going to have to go to your father's apartment here in Cairo."

"Why?" Danny asked.

"We're not sure, but we need to go there."

Danny shrugged. More than likely it had been cleaned out, but if the twins thought it was a good idea to go there, they would do it.

"And we need to go to the Giza Pyramids," Ernie said.

"So you can see something your father found and understood," Ed said.

"Was my father's last work site there?"

"No," Ed said. "His dig was farther to the south."

Now Danny was really puzzled. "Why go to Giza then?"

"A clue to the Hydra Journal is there," Ed said. "We think you should see it."

"Wouldn't my father have taken it with him, or the Hydra League hidden it after they took him?"

"No," Ernie said, pointing to a place in the notebook that was written in hieroglyphs. "Because it's been in plain sight for years. Every tourist looks at it without understanding what it is. Your father finally put meaning behind what everyone sees."

> *"A clue to the Hydra Journal is there," Ed said. "We think you should see it."*

"Oh," was all Danny could say.

The twins both went back to writing at full speed, so Danny decided he would get them all some breakfast.

"We're not going to either of those places without me checking out the area first," Bud said before Danny could stand. "And right now, I need to scout this hotel again. No one leave until I get back."

Bud moved quickly and went out the door, closing it carefully behind him.

Danny stayed in the chair he had been sleeping in and watched the twins work. He was very glad they had suggested making a copy of the notebooks and hiding both. That way, if the League did catch up to Danny, he could surrender the originals and still have what they needed to start their journey toward the Fountain and his father.

"Done," Ernie said.

"As am I," Ed said a moment later.

They quickly wrapped the original notebooks and put them back in their pack. Then they quickly took the four notebooks they had written in and hid them under their robes, in pockets that didn't seem to show the books at all.

"We have company," Bud said, coming back in quickly and closing the door.

"These guys are good," Craig said, sitting up and rubbing sleep out of his eyes. "Only two days to find us here."

The sound of the shot killing Professor Davis came back clearly in Danny's mind, but he pushed it away. "How many and where?"

"Only two, and they are at the front desk," Bud said. "But they have a picture of you, Danny, and the front desk clerk is chattering like a bird at sunrise."

"You three go out the window," Danny said, handing Bud a fifty Egyptian Pound note. "Circle around to the front and take a cab back to the bazaar and wait for us. They don't know you, so you'll be safe."

Danny grabbed his bag and then put his father's backpack over his shoulder.

Craig grabbed his suitcase.

"How are you two getting out of here?" Bud asked, a worried look on his face.

"Right through the front lobby," Danny said. "We're even going to check out and everything, then head for the airport."

Bud smiled. "I'm starting to like you two more and more. You have some courage."

"That is taking a great risk," Ernie said.

"They know what we look like already," Danny said as he opened the window to hold it for the three new friends. "They won't dare confront us in a public place. We'll try to lose them at the airport, but if we don't we're going to need cover when we reach the bazaar."

"You'll have it," Bud said, going out the window right behind Edward.

"Good luck," Ernie said and ducked out as well.

"We're going to need it," Craig said as Danny closed and locked the window, then turned and headed for the door, glancing around the room as he went to make sure that they hadn't missed anything.

Danny was happy that at least now copies of his father's notebooks were in the hands of two twins who would never be suspected of having them.

Danny knew his plan of escape rested on the two men staying in the lobby or outside waiting and not trying anything until they had privacy and red hoods, as they had done with Professor Davis. It was a gamble, he knew that.

And he was betting his and Craig's life that he was right.

# CHAPTER ELEVEN

*August 20, 1970*
*Cairo, Egypt*

**THE HALLWAY WAS** thankfully empty, so Danny led the way down the hall toward the front desk. The restaurant was on the right of the big lobby. There were plants, small palm trees, and a dozen places to sit.

The two men that Bud had described were still standing at the front desk. Both were white. One looked British and very

properly dressed in an expensive black suit. The other was of what looked like Italian descent, with big arms and a black suit that was two sizes too small. He looked mean, and his face had a nasty scar on the right cheek.

Clearly, the British-looking man was in charge. As Danny got closer to them, he could see that their skin had a weathered look to it all over. Not scarred, just weathered.

Danny had no idea if that was the same two who had killed Professor Davis, but if they were asking about him, he had no doubt they were with the same group.

"Remember," Danny whispered to Craig, "don't look at them. We don't know them. We're just checking out and heading home."

"You're nuts, you know that?" Craig whispered back as they crossed the open tile of the lobby and walked up behind the two men.

"Ah, Mr. Hawk," the desk clerk said loudly, looking over one man's shoulder.

Both men seemed to jump just slightly. Then one of them said to the clerk, "Thank you for the information. Please keep this to yourself."

"I understand," the clerk said, giving the man a sickly smile in return.

Danny wanted to just cut and run. He knew that voice. It was the man who had been in charge in Professor Davis's office, the man who had ordered the other to shoot the professor.

As the two men stepped off to one side, stopping close enough so that they could hear, Danny nodded to the clerk and gave him their room key.

"Checking out, going home," Danny said, pretending to be in a good mood.

"So soon?" the clerk asked, his voice trembling slightly. Clearly the two men had threatened him in some fashion or another.

"We've got to get ready for school," Danny said, trying his best to sound calm and relaxed, even though his heart was about to pound a new path right out of his chest. "It starts for us at the end of the month."

Craig stood beside him, pretending to read some sort of flyer that was on the counter. He had his back to the two men which, considering Craig's lack of a poker face, was a good thing.

"Where's your uncle?" the clerk asked as he wrote up Danny's receipt for the room.

"He left early yesterday," Danny said. "My mom needed his help. We wanted to stay and see the pyramids and everything yesterday, so he let us. Plus, we got my father's notebooks, which is what we came here to get."

He made sure his voice was loud enough that the men could hear him, and then to make it really clear, he patted the backpack he had on his shoulder.

Craig coughed and pretended to keep reading.

"Your father?" the clerk asked.

"Yes, he was an archeologist. These are his notes that I hope will help lead to where he is, but I can't read them. They're all Italian, Latin, and hieroglyphs. I figured someone back home can help me figure out what they say."

Craig coughed again and kept reading. Clearly Danny's little play was giving him a near heart attack.

"Well," the clerk said, glancing at the men, "have a good flight home."

Danny pocketed the receipt the clerk had given him and picked up his suitcase. "We will. Great food on the planes these days."

With that, he and Craig walked right past the two men who had killed Professor Davis.

Right past two members of the Hydra League.

Outside, in front of the door, was a cab that wasn't at the taxi stand twenty paces away. It had pulled up near the front door and had its back door open.

Bud must have set that up for them.

"Airport," Danny said as he started to climb in. A cab a few behind them honked long and loud, like a warning.

Danny suddenly realized that maybe Bud hadn't set up the taxi. Maybe it was the men inside, and the cab driver worked for them.

Danny quickly backed out, bumping into Craig and pushing him away. "Never mind," he said to the driver as he slammed the door.

The cab driver glanced back at Danny with an almost angry look on his face. Danny had a hunch they might have just escaped once again.

The two men came out the front door and watched as Danny and Craig moved toward the three cabs at the taxi stand.

Sitting behind the wheel of the second cab was Bud, smiling, a taxi driver's cap pulled down low over his head.

"Second cab," Danny whispered to Craig in case he hadn't seen Bud.

They quickly piled in the back seat, luggage and all, and before the door was even closed, Bud had the cab headed out of the cab line and toward the highway.

Danny glanced back as the two men got into the cab in front of the door and started to follow.

"Okay," Craig said to Bud, laughing, "how did you get this cab?"

"Driver had to use the bathroom and he got a little tied up," Bud said, shrugging as he focused on driving. "So I just thought we'd borrow it. We'll leave it at the airport, blocking traffic, of course. The twins took another cab and they will be waiting for us at the bazaar."

"The two men are in the cab behind us," Danny said, glancing back as if he were looking at the sights, not at the cab following them. His heart was still racing, and even though it was cool in the early morning hours, he was sweating.

"I know," Bud said. "Don't worry, we'll lose them in traffic or at the airport."

"You had me scared to death with that act at the front desk," Craig said, sitting back and shaking his head at Danny. "I thought they would just step up and grab the journals right there."

"I knew they wouldn't, once I had them convinced we didn't know they were following us. They'll wait for the right time."

"Was it the men in Professor Davis's office?" Bud asked.

"It was," Danny said, trying not to shudder. "I recognized one of their voices."

"They are mean-looking, that's for sure," Craig said. "Cold eyes."

"Very cold," Danny said, forcing himself to breathe evenly. It was one thing to talk about going after his father and risking his life, but it was clearly another matter to actually be in danger.

"And nice job telling them we hadn't read the journals yet," Craig said.

"You did?" Bud asked, glancing back with a smile. "Nifty trick."

"You think that might save our lives when they do catch up with us?" Craig asked.

"Probably not," Danny said, sinking into the seat. "But it was worth the try just in case."

# CHAPTER TWELVE

*August 20, 1970*
*Cairo, Egypt*

**BUD, EVEN THOUGH HE** was barely tall enough to see over the dashboard, wound the cab through the thick Cairo traffic like a racecar driver trying to gain on the lead.

As Danny watched, the cab with the two Hydra League killers behind them was cut off time after time, falling farther and farther behind in the thick traffic as they got closer to the airport.

Finally, they were so far back, Danny wasn't even sure which cab they were in in the sea of black and white cabs heading for the International Airport.

"When I pull up at the terminal," Bud said, "open both doors, then close them and duck down so you can't be seen. And stay down until I say otherwise, even if we're moving."

"Got it," Danny said. He was trusting Bud completely with his life at this point.

Danny tossed his suitcase over the seat and onto the front seat floor as Craig crammed his suitcase down onto the floor.

"Okay, get ready," Bud said.

He swung across two lanes and into a spot against the curb just in front of a small van. The sidewalk was crowded with passengers and their luggage going into the international terminal.

Craig opened the side door and Danny opened the door on the road side.

Then they both slammed them closed and ducked down onto the floor, trying to get as low as they could. The backseat of the taxi was cramped, but unless someone looked in, Danny was sure no one passing by in another cab would be able to see them.

"They're going past us," Bud whispered, sitting up on his legs so that he looked taller than he really was.

The seconds seemed to tick past as Danny held himself in the cramped position tucked down low.

"I'm going to ache in the morning from this," Craig whispered.

"Better than being dead in the morning," Bud whispered back.

"They have seen me," Bud whispered, pretending to count cash. "The cab is pulling in three cars ahead of us and the two men are getting out. Stay down."

Bud suddenly pulled the cab back out into traffic and moved over two lanes.

"The two men are going into the terminal," Bud whispered. "And the other cab is waiting for them. Stay down a little longer, until we get out of sight completely."

The cab bumped and jerked, and in the position Danny was, crammed on the floor of the back seat, his head down against his knees, he had no doubt that Craig was right, they were going to be very sore from this in the morning. And bruised from every bump that Bud hit.

The cab jerked right, then picked up speed.

"Clear," Bud said.

Danny tried to stretch his cramped muscles as he climbed back onto the seat.

"Great work," Danny said to Bud, reaching forward and patting him on the shoulder. "I'm really glad you're with us."

"Yeah, me too," Craig said.

Bud laughed. "Makes the days interesting."

"What, trying to stay alive?" Craig asked, laughing.

"I've been doing that for five years," Bud said. "But I will admit, this is new."

"Next stop, while we have them busy searching the airport, is my father's apartment," Danny said. "We need to know if the twins are right in there being something in the apartment that we need to see."

"Address?" Bud asked, like a regular driver would do.

Danny gave it to him, then sat back and tried to once again get his heart to calm down and stop racing. He really wished he had spent more time in training with his grandfather. Staying calm would come in really handy right about now.

*Continued in the next issue…*

# DEAN WESLEY SMITH

They Found Each Other
Through Luck...
And Across Lightyears.

# THE LADY AND THE SEEDERS

## Introduction to THE LADY AND THE SEEDERS

*About a year ago I had an assignment from editor John Helfers to write a story for his* Fiction River: How to Save the World *anthology. Now understand, I am one of the executive editors on the* Fiction River *line of anthologies. But the editors of each volume have the final call on the stories in each volume (within reason).*

*John had been pretty clear on what he wanted, but I had written "The Lady and the Seeders" a month before, starting it from the title and hadn't done anything with it. And the anthology was about saving the world, after all. So I sent it to John just to see if he was going to expand out his directions enough to include it.*

*He wasn't. He liked the story, though, and Kris liked the story, and I was kind of fond of it as well. But in his rejection letter to me, he said it felt like a novel.*

*Now, as an editor, I say that to writers at times myself. Often frustrating to the poor writer, but in this case, John was right. It did feel like a plot of a novel. Sort of. So I put the story away and as I started into this* Smith's Monthly *process, I decided to write the novel from the short story.*

*It's called "Against Time" and it was in* Smith's Monthly #3.

*There are tiny parts of the story in the novel, and characters have shifted around, but the core of the book is similar to the short story. So here in this fourth issue, I thought it would be fun and interesting to readers to show the short story that started the novel you read last month.*

*Enjoy.*

# THE LADY AND THE SEEDERS

## ONE

**I SAT IN MY BIG BLACK INERTIA CHAIR,** holding on for dear life as we came from deep space way too hot and directly into orbit insertion around a big, green-and-blue Earth-like planet we had named N-21-7. I had no doubt my fingers were going to have to be pried from the soft foam of the armrests and it tasted like my stomach might revolt from the sharp garlic on artichoke pizza I had baked us for lunch.

Doc, sitting to my right in his inertia chair, had us braking like crazy to hold the orbit as the features of the planet flashed by far, far too fast for me to even catch a glimpse. You would have thought we had someone with damn big guns on our ass.

Doc's fingers were flying over his control panel. My job was to watch for anything in front of us in orbit, but as fast as Doc had us braking, our orbital trajectory just kept changing, so I had no clue what was coming up, let alone be able to watch for anything.

We might hit something before we even had time to blink, and if the object we plowed into was too large, our screens might not block it.

This stunt was all my skinny partner's idea. Doc wanted to test out a new theory. He wanted to see how close to a planet we could drop out of a trans-tunnel and still control slowing into an orbit. He convinced me to give it a try by saying, "Just never know when it might come in handy in the future."

I was big on being prepared for just damn near anything, and we had been chased more than once in the last few years of roaming around through space. And more than likely it would happen again. Besides, I figured that if we didn't plow into something large, the worst that would happen was that we would just sling off the orbit like a flea off a dog's back and then have to backtrack.

Doc was convinced that wasn't going to happen, and he tried to show me the math. I nodded like I always do when he gets into the math on anything concerning orbits and trans-tunnel speeds and finally he stopped and said, "You'll see. It will work."

"Just don't hit the damn planet square on."

"No worries, Skip," he had said.

And that always made me worry. Especially when he called me "Skip" which was short for "Skipper." He never did that unless he was worried as well. My actual name was Fisher, Vardis Fisher, but everyone called me Fisher. I owned The Lady, as I called this deep space exploration ship.

Most of the time Doc just called her "The Ship."

We had built her in two years in a huge warehouse on my parent's estate just north of our hometown, right after we both finally finished with far too many advanced degrees in college.

I had the family money in my trust, more than enough, actually, to build a couple ships. And I had patents on a dozen devices I had invented that drew energy from dark matter.

Doc had the idea for the gravity drive that allowed us to not only just float out of a gravity well, but jump long distances very quickly in what Doc called "Trans-Tunnel Flight."

Basically it was a form of time-bending warp drive, but when we were in it, space looked like it had become a tunnel, so Doc named it the "Trans-Tunnel Drive."

"Better than "Warp Drive" he had said.

In the planning stage, we decided to make the ship really huge and really cool, right out of a 1950's science fiction movie. We even had painted it silver and put fins like a nifty plane and a pointed nose on it so it looked like a cross between a very fast plane and an old rocket ship. The fins were worthless unless in the atmosphere if the drive went out, and the pointed nose housed nothing but sensors.

We each had huge five-room suites on board, since the ship was the size of a hotel that flew. It was so big, there were parts of this ship I hadn't been in for over a year.

It actually didn't need to be this big, but both Doc and I had figured we never knew what we might run into out in space, or how much room we might need, or who might be riding along. The actual engine itself took up the room of a small closet and a large warehouse area was filled with many, many spare parts. The rest was a game room, an exercise room, a small gym, a massive kitchen with a dozen freezers, and numbers of spare bedrooms for a future crew or guests. So far, those guest rooms had not been used.

Before we took off, we had stocked more food than we would be able to eat in five years, even though, from darned-near-anywhere in this area of the galaxy, we could jump back to earth in a matter of a day or two.

Food is my passion. Somewhere back in college, after getting my first doctorate, I got close to three hundred pounds on my five-foot-ten inch frame. Back then people said Doc and I looked like the old comedy team of Laurel and Hardy, but I was larger back then than Hardy ever got.

And I loved cooking. Especially really rich foods. But a couple doctors told me that if I didn't lose some weight, I was going to have to cut down on many of the dishes I loved to cook.

So I went exercise crazy. Right before we left, I had run in my tenth marathon and I had been training for an Iron Man competition. I now weighed just under one-seventy and that was all muscle. And I could eat anything I damn well wanted.

Somehow, Doc ate everything I served him with relish and never gained a pound and spent only a minor amount of time in the gym, usually when he wanted to talk to me about something and knew I was a captive audience while in an exercise routine.

I didn't feel right if I didn't exercise, just as I didn't feel right when I didn't eat decent food.

One of the most enjoyable aspects of this exploring around space was discovering new types of food and ways of cooking it. I was stockpiling the

---

recipes with hopes of doing a number of cookbooks when we got back to Earth.

I could spend two or three hours a day in the kitchen just testing new foods and writing it all down.

I doubted anyone would give my books any credit, just as they didn't give my energy inventions even a second look. The power for everything on this ship and Doc's drive came from the energy floating around between matter and dark matter.

For some reason I had the ability to understand when something hidden was between two obvious things. I had perfected the idea of using the energy between the two states of matter while in school and applied for patents, but no professor would let me write it as a thesis. No one really gave my ideas any credit at all, actually, just as they didn't give Doc's trans-tunnel drive and anti-gravity work anything but laughter.

If they could only see us now.

Finally, Doc had us slowed enough that the orbit we had settled into seemed stable, even though we were still braking.

"Told you it would work," Doc said, smiling at me, his thin face twisted into mostly bright white teeth and wide blue eyes.

I just shook my head and worked my fingers off the armrests of my chair. "Only emergencies," I said as my stomach started to settle.

"Exactly," he said, nodding and going back to continuing to brake us into a stable orbit. "At some point I hope to figure out how we can come out of a trans-tunnel without forward speed. It should be possible."

"Make that a priority," I said.

Suddenly the warning lights on my heads-up panel flashed into a display that would do a Christmas tree proud.

The orbit we had dropped into had us hitting a large orbiting object in about five seconds.

I kicked off Doc's controls and cut the braking, which allowed us to move out higher away from the planet. On my screen our orbit around the planet changed from a nice circular pattern into a big egg-shaped elliptical orbit.

We flashed past what looked like an orbiting station far too fast to get a good look at it.

And far too close for my stomach to be happy. I had long ago lost the desire for near-misses on anything. And if we had hit it, we would have put a very, very large hole in it. Our screens would have kept us safe, but the station and everyone on it would have been in trouble.

"Wow, good catch, Fisher," Doc said. "Looks like we have a space-faring culture on this planet."

"Great, just great," I said. "Someone to chase us again after we almost destroyed their space station."

Doc laughed. "Yeah, we have a way of making an entrance, don't we?"

# TWO

**AS DOC BROUGHT US AROUND** the planet again and worked to match the orbit of the space station, I scanned the planet. It felt a little like scanning Earth from a low orbit. Evidence of human activity everywhere, large, sprawling cities on all of its major continents, and thousands of roads and smaller cities and towns.

It looked the same as many of the Earth-type planets we had visited. Humans had clearly been seeded on every Goldilocks zone planet that we had come to at some point in the distant past. We had run across no aliens, but humans were everywhere. At least in the small area of the Milky Way Galaxy we had explored.

At last count, we had found over two hundred Earth-like planets and every darned one of them had either had human life on them at one point or still did have thriving civilizations.

And not many of them seemed very far beyond or behind Earth's level, as if they had all started at the same time in history.

Very, very strange and it had bothered us both for the first fifty or so planets, but now we were growing used to the idea.

The human civilization on the planet below also seemed to be around Earth's level of growth and expansion.

But as we went around the dark side in our orbit, I noticed one major problem: Nothing was moving.

And the planet was slowly dropping silent and dark. Only basic recorded sounds were coming from the surface.

In very short order it would be ghostly silent. And very, very dark.

"Doc, we have a problem," I said.

"They can't be coming after us already," he said, not looking up from his board as he brought The Lady up slowly on the orbiting space station. "We missed them, didn't we?"

"No one is coming after us," I said.

"That's good," he said, still not looking up. "So what's the problem?"

My fingers were moving as fast as I could get them to move over my controls to confirm what I feared.

All the readings came up the same.

"Everyone down there is dead."

At that, he looked up.

# THREE

**WE DID TEN ORBITS** over the next few hours, recording and studying everything we could. There was no doubt the planet below us was just flat dead. Actually, the planet was fine, but all the humans and a bunch of animal life had died very, very suddenly.

And very recently.

There were numbers of smaller animals and some larger ones still alive, but human bodies lay everywhere, in every building, in every street.

Something had killed everyone on the planet and it had done it quickly, where they stood, as they walked, as they drove cars that looked frighteningly like cars from Earth.

"You see anyone alive?" I finally asked Doc.

"Not a one," he said, his voice unnaturally soft.

He looked over at me, his eyes looking as haunted as I had ever seen them. We had run into a couple of Earth-like planets with no humans and only signs of a civilization in the distant past. That was one thing, almost a scientific curiosity as to what happened.

But it was a different thing when you could see human bodies littering the streets and filling the buildings.

Recently dead human bodies.

Millions and millions of them.

A vastly different thing.

And what worried me more than anything else was that this could happen to Earth. We somehow needed to find out what happened here.

"The station," I said.

He nodded. After this many years together, we often didn't have to finish sentences or thoughts.

We both knew that the instruments there might give us some sort of understanding of what had killed the population of this planet.

His fingers again flew over the control board, bringing us even closer in to match the orbit of the large space station.

I was feeling stunned and not really looking forward to going into that station when suddenly space around the planet was filled with a hundred huge ships.

They just appeared out of nowhere and at a dead stop. They made The Lady look like a kids ship in a bathtub compared to an aircraft carrier.

"What the…" I said, pushing back in my chair as if I needed to get farther away from those clearly alien monster ships.

Doc glanced up and jerked, also pushing back.

Then suddenly, on my sensors, I started reading humans again on the planet below.

Some alone, some scattered in groups.

I pointed to the readings and tapped Doc who glanced at it and nodded.

"They are transporting humans to the planet below," he said. "Looks like we found our seeders."

"We are not the originals," a voice said clearly inside the control room of The Lady. Only it wasn't my voice or Doc's.

Then everything around us shimmered for a moment and stabilized again.

The Lady was no longer floating in space near an empty space station. It was now seemingly sitting on a huge landing dock inside another ship.

"Oh, man," I said, trying to keep the last bit of control I had. Somehow I managed to not scream and run to the back of the ship.

"Now what are we going to do?" I asked.

Doc shook his head slowly, clearly as shaken as I had ever seen him before.

Then he turned to me and with a half-smile said, "Go and say hello?"

# FOUR

**WE DID SOME QUICK CHECKING** and the atmosphere outside the ship in the huge space dock was normal, no bad things in it that could kill us. And the gravity seemed to be Earth-normal as well.

Beyond that, we couldn't tell much of anything about the ship around us past what we could see in the huge room. The dock had to be as large as a football stadium and could have easily held three or four ships The Lady's size.

We tested, but every control we had was locked down solid and our engines were offline. We were going nowhere under our own power.

"You ready, Skip?" Doc asked, standing and pretending to stretch like he was relaxed about meeting the owners of these huge ships.

I just shook my head and stood as well. "Seems like we have no choice, doesn't it?"

A good minute later we were standing on the deck looking around. The sides of the room seem to vanish in the distance and I was clearly wrong. This room could hold twenty ships the size of ours, and have room between them all.

And we thought we had built a large ship when we built the Lady. Everything in space was relative it seemed.

Then, just as the first time we were grabbed, everything shimmered and we found ourselves in a meeting room with tables full of meats and vegetables and breads that that looked like they had been worked over by starving hordes.

I turned slowly around, surveying the large meeting room. The place was littered with a bunch of blankets and chairs and cots. One wall was filled with a huge view port that looked down on the greens and blues and whites of the planet below.

"Looks like we are late for the party," Doc said.

"If you had come to this planet ten minutes earlier," a voice said from behind us, "you more than likely would have been as dead as most of those on the planet below."

Doc and I spun around to see a man about my height and weight walking toward us, smiling. He had brown hair, wore jeans and a green short-sleeved shirt tucked into his pants. He looked as normal and as human as anyone from Earth.

And as far as I could tell, he was speaking perfect English. We had met a few human cultures that had perfected some sort of translation devices that just made it sound like they were speaking English. But this was even more advanced. His lips seemed to match what he was saying.

Considering the size of this ship we were in, I think I would have been less stunned if an alien had joined us spouting six arms and a beak and squeaking our national anthem.

He extended his hand for me to shake. "I'm Benson."

"Fisher," I said, carefully shaking his hand back.

It felt as normal as any human handshake, which bothered me even more.

"Doc," my stunned partner said softly as he shook Benson's hand next.

"So you are the two explorers we've been hearing about," Benson said, smiling. "I understand you have had some adventures."

"A few," I said, even more shocked that anyone had followed us around this area of space. Granted, it was a tiny area in comparison to the entire Milky Way Galaxy, but we had still covered a lot of light years and visited a few hundred Earth-like planets. And tracking us through open trans-tunnel space wasn't like following footprints in the mud. Or at least I didn't think it was.

"So where are you two from?" Benson asked.

"Earth." I gave him the answer I knew would make him smile and at the same time give him no information at all, since most of the human planets we had visited had called their planets Earth. In fact, every one of them had.

He did smile. "I don't blame you for not wanting to tell me. How about I show you around and tell you what we are doing and then maybe you'll feel more like talking. I find it fascinating that a human culture in this area has advanced as far as you have."

I almost told him that the rest of our planet hadn't just yet, but instead just nodded and said, "Lead the way. But first off, what happened down there?"

I pointed at the planet that could be seen out of a large view port on one side of the room.

Benson tapped something on his wrist and in the air near us an image of the Milky Way Galaxy came into being, spinning in the air.

Impressive three-dimensional image. Then like focusing in, the view shifted down to this spiral arm of the galaxy and then to this small section of space. There had to be five hundred suns represented by nothing more than bright colored lights floating in the air.

One light was suddenly circled in the air by a red ring.

"An explosion in this sun caused rays of extreme electro-magnetic energy to be sent out into space."

From the circled star a number of white rays seemed to expand outward. Benson went on. "By the time we noticed the explosion and calculated the frequency of the energy and then traced its path, we were too late to get here to save the people of this planet."

"EMP blast killed them where they stood," Doc said, nodding. "The right frequency would short circuit human brains like that."

Benson nodded. "About three million of the population survived by accidentally being in different forms of shelters or underground or inside something that shielded them. They didn't know it was coming.

Then I understood finally what we had seen. "But there was a second blast of energy following the first."

Benson nodded. "We got here ahead of that with a large enough fleet and got the survivors out of the way. What you witnessed was us putting them back."

"We arrived right behind the second wave?" Doc asked.

"About two minutes after it passed," Benson said. "Your shielding might have sheltered you, but it might not have either. Before you leave we will help you strengthen that shielding some for the future."

I looked at Benson and then nodded. "Thanks."

"So you go around rescuing planets full of humans?" Doc asked.

Benson shook his head sadly. "First time. But after this we will be more vigilant. Millions died down there before we got here."

He seemed actually deeply affected by that, so I tried to change the subject.

"So you know who seeded humans on so many planets in this area of the galaxy?" I asked.

"In every area of the galaxy," he said so matter-of-factly that it bothered me. "There are hundreds and hundreds of thousands of human civilizations in different stages of development in the galaxy. And no one knows much about the people or race who did it except that it took them over fifty thousand years to complete the task."

"Your planet was seeded as well?" Doc asked. "How come you are more advanced than any we have seen?"

"We were all seeded," he said, nodding. Again the floating map of the Milky Way Galaxy came into being in the air beside us. "My home planet is there, also called Earth."

A circle appeared around a dot a third of the way around the galaxy. Then another appeared around a dot I knew to be the sun we were orbiting.

"We are here at the moment," Benson said. "My area of the galaxy was seemingly seeded first, so civilizations that survived in that area are the most advanced. This arm of the galaxy was next, and as you move around in a clockwise direction, each human civilization gets more primitive."

"Wow," was all I could say.

Benson went on. "Our area of the galaxy has formed a large organization of aligned planets and about fifty worlds work together. That's why we could mount such a large fleet on such short notice."

"And no alien life at all?" Doc asked.

"Nothing above basic animal level," Benson said. "The Seeders, as we call them, not only seeded humans, but all the plant and animal life it would take to sustain human civilizations in the growth years."

"All the same on every planet?" Doc asked.

"All the same. Exactly."

I stood there shaking my head and just staring at the image of the galaxy floating in the empty meeting room air. I remembered how stunned I had felt every time we came across another human civilization during our first year exploring. But after a while I had just come to expect it.

Now I was feeling that same feeling again. It was just too much to grasp.

Humans always thought we were alone in the galaxy. It seems we were. But not in the way people back home might think.

Finally I shook my head and glanced at Benson, who looked almost haunted as he stared out the view port at the planet below. For some reason he clearly felt responsible for all those deaths.

I decided that our only hope in learning even more from Benson and his people was to confide in him.

"Could you focus this image in again to this area of space?" I asked, pointing to the floating galaxy.

He nodded and the floating image focused down and I pointed to a yellow star about sixty light years from this sun. "That's our Earth. And we are the only two that have this kind of technology at the moment."

Benson nodded. "I figured as much," he said. "On a couple of the planets in our area single explorers were the first out between the stars as well."

"So we are the first in this area of space," Doc said.

Benson nodded. "But after some of your visits to a few of the planets, I have a hunch those won't be far behind now that they know it's possible."

How in the world had he traced us? I was about to ask, but Doc got a question in first.

"So is your drive the same technology as ours?" Doc asked as I turned to stare back out at the damaged planet below.

Out of the corner of my eye I saw Benson shrug. "Just more advanced, but the same principles. If you want, I'll get some of our scientists to explain some of it to you?"

"You'd do that?" I asked, turning to Benson. I was again as stunned as Doc looked.

"Why not?" Benson asked. "We're all out here together. If we can't help other human civilizations, what's the point?"

Doc opened his mouth, but nothing came out. He was like a kid that had just been offered everything for free in a candy store.

I just shook my head and turned back to the view port. "So how do we help all those people down there?"

"We can't do much," Benson said. "At least not right now. Not until they get through the rebuilding stage, which the experts tell me is going to take a few hundred years at least."

"They have enough population to survive?" I asked.

Benson nodded. "More than enough. The Seeders only put a hundred and forty-four thousand humans on every planet and all but a few populations managed to keep going. There's almost three million alive down there still."

That exact number bothered me as well. A lot about this was bothering me, but I was in such shock, nothing was fitting together.

"You saved millions," Doc said. "That's impressive."

"And we didn't save many millions more," Benson said, his voice soft. "But the one thing we know about humans, we survive. And they will as well. The Seeders made sure we all had that trait."

# FIVE

**WE SPENT THE NEXT** two months on the big ship, getting The Lady refitted with the most advanced technology and screens. Doc was like a kid let loose with a million new toys. He was soaking in more information than I could ever imagine and said that The Lady would be the fastest thing in the galaxy when he got finished with it. And the safest.

I was happy to hear that second part.

At first I spent about half my time with him learning everything I could about our new upgrades, especially the ones that were in my areas of expertise. The rest of the time I explored Benson's vast ship that he called The R-12. He said it was so new, rushed into service for the big evacuation, that it hadn't been officially named yet.

It turned out Benson was actually the captain of the thing. But it seemed the big ships of his world were run more like huge corporations and he was the Chairman of the Board. Everyone called him "Mr. Chairman" instead of Captain.

Their corporate system sure seemed to work. There had to be a thousand people on board of all ages and sizes. And many had families, including newborn babies.

"Nice thing about space," Benson said one day when I commented on the size of the ship while sitting in his office. "Materials are plentiful in space, power is limitless, and size is easy."

At first, after the second day we were on Benson's ship, there were still four of the original hundreds of the big ships in orbit around the planet. But as the month wore on the other three ships left when it became clear that there just wasn't anything more anyone could do to help the people on the planet. Those people down there were starting over in the bones of their own civilization. But it was clear even after a month that they would make it.

Benson said his ship had been picked to remain in orbit watching them for at least six months. He said it gave him and his crew time to settle in to their new ship.

At the beginning of the second month, I finally decided to flat ask Benson a question that had haunted me since we had been on board.

"Has anyone ever gone looking for the Seeders?"

He laughed. "Just about every day from every planet out there that has figured out space travel."

"And no trace?"

"Not one item left behind by the Seeders. Nothing. They seeded the galaxy with humans and plants and animal life that took over on each Earth-like planet in the Goldilocks zone of each sun and then seemingly vanished."

He tapped what I had come to learn was a form of computer panel on his desk, then scribbled something on a note pad that everyone on the ship seemed to have and leave around like paper. He then handed the pad to me.

"Doctor Jenny Sins, the top scientist in the department focused on the Seeders search. Go talk with her. Tell her I sent you."

"You have an entire department on the ship for this?"

"Every ship does. The question you asked is that important to all of us. We all know how the universe started. That's just science. None of us have a clue how we got here. Or for that matter, why?"

# SIX

I WAS STUNNED when I entered the Seeder Research area of Benson's big ship. There had to be fifty people working in the large room at different stations. I had no idea what they might be doing.

An elderly man with white hair and a formally white lab coat that seemed smeared with some sort of strawberry jam sat at the first desk closest to the entrance. He glanced up and then smiled with a perfect set of teeth. The smile made his face turn into a mass of loose flesh and wrinkles. "You're one of the explorers from this sector, aren't you?"

"I am. Doctor Vardis Fisher," I said, extending my hand. "But everyone just calls me Fisher."

The older man took my hand and shook it, but before he could say anything a woman's voice behind me said, "Well, Doctor Fisher, The Chairman warned me you would be coming."

I turned around to face one of the most beautiful woman I could have ever imagined wearing a white lab coat. And trust me, over the years I had imagined some pretty amazing women in white lab coats. Never met one, but imagined many.

"I'm Doctor Jenny Sins," she said, extending her hand and smiling and melting me down even more. The smile reached her pretty green eyes and made her seem radiant. She had long brown hair pulled back into a ponytail, and seemed to be about my height.

And she was my age as far as I could tell. I was far, far, far from an expert on anything to do with women. Most of them over the years had just ignored me, and to be honest, most of the time I had been too busy with research and work to pay much attention to them in return.

That didn't mean I didn't want a relationship some day. It just had never come to the top of the priority list.

I took her hand and managed to choke out that I was pleased to meet her.

More pleased than she would want to know I imagine.

She held my hand for a few seconds too long while she stared into my eyes, then nodded and let go and turned away. "Let me show you what we do here."

Somehow, following her and her flowing brown hair and white lab coat, I managed to pull myself back together a little. But for a climate-controlled ship, it was sure hot in this Seeder Research lab.

After introducing me to three others, we finally ended up in a large open office built into one wall of the large room. It was clearly her office and from it she could pretty much see the entire room.

She went around and sat behind a large desk that had seemed to have grown out of the floor. She indicated I should take the chair across the desk from her, which I gladly did. Anything at that point to stay talking with her.

She smiled at me again and once again the room got far too hot for normal climate control.

"Well, Doctor Fisher, ask me anything and I'll see what I can tell you."

"It's just Fisher," I said.

She smiled again. "Jenny."

I think I smiled in return and then tried to gather my wits enough to ask something logical about the Seeders.

"So is it clear where they started and where they stopped?"

She nodded and with a few quick taps on a control panel on her desk, an image of the Milky Way Galaxy appeared on the wall to the right.

"They started in this area," she said, and on the map an arrow appeared pointing at some stars on the outer edge of one of the spiral arms of the galaxy.

"They went around the galaxy clockwise, working inward and then outward, and ended in this area."

Again on the image of the galaxy another arrow appeared near the edge of the galaxy.

"Looks like they came into the galaxy," I said, "did their work, and then left."

She nodded. "Sure seems that way."

"How far into the core of the galaxy did they push?"

"Only as far in as human population could stand the radiation levels," she said. "But very few of those civilizations in close have survived for very long. Just too much going on that causes planet-wide destruction."

"Like what we saw below," I said.

"At a vastly more frequent and violent scale," she said. "The closer to the core of this galaxy, the nastier it gets for human life."

"So where do you think they went?"

"Andromeda Galaxy," she said without hesitation.

The map of the galaxy shrunk down to the size of a small dinner plate on the wall allowing the closest neighboring galaxies to be shown. "Looks like they came in from the Large Magellanec Cloud and then headed to Andromeda and all of its satellite galaxies."

I had to admit that it looked that way.

"Anyone go after them?"

"Not that I know of," she said. "Our ships don't have the speed to cross that much distance in a time that would allow us to catch them, even if we were sure where they were headed."

"So how did they do it?" I asked. "Are we all genetically the same? Everyone on every planet?"

"We all started from the same basic gene pool," she said. "And no degradation over time. Every planet's human and animal population started with the same genes, the same diversity, the same numbers. One hundred and forty-four thousand."

There was that number again. I just couldn't seem to make any logical sense out of any of this. There was something very clear I was missing. I knew that feeling. I just had to find what was between the obvious.

"Did they grow our ancestors or something?"

She shrugged. "Lots of theories on that. But what we do know is that it took them six major visits to each planet to accomplish what they did."

"Six?"

She nodded. "On the first visit they shoved some asteroid or something large into every planet that caused a vast extinction event of most of the animal and plant life that was natural to the planet."

"You're kidding?"

She shook her head no. "On the next four visits they covered each planet with new plants at first and then stages of animal life that quickly took over, including early primates."

"How long between that last animal seeding and the introduction of humans?"

"About three thousand years," she said, not even breaking into a smile.

I shook my head. "That is so against all science I know that it's scary."

She nodded. "We are convinced they also seeded historical evidence on every planet of both human, plant, and animal history."

I started to open my mouth to object, then realized where I was sitting and that I was talking to a beautiful human scientist I was very attracted to on a spaceship light years from my home and even farther from her home.

Historical evidence could be planted. Sitting here was very real and hard to discount.

I closed my mouth and just sat there.

"Hard to get a grasp on it all, isn't it?"

I laughed. "I imagine you grew up with this knowledge. I've just been coming to grips with it over the last two years that we have been out here exploring."

"That would be difficult," she said, a look of worry suddenly in her green eyes.

"I'm sure I'll come to terms with it," I said, even though I wasn't so sure. "So how long do you think the Seeders were in this galaxy?"

"Only about fifty thousand years," she said.

That number made no sense to me. "How many planets did they do this to?"

She shrugged. No firm count. "Maybe upward of a million. No one really knows."

"In fifty thousand years? Holy smokes, how many Seeders were there?"

She shrugged. "No one knows that either, but they just finished about five thousand years ago as far as we can tell."

That stunned me even more.

"How long have the races in your sector been in space?"

"About two thousand years," she said. "We just missed them."

"And they didn't leave a trace?" I asked, stunned at what she had told me.

"Just us," she said. "Just us."

# SEVEN

**I SPENT A LARGE AMOUNT** of time over the next few weeks with Jenny, not only learning more about the Seeders, but about her as well.

She was single, had been married once and divorced when she left for space on this rescue mission. She liked my sense of humor and she loved my cooking. Luckily she was also an exercise buff.

She also made a room heat up around me with a single touch of her hand on my arm. I was smitten, of that there was no doubt. And surprisingly, she seemed to like me in return.

During that time Doc had also met a woman named Xin in the engineering department. He had been spending a lot of time with her as well.

She was as tall and as thin as he was. She had bright brown eyes, dark skin, and a set of white teeth that could light up the blackest of nights when she smiled.

At the start of our third month on the big ship, I cooked the two of them dinner on The Lady. Jenny had to work to finish an experiment and get in her exercise, but she made me promise to save her leftovers.

Most of the conversation was about the new drive they were working on together. Even with my science background, I only understood about half of what they were talking about. Xin was as smart as Doc and they clearly spoke on their own level,

sometimes only in half-sentences.

Clearly Doc had been soaking up all the technology of a civilization a thousand years ahead of us and having no problems at all. In fact, it seemed, he was helping advance it.

Somewhere in that conversation I asked Doc about The Lady's new speed. Both Doc and Xin lit up like high school kids getting to talk about their favorite science fair project.

"It seemed that because of The Lady's small size," Doc said, "compared to the huge ships like the one serving as our host, it is possible to go faster. Much faster."

"The size of the large ships takes too much energy to drive it forward through a trans-tunnel conduit," Xin said, smiling at me with those bright teeth.

Doc and Xin had come up with what seemed like a brand new idea of putting a trans-tunnel drive conduit through space inside of an already opened trans-tunnel conduit.

In other words, we would jump like we normally did and then while in transit open up another trans-tunnel conduit inside the original and jump again to increase our speed by some factor.

Doc and Xin were leading a research team on the idea and it seemed likely it could increase speeds to levels I didn't want to much think about. Doc and Xin both said The Chairman was behind them all the way and had been diverting resources to their new department.

"So how fast could we get home?" I asked.

I knew by our old drive that the time was about thirty hours from this place in space. We really didn't have much to go home for at this point except to report into parents that thought we were on a remote research station for a few years and out of touch.

"Six hours," Doc said, smiling.

"Six hours? That's a lot faster than thirty."

Doc smiled. "And if we can figure out a few more details, we might be able to open up many, many trans-tunnel conduits inside each other. If we figure that out we could be home from here in minutes."

"Wow," I said.

Then the two of them went off into the details and I was soon completely lost.

I picked at the peach cobbler I had made for dessert while I half listened and half watched them talk.

Then, suddenly, out of the blue, what had been eating at me since we came aboard finally came to the surface like a dolphin jumping.

"Culture," I said out loud.

Suddenly I could see all the details right there between the pieces of information just as I had found all the energy between matter and dark matter.

Both Doc and Xin stopped talking and looked at me with almost identical puzzled frowns.

"Xin, what planet are you from?"

"We called it Earth like most every other human planet."

I nodded. "And Jenny is from an Earth as well."

"So?" Doc asked. "Common term in all languages."

"Xin, your culture is pretty much capitalistic and democratic, right?"

She nodded, frowning.

"As is most of our planet and all of Jenny's and most of all of the planets we visited."

Now Doc clearly saw where I was heading. And he was frowning.

"How is that similar growth possible," he asked, "when one-hundred-and-forty-four-thousand humans were planted at a caveman level and left to develop over centuries?"

"It's not," I said, "without guidance."

"And who did the guiding?" Xin asked, frowning as well.

"The Seeders," I said, smiling and shaking my head at how really, really simple it was. "They're still here."

"So how come there is no evidence of them anywhere?" Xin asked, her frown covering her entire face. Clearly I was questioning something she didn't like to look at too closely.

"Oh, there is," I said, standing. "We're just not looking in the right places. Sort of like finding energy where there isn't supposed to be any."

I headed out the airlock and into the big hanger. I had to talk with Jenny.

Behind me I heard Doc shout. "Thanks for dinner!"

# EIGHT

I PAGED JENNY once I got off the landing deck and she agreed to meet me in her office.

She showed up only a minute behind me, her hair pulled back and a white towel draped over her shoulder. She was dressed in her exercise clothes, a gray tee-shirt under a dark sweatshirt. She had on sweat pants as well and tennis shoes and still looked like she had a slight sheen of sweat on her neck.

She looked even more stunning that way than in her white lab coat.

"How was your dinner with Doc and Xin?"

"Over my head, mostly," I said, laughing. "Those two are really making some trans-tunnel breakthroughs with speed."

"How much speed?" she asked, suddenly very interested.

"They tell me that it could be factors of thousands of times faster," I said. "Maybe more."

"You're serious?" she asked, leaning forward.

I knew exactly what she was thinking. With that kind of speed, it would be possible to follow the Seeders.

"We can talk to them later," I said. "But they seem sure and The Chairman is backing them with a department full of help."

"Wow," she said softly, leaning back and wiping off her face with the towel.

"But we may not need that kind of speed to actually talk with the Seeders," I said.

Now she put the towel aside and leaned forward. "Too much to drink or just a new theory?"

"Nothing to drink and not so much a theory," I said, smiling at her. "More just observed facts that the Seeders, at least some of them, never left."

She just shook her head. "Then where are they?"

"Right here. We're Seeders. Or we will be when we get a little more advanced."

She shook her head. "That theory has been considered and discarded a number of times over the years."

"No hard evidence, right?" I asked.

She nodded.

Even though your culture has pretty much invented everything needed to be a seeder. And you built ships that held over three million humans on short notice."

Again she nodded, a little more slowly.

"Looking for Seeders seems to have always been an outwardly directed hunt. But all of us looking didn't know where to look. One of my specialties is being able to see things where there isn't supposed to be anything."

"So what evidence have we all missed for a thousand years of studying this?"

I could tell I was on the edge of insulting her, but I kept on.

"Assume the Seeders are humans just like us. Any evidence would be human evidence."

"We've thought of that," she said. "I can give you some of the papers discounting those theories."

"Written by Seeders, of course," I said, smiling at her frown.

Then not giving her a chance to go on, I said, "Just look at the cultures. Now I know math, and I wouldn't want to even try to calculate the chance that every culture on every Earth-like planet would become over centuries of war and fighting democracy and capitalism based. Or that every planet would develop along the same exact lines and at the same speed."

"They were directed and helped," she said. "That's your theory?"

I laughed. "It's the only thing that explains anything I've seen in the last two years. They are still here and still helping and you've met them."

"And just how are you so certain of that?" she asked, clearly upset.

"Because I've met one as well."

I glanced up at the ceiling and said just slightly louder, "Am I correct, Mr. Chairman?"

At that moment Benson shimmered into view, pulled over a chair and sat down next to me.

"What gave me away?" he asked, smiling and ignoring the completely shocked look on Jenny's face. Her mouth was opening and closing and nothing was coming out, sort of how I felt when I first met her.

"A couple of slips," I said. "You knew about me and Doc ahead of time."

He laughed. "I had hoped you had missed that. Not sure what I was thinking on that."

"And the look in your eyes when you looked at the planet below. It was a personal failure to you."

He nodded, his eyes again filled with sadness. "It was. This area of the region is mine to watch and I just couldn't mount a rescue operation fast enough, get the right people on advanced enough planets involved quick enough, get them here fast enough. At least we saved some of those poor souls."

"How long ahead did you know what was going to happen?" I asked, my voice respectful.

"A good three hundred years," he said, his voice soft.

Then he looked directly at me and shook his head. "I knew from the moment you two started building your ship that you would be problems."

I laughed. "Your secret is safe with us. But I'm betting the problem is Doc and Xin, right?"

He nodded. "They are a rare combination and very advanced. This galaxy isn't supposed to develop that kind of speed for another two thousand years. It's about then we'll be needing help in Andromeda."

"Can't use a little help a little earlier?" I asked.

He laughed. "Seems like we're going to get it even if we don't need it, huh? But before then, we could use a little help here in the Milky Way. There are a lot of wars going on right now on the developing planets. And there's only so many of us to go around who stayed behind to help here."

"So how long until you teach us that teleportation trick and the long age secret?"

"You agree to become a Seeder and it might be a lot sooner than later," he said, smiling.

With that he smiled at Jenny's open mouth and stood. "I'll let you explain what just happened to Jenny," he said. "I've got a war to try to stop about fifty light years from here. We can talk tomorrow if you want."

With that he vanished.

I turned to face Jenny and her shocked expression. "I told you that you had met some Seeders."

"But…"

"That's all right," I said, laughing. "Let's go find you a shower and some dinner and we can talk about being recruited by the Seeders."

She let me lead her back toward her apartment without saying a word the entire way. I knew what it was like to have my entire worldview shaken up.

Visiting Earth-like planet after Earth-like planet had done that to me.

Watching Benson and his people save an entire planet of people had done that.

And meeting Jenny had done that to me as well.

She would recover, just as I had done, as soon as she realized that what she had searched for her entire life had always been right there in front of her.

# DEAN WESLEY SMITH

USA Today Bestselling Author

# MONUMENTAL SUMMIT

A SCIENCE FICTION NOVEL OF THE OLD WEST AND TRUE LOVE

USA Today *bestselling writer Dean Wesley Smith returns with a second novel in the world of* Thunder Mountain *from the second issue of* Smith's Monthly.

*Historical interior designer April Buckley and architect Ryan Knott are hired to design and furnish a huge lodge to the year 1900 standards. The two that hire them are Bonnie and Duster Kendal, two of the world's great mathmaticians.*

*Only problem: The lodge can't be built. It can't exist. Yet somehow it does because they built it. And fell in love in the process.*

# MONUMENTAL SUMMIT
## *A Science Fiction Novel of the Old West and True Love*

## PROLOGUE

*July 21, 2015*

**BONNIE AND DUSTER KENDAL** sat at a wooden lunch table on the large wooden deck of the Monumental Summit Lodge in the Central Idaho Mountains.

The July day was almost perfect in temperature, the air dry, with a slight breeze through the pine trees on the hills around the lodge. A thousand feet below them was the Monumental Creek Valley. And on a clear day like this, they could see east over varied mountain ranges all the way to the Montana border. It was very clear where the Middle Fork of the Salmon River cut through the center of the mountains.

On either side of the lodge rose tall rocky peaks that gave away just how high in the mountains this lodge really was. The one to the right was called Thunder Mountain, the peak that gave the entire region its name.

Duster had on his standard long oilcloth dark-brown coat and cowboy hat and Bonnie wore a silk blouse under a light dress jacket over jeans. Duster wore cowboy boots and looked like he had stepped right out of the past, while Bonnie wore comfortable tennis shoes.

Both had dark-brown hair, Duster's short, Bonnie's long and tied back off her face. Looking at them, you would have never known they were two of the greatest mathematicians alive.

All the rooms in the lodge were booked for most of the summer, but that didn't matter to them. They had to see this, so they had left early in the morning and had enjoyed the drive up here on the narrow, one-lane paved road that wound its way through the trees up the side of the mountain.

It had been an easy four-hour drive from Boise in their big Cadillac SUV and got them to the lodge just in time for lunch.

The Forest Service had taken over the lodge back in the 1960s and maintained it in its original condition, as were the instructions of the trust funding the lodge's upkeep.

Duster and Bonnie had taken a tour and were surprised that where possible, all the original 1901 furnishings and decorations had been kept. The lodge and everything around it was now designated a historical monument, sitting as it did on the edge of the largest primitive area in the lower forty-eight states.

Duster looked around and just shook his head as a waiter took another table's lunch order.

"This can't be here," he said.

Bonnie knocked on the top of the wood table. "But it is here and is very real. It seems we have some calculations to run before we dare go any farther."

"Yeah, it does," he said, shaking his head. "Somewhere, we have an assumption wrong."

"Very wrong," Bonnie said, nodding.

They ordered lunch and ate mostly in silence.

After lunch, they took a drive down the one-lane paved road into the Monumental Valley to where one of the now famous Idaho ghost towns existed.

The town had been submerged by a landslide and flood in the spring of 1910, just nine years after the lodge had been built, killing most of the traffic to the lodge.

But the original owners of the lodge and their children had kept the lodge in shape and accepting guests until the Forest Service took over, running it with the money from a trust. Now it was considered one of the great destination resorts of the summer.

Down in the valley, Duster and Bonnie drove along until the main road left the valley and headed up a side valley. There they parked in a large paved lot with a dozen other cars. Signs pointed down the valley to Roosevelt Lake. Through those waters you could still see the foundations of the old mining town.

But Duster and Bonnie had no desire to see it again. They had seen the lake and the ruins once. That was enough.

Instead, they took lawn chairs out of the back of their car and walked over to the bridge over Monumental Creek and sat the chairs in the middle of the bridge.

Then, facing back the way they had came, they both sat and looked up the valley.

There, dominating the top of the summit at the end of the valley was the big Monumental Summit Lodge.

"That's just not possible," Duster said, staring at the lodge.

Bonnie put her hand on her husband's arm.

There was not a thing she could say because as Duster had said, what she was seeing wasn't possible.

But yet there it sat, the fantastic Monumental Lodge that she had come to love so much.

# PART ONE

# CHAPTER ONE

*Two Months Earlier…*
*May 19, 2015*

**APRIL BUCKLEY STOOD** behind the big dark-mahogany captain's desk in the back corner of the ornate parlor room and stared at the two couples as they entered the Sandford House Museum, ambling into the living room from the entrance. They were clearly not from San Francisco.

In fact, she couldn't begin to even venture a guess as to where they were from exactly, and that bothered her a lot. She could usually tell at once the background of a person.

Not these four.

One man, the tallest, wore a cowboy hat and what looked like a light duster made of some sort of oilcloth. He had on cowboy boots and jeans and was nodding to things the tall woman with him was saying as she pointed to various areas of the house.

The woman had long brown hair running down her back and was dressed perfectly for any modern city in a light silk jacket over a tan blouse tucked into jeans, yet it was clear she was with the man in the duster. She was tall, maybe three inches taller than April's five-eight.

April never let her hair down like the woman wore hers except when at home. She liked hers pulled back and sometimes on top of her head. Today, since she was dressed up for the museum opening week, she had her hair up and styled, with an 1890's whalebone comb holding it into place.

The other two arrivals were clearly a couple as well. He wore jeans and a long-sleeved dress shirt with the sleeves rolled up in such a fashion that it looked normal for him. He was clean-shaven and his hair stylishly cut short.

The woman with him also had on jeans and a long-sleeved silk blouse and had her long hair also loose down her back. Both she and the guy she was with wore comfortable and expensive tennis shoes.

And both of them looked completely at ease and were nodding at what the woman with the long brown hair was saying as she pointed to varied aspects of the museum as if giving a tour of the place.

All four of them seemed to be about April's age—in their mid-thirties—and they carried themselves with an air of confidence that April rarely saw except among the super rich. Yet these four did not strike her as super rich. Yet they were here, in the Sandford House Museum together, on a Monday, in the middle of the afternoon.

Middle class didn't do that sort of thing. They didn't seem to be working class either. Not by a long ways.

It really bothered her that she couldn't get a read on these four. It was her job to observe details in both people and environments. She had a master's degree in interior design and before that had finished a doctorate in psychology. She seldom used the psychology training except when working to find out what a client really wanted. Her passion had become historical design and she had written two books on the subject and became one of the top authorities in the country on historical interior renovation and construction.

Finally, as the group got a little closer, on the edge of the parlor, April pretended to study a museum brochure on the desk in front of her as she tried to listen. The big old house held the city sounds of San Francisco away.

What she heard startled her.

The woman said, "The lighting fixture in the front area is very different from the one I had. Mine was a six-post white-china glass with flowers hand-painted on the china. It was designed by Fillan Glass, a small glass shop out of Italy. The room doesn't feel right without it, to be honest."

The man with her and the other two nodded.

April looked up and caught the eye of the woman talking, who smiled at her, knowing full-well she had been overheard.

"How do you know about the old light fixture?" April asked, smiling and moving out from behind the big old desk. "It hasn't existed since 1937. It was taken down and supposedly stored and no one knows exactly where. There are no real pictures of it."

The woman laughed and said, "You wouldn't believe me if I told you."

That got nods from the other three.

"You've done a fantastic job with this place, Doctor Buckley," the woman said, stepping forward and extending her hand. "I'm Bonnie Kendal."

April was too stunned to say anything except "Nice to meet you." No one knew her name or background in here. She didn't even have on a nametag since she didn't officially work as a guide for the museum. She just wanted to see how her hard work in detailing out the museum to 1880's furnishings went over with visitors, so she had decided to hang out for a week or so before heading home to Denver.

The interior design firm she worked for in Denver could go on just fine without her. The three other historical renovation projects they had taken on, one in Denver, two in Kansas City, didn't interest her. It was this project that had really held and challenged her and she was sorry to see it end. She really had no desire to go back into the grind just yet.

Bonnie Kendal turned and indicated the big guy in the cowboy hat. "This is my husband, Duster."

Duster had moved off a few steps to look at the edging on a mirror and just nodded, smiled, and tipped his hat to April as a gentleman would have done a hundred years before.

Bonnie went on, indicating the couple that stood beside her. "These are my two close friends, Professor Dawn Edwards and Professor Madison Rogers."

Now April was really stunned. Two of the greatest western historical writers and researchers of the time had just walked into her museum. They were normally in Idaho. Not down here in San Francisco.

"Wonderful meeting you both," she said, trying to calm her stomach as she shook their hands. "I've read all of your books."

April turned to Professor Edwards and smiled at her. "Your book, Thunder Mountain: The Brutal Magic of America's Last Gold Rush is my all-time favorite historical book. Just stunning work."

Professor Edwards smiled in return and seemed actually embarrassed. "Thank you. That's high praise coming from you, Doctor Buckley. I've read and loved your books on interior design as well."

Now it was her turn to be slightly embarrassed. "April. Just call me April."

"I go by Dawn," Professor Edwards said. Then she turned to Professor Rogers. "Is this going to be the kind of comfort and elegance we are looking for?"

"It's wonderful," he said, nodding and looking around the museum.

"It is wonderful," Bonnie Kendal said, nodding. "I honestly am stunned."

Her husband, Duster, came over as she said that and put his arm around her and hugged her. "Miss it?"

She nodded. "I do. After seeing this, I really do."

April had no idea what Bonnie was talking about. This home had almost been torn down and for decades had been used as a halfway house and before that it had been divided into apartments. She had been the one to restore it to this look now, as close as she could come to how it looked in 1880.

"Would you be interested in a very large job?" Dawn asked before April could ask what Bonnie was talking about.

"Depends on the job, of course," April said.

"A large resort lodge," Dawn said, her dark-brown eyes almost twinkling as she smiled at April. "Built on a high ridge on the edge of the Idaho Wilderness. And furnished completely to the year 1900 standards."

April stared at Dawn for a moment, then glanced at the other three. All seemed to be waiting for her answer.

"How big?" April asked.

"At least twenty guest rooms, a number of them suites, large dining, living, card room, and other areas," Dawn said. "But you will have to spend some time in the Idaho Central Mountains on the project."

"I love hiking," April said, smiling.

And she did. With a passion that few others could understand. In the six months she had been out here, almost every spare moment had been up around Lake Tahoe. And when home in Denver, she spent a lot of time up on the trails along the Front Range.

In fact, her love of hiking always seemed to get between her and any man she met. They all pretended to like it for a short time, then they would try to get her to stay in the city when all she wanted to do was escape to the beautiful trails and primitive nature of the mountains.

She had no doubt she had been born just about a hundred years too late for what she really loved.

"We had heard that you loved the mountains," Duster said.

Again April felt surprised. These four clearly knew a lot about her when the walked in the door.

"You like the idea of this monster-sized project?" Dawn asked. "We could really, really use your help."

"It would all be authentic?" April asked, working to keep her business side in control.

"Every detail," Dawn said.

The other three nodded.

"A project of that size will cost a fortune," April said, now worried about these four having the money.

"Not an issue," Duster said with a shrug.

April took a deep breath to try to calm the excitement building inside her. "A large resort to historical 1900 standards in the Idaho Mountains?"

Dawn nodded.

"It sounds like my dream job," April said, doing her best to not get too excited at the idea.

"It will seem like a dream at times," Dawn said. "I can promise you that."

"And you'll have time to write as well," Professor Rogers said, smiling and hitting her in one detail she always worried about.

Dawn nodded.

"I'll need to clear it with my boss," she said. "But it sounds like a perfect challenge for me."

"No need to clear it with your boss," Duster said and Bonnie laughed.

"I don't understand?" April said, suddenly very worried that this was all some sort of stupid joke.

Duster stepped forward and shook her hand. "You just got a very large raise, Doctor Buckley. I bought the design firm that you work for two days ago. I figured we'd need all hands in your firm for this project. Glad you want to be on board because you're the reason I bought it."

April shook Duster's hand, her mouth opening and closing.

She had no idea what to say.

# CHAPTER TWO

*May 21, 2015*

**RYAN KNOTT SAT** in the passenger seat of the big, white Cadillac SUV as Duster Kendal took it through a small streambed that cut the hairpin turn down the middle. Ryan liked the car because it was more than big enough for his six-foot frame and long legs. And even on rough roads, it seemed to have a really smooth ride.

The entire back of the car was full of gear. Ryan had been told to only bring a backpack with his clothes and personal items. Duster would furnish the rest.

They were headed up to a place called Monumental Summit on a road that didn't seem much more than a wagon track. So far Duster had been forced to back the big SUV up twice to make a corner as they worked their way up the hillside in the deep forest. This corner might turn out to be another one from what Ryan could tell.

It was the middle of May and snow still remained in piles along the road and under the trees. And the small streams running over the road were still running pretty good with snow melt. There was little doubt the season up here was very short.

They had left Boise, Idaho, five hours ago, stopping in Cascade for a late breakfast after just over an hour, then stopping in a small town in a remote mountain valley called Yellow Pine for lunch in an old bar that looked like it had been in existence since the gold rush days in the region.

As they left the old bar, Ryan had asked Duster about that and Duster had said the bar had been there from the time of the Roosevelt gold rush in 1902.

"Doesn't look much different at all, actually," Duster said.

Ryan just assumed that Duster had seen old pictures of the place. He had learned quickly how good at research and preparation Duster and Bonnie and the two professors were.

From Yellow Pine, the roads had turned just flat ugly and had remained that way as they wound their way through an old mining ghost town called Stibnite and then up the hill. Even the Cadillac's smooth ride couldn't smooth most of the road bumps out.

Their destination, Monumental Summit, was on the border of the Idaho Primitive Area that contained The River of No Return.

Duster again had to back up the big SUV to make it around the sharp turn, then managed to get up to almost twenty miles per hour before coming up on another turn.

Ryan desperately wanted to ask how much farther they had to go, but he didn't want to sound like he wasn't enjoying the trip. Actually, he was.

He loved this area of his home state and had read all the books studying the area's history and geological formations. He had taken raft trips down both the Middle Fork of the Salmon and the Main Salmon River, called The River of No Return.

And twice, with two different girlfriends, he had tried to hike into parts of this area. Both times his girlfriend of the moment had freaked out at the isolation and left him a short time after returning to civilization.

So now, being paid to take a trip to the edge of the big primitive area was a joy for him. If he didn't have to make a living, he would be up here in these mountains all summer.

But since he was an architect, his main building season was in the summer in Idaho. So that limited his trips in here.

But now Duster, who had been a friend back in college down at Stanford, had come to him to design a huge lodge out of natural materials on the top of an 8,000 foot ridgeline on the edge of the Idaho Primitive Area.

It sounded like a challenge and Ryan loved challenges.

Duster now seemed different than he was back in college. Older, sure, but more than the ten years that had passed. And he seemed calmer and far more mature than the math geek that Ryan had known. Duster had always been the smartest person Ryan had ever met, but now Duster seemed to also be the calmest.

And the richest.

Ryan had no idea where Duster got all his money and hadn't asked.

Duster had offered Ryan more money than Ryan could ever imagine to design the lodge. And to spend the summer with Duster and the rest working on the lodge to get it started.

Ryan had done some research on the site Duster was talking about and he knew, without a doubt, that this entire project was a fool's errand. The government owned the land and no amount of money or influence was going to get it into private hands.

Or allow any kind of construction on it.

But Duster had assured him that the project was very real.

And Duster's money had been real. So that was enough for Ryan for take on the fun project, even if it never got beyond the planning stages. That wasn't unusual in his business.

He had also gotten to meet Duster's wonderful wife, Bonnie, and the two professor friends who would be working on the project as well. He knew both of the professors by reputation and from their many books on the history of the west.

He had been honored to meet them both and they seemed very nice and were happy to meet him as well.

They would be coming up tomorrow with an interior designer from Denver they had hired. An April Buckley. He also knew her by reputation as one of the top historical designers in the country. He knew nothing else besides that about her and until now hadn't had the privilege to work on a project with her.

Clearly Duster was hiring some top talent on this crazy lodge idea. Even if the lodge never got built, it would be fun designing it. Especially with the challenge Duster had given him of only using the natural stone and trees from the area.

Ryan liked challenges.

And he liked working with good people like Duster and Bonnie and the two professors.

Duster got the big Cadillac up to almost thirty along the single-lane dirt road. The trees seemed to flash past the window.

Ahead Ryan could see some light through the trees and clearly it seemed they were almost to their destination.

A few more corners and the road came out onto a flat, forested area between two high ridges on either side. It was called a "saddle" because it was the low area between two higher mountain areas.

This one didn't seem to be much more than a hundred paces across.

Duster pulled off the road and shut off the engine.

"We're here."

With that, Duster put on his cowboy hat and slid into his oilcloth duster as he climbed out of the car.

Ryan climbed out on the other side and was instantly struck by the fantastic fresh air, slightly crisp from the coolness of the May day, with a fresh smell of new grass and pine trees.

The engine of the big car pinged a little, but otherwise there was no sound except for a faint breeze through the pines.

Ryan was wearing only a light dress shirt with rolled-up sleeves and jeans and tennis shoes. He reached back inside the car for his light cloth jacket and slipped it on against the chill of the crisp air.

"Take a look at this," Duster said, heading toward one side of the ridgeline.

As Ryan followed Duster through widely-spaced pines, the view of what seemed like a thousand miles of mountains and valleys sudden spread out below him. To his right was a high peak and another to his left, but the view in front of him and to all sides of the peaks caught him by surprise.

Duster stopped on the edge where it seemed the ridge just dove straight down a thousand feet.

Ryan had seen a lot of mountain vistas, but never one like this.

He just kept staring at it, shaking his head.

Duster pointed to the peak to their right that climbed about a thousand feet higher than they were. "That's Thunder Mountain, the peak that this entire area is named after."

Ryan just nodded.

"Monumental Creek drainage," Duster said, pointing down.

"The town that's under water is down there, right?" Ryan asked.

"Roosevelt," Duster said, nodding. "Now called Lake Roosevelt. About a thousand feet downhill and five miles in that direction is the lake. We can take a trip down there in a day or so if you are interested."

"I am," Ryan said. "I read Professor Edward's book about it, would love to see it."

The two stood there for a moment in silence, just staring out over the mountains.

Ryan knew exactly where he was at now.

Monumental Creek drained into Big Creek, which drained into the Salmon River. He could follow the line of the valley down to the big river where he had rafted.

He could almost visualize a map over what he was seeing. It was all so clear.

"How about this for a view from a lodge?" Duster asked.

"It would be stunning," Ryan said. He stepped back from the edge and looked around the fairly flat ridgeline. Through the thin pines he could see about a hundred yards to his right, but to his left on the other side of the road, the ridge just cut up dramatically toward the peak of Thunder Mountain.

"Is this the site?"

Duster laughed. "This is it. Come on, I'll walk you around it."

They went through the trees to the right, away from the road and along the edge of the cliff dropping down into the valley below.

Suddenly the ridgeline climbed, with some scrub trees, but almost all rock.

At that point the ridgeline itself was not more than thirty paces wide.

They moved through the trees, avoiding snowdrifts that were still remaining from the winter to the other side of the ridge.

Ryan could see that the view of that side was just as spectacular looking out over a different part of the Idaho Central Mountains. The hill didn't drop off as fast, but fast enough to not make anything beyond the edge worthwhile except secondary buildings.

They then worked their way back toward the road.

From what Ryan could figure, his task was to design a huge rugged lodge made out of stone and large logs on what felt like basically the top of the world, on an area about as big as three quarters of a football field.

"Well, what do you think?" Duster asked as they got back to the big SUV.

"It can be done," Ryan said. "A real challenge."

Duster laughed and started unloading camping gear. "I expected you to tell me it would be impossible."

Almost impossible, he started to say, then didn't. He really wanted the challenge of the design. "Nope, not completely impossible, but almost."

Ryan knew that the design of this lodge would be his biggest challenge ever. And he would make the lodge the most spectacular place to match the spectacular views.

Too bad it would never be built.

# CHAPTER THREE

*May 22, 2015*

**BY THE TIME BONNIE** pulled the big van up on the ridge beside a Cadillac SUV and shut off the engine, April was more excited than she had ever remembered being.

She had hiked a lot of mountains in Colorado and Nevada, but she had never seen anything as rugged and beautiful as these Central Idaho Mountains. And the road up the side of this mountain had taken them almost an hour with numbers of places where Bonnie had been forced to stop and back up to make a tight corner.

April had been in the passenger seat from the time Bonnie and Dawn and Madison had picked her up at her hotel near the Boise airport just after six in the morning. She had flown in the night before and gotten a good night's sleep as Bonnie had told her to do.

She was rested and excited to see an area of the country she knew little about beyond books.

For the first hour or so of the drive, Bonnie and April just sat, not really talking. In the back seats, Dawn and Madison were sound asleep, sort of leaning against each other as much as their seat belts would allow.

They were clearly a very cute couple and loved each other dearly. April admired that and hoped that some day she would find someone who could share her likes and dislikes as well.

So far, her three major relationships had led to nothing but relief when they were finally over.

On both sides.

She remained friends with all three men, and all three were now happily married to very nice women.

April had never been up the road out of Boise into Central Idaho and she was surprised it was only two lanes. At one point, where the pavement got so narrow between a river on one side and a rock cliff on the other, she couldn't imagine meeting a truck coming at her on that stretch.

She said something about that to Bonnie who laughed. "This is the only major north-south highway in the state. This is as good as it gets."

"Oh, joy," was all April said, which made Bonnie laugh.

At a small town called Cascade, they stopped for breakfast and Dawn and Madison began to wake up, with the help of some greasy bacon and eggs and two cups of coffee each.

April just felt excited about the entire adventure.

And she flat loved the mountains around them.

For the rest of the trip they talked about the history of Idaho and the west. They had a lunch at an old bar in a tiny town called Yellow Pine where history just kept staring at April from every direction.

At one point, April asked Bonnie how she had known about that light fixture in the museum. Again Bonnie had only laughed and said, "Right now you wouldn't believe me. But we'll show you. Honest."

There were other offhanded comments that the three of them made at times about something from history that made April just frown. But she was so amazed at the beauty she was seeing around her on the mountain roads, she just let it all go by, filed in her mind as questions to be asked about and answered later.

"We're here," Bonnie said after almost a two-hour drive from the lunch in Yellow Pine, up some of the roughest single-lane roads April had ever been on. Bonnie turned off the big van and stretched. "Just about five hours from Boise. Not bad."

"Not bad at all," Madison said from the back as he slid his door open.

April climbed out into the brisk afternoon air, stretching as she went. She had enjoyed the ride up here, but it had still been tense and rough.

The sun was almost directly overhead, but there was snow all around under the trees. The air smelled of pine trees and not much else.

In a wide area on the ridge, there were four tents set up, scattered around a campfire ring and a stove set up beside the ring. All four tents looked very modern and large, like small bedrooms.

When April hiked on her own or with friends, she either slept out under the stars or in a very small lightweight tent barely big enough for her to crawl into.

Those four tents you could stand upright in. The value of car camping, of that there was no doubt. She wouldn't mind.

It seemed that nothing Bonnie and Duster did was second class.

April stretched again, looking around at the incredible forest and just letting the crisp, clean mountain air fill her lungs and clear her head.

"Take a look at this," Bonnie said to April as Madison and Dawn went around to the back of the van to unload supplies.

She led April through some of the trees and to the edge of a cliff.

Spread out in front of her was the most spectacular view April had ever seen, and she had seen some amazing views in her years of hiking mountains on the Rockies front line.

On this clear May day, she felt like she could see hundreds of miles. And more than likely could.

"The town that Dawn wrote about in her book is down in this valley below us," Bonnie said.

"Can we go down to it after we're done here?"

She couldn't believe how excited she was at the idea, even though she knew she would only see a small lake and some ruins. It was the idea that the town had been destroyed and then forgotten by history. She wanted to be one of the few to actually see the site.

"I can't imagine how we won't," Bonnie said, smiling.

"So where is the lodge site from here?" April asked.

"You are standing on it," Bonnie said.

"Oh," was all April could manage.

Stunned didn't begin to describe how she felt. She had been involved with a lot of building projects, but never one on such a fantastic location.

"Come on," Bonnie said, turning away from the spectacular view. "Let's get your stuff in your tent and a fire started. I imagine Duster and Ryan are exploring along the ridge looking for materials to use to build the place."

With one more look over the vista of mountains and valleys, April turned and followed Bonnie back to the van to help unload her stuff and the supplies.

The tent Bonnie said was hers was amazing. It really was the size of a small bedroom, with a small heater beside the raised bed. And sheets and two quilts on the bed. Plus a few bottles of water near the top of the bed.

Stunning, just stunning comfort for being so far into the middle of nowhere. In fact, they hadn't seen another person since leaving Yellow Pine.

When she came out of the tent, Bonnie pointed her toward a group of trees about fifty feet away. "Duster dug a latrine over there. Shovel and paper are beside it."

April used the latrine, then came back to see what she could do to help. But Dawn and Madison and Bonnie were so good at everything and moved so efficiently, there was nothing she could help with at all as they got the fire going and started some water boiling and set up two tables to work on to prepare dinner.

"You three have certainly done your time camping," April said at one point after standing and watching them for a few minutes.

"It becomes a way of life," Dawn said to her, smiling.

"That it does," Madison said.

After a short time, April went back into her tent to dig out a sweater and light jacket from her pack. Even though it still was early afternoon, the air had a bite to it.

As she slipped into the jacket, she heard Duster's voice outside, along with another man's deep voice. That had to be Ryan, the architect's voice, since he was the only other one on this trip today.

She stepped out of the tent and looked up at Duster and another man dropping a few rocks beside the campfire.

She thought the view of the valleys had taken her breath away. No one had warned her that the architect on this project was the best-looking man she could remember seeing.

Ever.

She stopped cold and tried to just breathe the crisp mountain air as she watched him talk with Duster and Madison, laughing about something, his back slightly to her.

He was about six feet tall, with a thin runner's body and short brown hair. He looked to be about her age, in his middle thirties. He had on a light jacket and jeans and tennis shoes.

And he seemed perfectly at home with the mountains, like he belonged in them.

"Ah, April," Bonnie said, seeing her standing just outside her tent. "Come and meet Ryan."

April noticed that both Dawn and Madison stopped their work on dinner to look up.

Bonnie was smiling.

April managed to get her feet moving and not stumble over the rough forest floor, moving toward the fire.

Ryan, at that moment, turned around and looked into her eyes.

Damn.

Once again her breath was gone.

How could one man be so damned good-looking?

She hadn't felt like this about meeting someone since high school. What the heck was going on?

Ryan was just staring at her, a slightly shocked expression on his face, his deep hazel eyes wide.

Looking at him directly, she could see how perfectly his face was shaped and his strong chin.

She managed to take the last few steps and extend her hand. "Nice meeting you, Ryan."

He took her hand and the feeling felt wonderful to her.

She really, really needed to get it together or she was going to make a complete fool of herself very shortly.

"Nice meeting you as well," he said.

His voice was deep and slightly husky.

Oh, crap, she was in trouble. A perfect body, a solid chin, a deep voice. She was in deep trouble.

They stood like that for clearly a moment too long, but she didn't care. She didn't want to look away from him.

And she sure didn't want to let go of his hand.

At least not for a long time.

"Okay," Bonnie said, "tell us what you found, guys."

Ryan let go of her hand with a slight nod and slight smile and turned away.

April moved over beside where Bonnie stood working at a table chopping some carrots.

"A real looker, isn't he?" Bonnie whispered to April.

"Just looking isn't half of what I was thinking," April whispered back to Bonnie.

And Bonnie burst out laughing.

April worked to help Bonnie where she could and watch Ryan and Duster explain about the rocks up the ridge to the left that could be used for the foundation and fireplaces. And how down the hill on the side they came up there was enough lumber that could be hauled back up the hill to build the lodge.

Then suddenly, as they talked about construction, one obvious fact dawned on April that she hadn't put together on the way up here on that rough, long road.

Every bit of furniture and fixtures and carpet and wall coverings were going to have to be hauled up that road or flown in.

An entire lodge's worth.

# CHAPTER FOUR

*May 22, 2015*

**RYAN MANAGED TO KEEP** his mind as much as possible on explaining to everyone about how the materials were all close enough to build the lodge with enough manpower.

But every so often he would look up at April and he would have a hard time catching his breath. He hadn't been so instantly attracted to a woman since back in high school. And meeting her made him feel like he was seventeen again. Luckily, he had managed to not stammer and he actually had let go of her hand when it was appropriate, even though he hadn't wanted to.

April looked to be a few inches shorter than he was and clearly knew her away around mountain camping. She had on a light jacket over a sweater and jeans. Her long brown hair was pulled back and tied. Her face was a sort of classic beauty, with high cheekbones and a wide smile and white teeth.

And she laughed easily. He loved the sound of her laugh.

He had no idea if she was married or not, but she wasn't wearing any rings.

Or if she was even interested in men.

She had seemed to be interested in him, but he had read women's reactions wrong before.

Last night he and Duster had set up the tents and the camp and Duster had explained a little about April while they ate. She was a specialist in historical interior design and worked out of Denver. But past telling him how good she was in her field, Duster had said little else about her.

And Ryan had no idea how much she knew about him. More than likely, as little as he knew about her.

This was going to get interesting, of that he had no doubt.

Everything about this project was interesting.

Madison brought out six lawn chairs and put them at a safe distance back around the fire and then set a television tray in front of each one for dinner. And he was the one who seemed to be directing all the cooking.

"Wow," April said, looking at the set-up. "Fancy camping. I'm more used to sitting on rocks and eating out of the pan."

"Actually," Dawn said, smiling at her. "So are we, but when you get the chance to go first class, why not?"

Ryan had nothing at all he could say to argue with that. But he loved the fact that April said she was used to regular camping.

The later afternoon air had gotten colder and Ryan was glad for his jacket.

Everyone now had on sweaters and light coats. And, of course, Duster still had on his long coat and cowboy hat.

As the sun had dropped, Duster had sat up lanterns around their camp, hanging from trees. Those lanterns and the low-level orange light from the fire made it seem almost like the campsite was inside, even though the sun was down behind Thunder Mountain peak and the shadows of the early evening were long.

There was almost no wind in the trees overhead, which Ryan guessed wasn't normally the case for this lower area in the ridgeline. From the looks of some of the trees and plants growing along the rocks, the wind could howl over this mountain. He would have to make sure that worked into his designs.

Bonnie and Dawn helped Madison fix the meal and served it to all of them. Ryan made a mental note to ask Madison where he had learned to cook later.

April sat on Ryan's left, Bonnie and Duster on the other side of her, and then Dawn and Madison, with Madison directly beside Ryan.

Everyone's face was clear in the lamplight and yellow light from the flames. And the smoke was going straight up, so it just made the area feel more comfortable. Ryan loved the smell of a campfire and the occasional crack of a burning log.

Camping in the mountains didn't get any better than this. And the weather was perfect as well.

Ryan felt slightly uneasy next to April, again like a date in high school, eating for the first time in front of a girl. But as he dug into the fantastic-tasting steak and salad with light vinaigrette dressing, the food made him forget about his nervousness.

Beside him, April was clearly enjoying her food as well.

After a short time, Duster looked over at Bonnie, who nodded.

"All right, we have some stuff to talk about."

Ryan noticed that Dawn and Madison just nodded and kept their gazes on their food. Ryan had a hunch that what was coming next was important.

Duster then, between bites, gave an introduction of himself and Bonnie, telling Ryan and April where they met in college and how many degrees in advanced math they both had.

Ryan was impressed. He only knew of the first graduate degree.

"In fact," Duster said, "Ryan and I met in college and have been in touch at times ever since."

"We have," Ryan said. "But I sure don't remember you telling me how you got so rich."

Everyone laughed and Duster said, "That will become very clear in time."

Then Duster turned to look at Ryan. "You know Bonnie and I love history, right?"

"Clearly," Ryan said.

"So we are going to have to ask both of you to trust the four of us a little bit," Duster said.

"Try a great deal," Madison said, laughing.

"All right, a great deal," Duster said. "We have some secrets to tell you."

Ryan sort of sat back in his chair. "Secret? Not illegal?"

"Nothing at all illegal," Duster said and the other three nodded. "That I promise."

"Is the project still building a big lodge here?" April asked.

"It is," Duster said. "Everything we have talked about has been accurate. And we really, really need both of you to help. We just haven't told you the entire scope of the project yet."

"I'm not following," Ryan said, clearly getting worried. Luckily he had finished most of his great meal because he didn't feel like eating much of anything at the moment. This felt like some very bad news was right around the corner.

Duster looked directly at him. "I told you the location of the lodge. About this ridge a number of days ago. Right?"

Ryan nodded.

"And knowing you, you researched this and came to the conclusion that nothing would allow us to get this property for such a project. For any project, actually."

Ryan nodded, relieved that Duster understood that as well. "Not a chance in hell."

"But yet I am spending a large amount of money for you to design and help us build a huge lodge on this site," Duster said. And he looked at April. "And I want you to furnish it with the best furniture and carpets and interiors. Right?"

Ryan nodded and out of the corner of his eye he saw April nod as well.

"So we can't own the property," Duster said, "but yet I want you to build a lodge right here. So I am crazy, right?"

"Starting to sound that way," Ryan said, smiling at Duster.

Madison laughed. "I still think I've gone crazy at times myself with all this."

"Now remember," Duster said, "that Bonnie and I have more degrees in higher math than I want to think about, or try to remember."

"We aren't that old," Bonnie said. Then she laughed. "Wait, we really are that old. Sort of."

> *"And knowing you, you researched this and came to the conclusion that nothing would allow us to get this property for such a project. For any project, actually."*

Duster smiled at his wife. "I still love you, old woman."

Bonnie smiled at Duster. "Marshal, you will pay for that later."

Duster laughed and turned back to face Ryan and April. Ryan had no idea why Bonnie had called Duster Marshal. He would ask about that later as well.

"You will not believe what I am about to say," Duster said, "but we want to build the lodge on this site in the year 1900."

Ryan just looked as his old friend and shook his head.

Beside him April had pushed her plate away on the television tray and was looking like she might make a bolt out of here. If she did, Ryan would go with her.

Dawn smiled. "Look, April, you said you liked my book about the history of that town down there."

April nodded.

"I could make it as real as you said because I wrote that book over a very difficult winter of 1902 living in that town."

Now April really looked like she was about to take off running. And Ryan felt like he might beat her to the first step.

"Duster's family has an old gold mine that broke into a very special crystal cave," Bonnie said. "We discovered that the cave was very, very special, a place where all branches of time exist. And using our math degrees, we worked out a way to travel back into the past in different timelines, different alternate realities, and live."

"Explain alternate reality," April said, her voice cold and low and clearly angry.

"If you had decided to not come up here with us," Bonnie said, "that would have started another alternate reality, a timeline or reality where you came along, one where you didn't. Every time a person makes a decision it starts a new reality splitting from that decision point."

Ryan knew and understood the idea of alternate realities. "Not sure I believe alternate realities can exist because that would mean there would be millions of constantly splitting timelines."

"More like unlimited numbers," Duster said. "Some lines fold back into each other when nothing changes, but many, like your decision to come up here or not, create splits in the millions and millions of universes you exist in."

Ryan just sort of nodded. Duster had been the smartest man he had ever known. If anyone could figure out what he was suggesting, it would be Duster.

"So what does this have to do with building a lodge?" April asked. "If we had gone back and built it, wouldn't the remains still be here?"

"In another timeline, yes," Duster said, nodding. "But our history in this timeline is set. So there are no lodge remains here in this timeline. We cannot travel back in this timeline. We can only go back in alternate timelines."

"This is the strangest campfire story I have ever heard," April said, shaking her head.

"Neither Madison or I believed it either last summer," Dawn said. "Bonnie and Duster had been our patrons for our research, helping us with information from the past that we needed. I just believed they were great fans of the past until they showed us and brought us here."

"We camped right here for the first time," Madison said, pointing to the ground, "in June of 1902. And we lived the summer in the boom-town of Roosevelt. Since that first trip here, we have lived almost eighty years in that town down there, from 1901 to 1910, in different timelines."

"We have been back here seven times," Dawn said, "and we love it here. More every time. Which is why we want to build this lodge."

Now Ryan just looked at them, shaking his head.

"When you travel into another timeline," Duster said, "you are only gone from this timeline for two minutes and fifteen seconds. That's why in one year they could travel and live so many years."

"You can live out entire lives in the past," Bonnie said, "over and over in various timelines. And only age just over two minutes when you come back here."

"My head is spinning," Ryan said, trying to contain some logical thoughts, but nothing was coming.

"You know I don't believe a word of this," April said.

"I know," Bonnie said. "But I told you that you wouldn't when you asked me about that light fixture."

"The museum?" April asked, her voice now soft.

Ryan looked at April directly, again stunned at how beautiful she looked in the light from the lamps and the flickering orange flame.

"That is always my home when I return to San Francisco," Bonnie said. "I always buy it from the Concords in 1891."

"The Concords sold it to the Frank family in 1891," April said.

Bonnie nodded. "In this timeline."

April started to open her mouth, then shut it and just shook her head.

"However, I do know where that fixture is stored in this timeline," Bonnie said, smiling at April. "When we get off the hill, I'll give you the address and someone from the museum can go buy it. The owners have no idea what they have, so it won't sell for much. Or I can buy it and donate it in your name if you like."

"Thank you," April said.

Ryan could tell that the response from April was only to stop that part of the conversation.

"So why are you telling us all this up here?" Ryan asked. "Is this mine close by?"

"Oh, heavens no," Bonnie said.

"It was Madison and my idea to tell you here," Dawn said. "When Bonnie and Duster first took us to the mine last summer, we both were scared to death and sort of feeling like we had been kidnapped. And even though they demonstrated it all, it took a long time to sink in."

"A real long time," Madison said, nodding. "We didn't want to do that to you."

"So we figured," Dawn said, "that even if neither of you wanted to help in the construction in 1900, we could still hire you now, tell you the truth, and design the hotel now. Then with your plans, Ryan, and April's furnishing selections, we can go build and furnish the hotel ourselves in any timeline we want, using both your plans."

Bonnie and Duster were both nodding to that.

"So we won't have to travel in time, if that's actually all you want us to do?" April asked.

"Nope," Dawn said. "We just want you to pick and lay out the furnishings

for each room that Ryan designs. And it all needs to be from furniture you know we can buy in 1900."

"So this is a here-and-now job?" Ryan asked, suddenly feeling relieved.

"Completely," Bonnie said, "unless you want to travel with us. But you can decide that at any point in the future."

Madison smiled. "We just need you both to design a hotel we can build right here, on this site, and furnish it as if it was built in 1900. That's the job."

"That I can do," Ryan said. "But you still didn't answer why you told us this story you all four knew we would never believe?"

"Because all four of us hate lying to anyone," Bonnie said.

The other three nodded to that.

"I wanted you to design this because I like your work," Duster said to Ryan, "I actually had them considering not telling you for fear you would run."

"Can't say I didn't think about running," Ryan said.

"I'm still thinking about it," April said.

Then she looked at Madison. "But if you promise me a breakfast as good as this dinner, I might stay until morning."

"Deal," Madison said, smiling.

# CHAPTER FIVE

*May 22, 2015*

**APRIL SAT AND LISTENED** to more of the conversation around the campfire, working to just keep her nerves level as she listened. Bonnie told them about her background and how she and Duster met in school. And then both Dawn and Madison told them their backgrounds.

Then April helped Bonnie and Madison with the dishes, drying as Madison washed.

She just let the entire time-travel silliness lay and they talked about normal stuff, including which book Madison was working on next.

Then Bonnie, as they were almost done, asked a very simple question of April.

"Did you ever find the secret basement entrance in the Sandford House?"

April glanced at Bonnie, so stunned she didn't know what to say.

"It's a wooden panel in the parlor, near the bookcase on the north side," Bonnie said, sealing up the remains of the salad and packing it into a cooler. "You have to push it exactly right at the top left corner and on the trim across the right side for it to slide open and show you the staircase."

April knew her mouth was open, but she couldn't force herself to close it. No one could know about that basement. It had not been on the plans and she had found it by accident one Saturday when she was there by herself and she had told no one. Not even the contractor, because it would have delayed the opening of the museum. Especially considering what she found down there in that small, damp basement.

Bonnie glanced at April, then smiled. "I see you found it. But didn't tell anyone because of the skeleton on the old couch?"

"There is just no way you could have known," April said, turning and staring at Bonnie.

"I have lived lifetimes in that house, remember?"

April just shook her head. That made no sense and she just couldn't let herself believe it.

"The skeleton is a guy by the name of Carson Lofts. In this timeline, he died of natural causes down there in 1938, during the Depression. He drank himself to death, but the house in this timeline was being remodeled into apartments and no one noticed, or if they did, they didn't report it."

"Impossible to believe, isn't it?" Madison said.

"Considering how many other logical explanations there are," April said, "Yes, traveling in time is hard to believe."

"We really don't expect you to," Bonnie said, smiling. "We just hope you'll design us the interior of the most beautiful lodge ever built in 1900."

"That I can do," April said, nodding.

She pushed the image of that skeleton in that basement out of her mind. And she didn't want to think about how Bonnie could have known about it.

When the dishes were finished, she went over to where Ryan was still sitting staring into the fire, clearly thinking.

He was so damned good-looking there in the light from the lanterns and the yellow flickering firelight, she almost said nothing and just sat beside him, letting herself enjoy the cool air of the mountains around a campfire. But he was in this with her and she needed to talk with him.

"Take a walk with me?" she asked him, managing to keep her voice level.

He glanced up, shocked, then smiled and stood, "I would be glad to. But if we're going to make a run for it, we'll need heavier coats."

Duster laughed, and April found herself smiling.

"Just a walk along the road," she said.

Ryan handed her a small LED flashlight and she put it in her jacket pocket. He took another and put it in his pocket, then he said to Duster, "Mind if I take an electric lantern?"

"Be my guest," Duster said.

April watched as Ryan took the lamp hanging on a tree farthest from the camp and turned it down so it was only a faint light, then said, "Lead the way."

She made her way the short distance to the cars and turned down the road the way they had come up. She knew that way was fairly flat for a short distance, far enough for a comfortable walk.

She had noticed earlier that the road going the other way looked really steep as it dropped into the Monumental Creek drainage. She was up for a leisurely walk, not a climb.

They walked slowly along the rough road, until the light from the camp behind them was only a glow in the tops of the trees and the lantern in Ryan's hand cast a soft-white glow over everything. The shadows in the forest on both sides of the road seemed to almost dance with his steps and the swaying of the light.

She could feel him beside her, and she was afraid to look at him at the moment for fear of being distracted. She was amazingly attracted to him and she had no doubt that would continue. But right now she needed to get her mind around all this craziness.

"So, what do you think?" she asked after a few minutes of silent walking.

"If it wasn't Duster and two of the most respected historians in the country," Ryan said, "I would think we had fallen in with four complete nut cases and should just keep on walking."

"I don't know Duster," April said. "But Bonnie sure knew things about that mansion in San Francisco I was working on that she shouldn't or couldn't have known."

"Don't forget the two major historians," Ryan said.

She nodded in agreement to that. Madison and Dawn were two of the most respected professors in western history in the country. Their books were hailed for their authenticity. They were far, far from nut cases.

"I'm so confused," she said.

"And that makes two of us," Ryan said.

She was very glad he said that, because she was going to feel horrid if she was the only one having troubles with this thing.

"Here's what I am thinking," Ryan said. "Duster has hired me for a summer to design this huge lodge out of the natural materials up here on this ridge. He has paid me more money than I care to think about to do that. With bonus payments if I finish the design within two months."

April nodded. "I also am getting paid a huge amount. In fact, Duster bought the design firm I worked for and said if he and Bonnie were satisfied with my work on the interior of the lodge, as a bonus he would give me the design firm when the project was finished."

"So basically," Ryan said, "we can consider this a job where we are working for eccentrics. And just ignore all the time-travel craziness for now."

April knew she could do that. In her line of remodeling old buildings, it was rare when a client wasn't an eccentric weirdo in one fashion or another.

"I can do that," she said after a moment. "Can you?"

"I've worked with far crazier people than those four," Ryan said, laughing.

She really liked his laugh and it sounded wonderful and almost relaxing echoing in the dark trees around them.

They reached a point where the road sloped down dramatically and both of them stopped.

She turned to look into his eyes. The light made them glow and she laughed.

"What?" he asked. "I got lettuce in my teeth?"

"Your eyes are glowing in this light," she said, shaking her head and laughing again.

"So are yours," he said, smiling at her. "And has anyone ever told you that you have a wonderful laugh."

She was sure she blushed like a silly schoolgirl. "Thanks."

They stood there on the road for a moment. She had to know if Ryan was available and at this age, playing games to find out was just annoying.

"I have a couple questions to ask you, since we will be working closely on this project."

"Fire away," he said.

She took a deep breath of the cold night air. "Do you have a girlfriend, wife, or married, or living in a committed relationship?"

He smiled. "No girlfriend, but I've had a number over the years, but I was always too busy for them. And they hated camping with me."

Her heart actually skipped a beat and she made herself take another deep breath.

"Sorry, just needed to ask," she said.

"Same question back at you," he said. "Do you have a boyfriend, husband, or married or in a committed relationship?"

"Had boyfriends over the years," she said, "but they hated my job as well and they hated that I loved to spend so much time hiking in the mountains."

"You are serious?" he asked. "You lost boyfriends because you liked to hike too much?"

She nodded. "I've summited all but the three highest peaks in Colorado in the last five years. I thrive outdoors. Not in that kind of luxury," she waved her hand back in the direction of the camp. "But in hiking-with-everything-on-my-back luxury."

He just shook his head and looked at her with his glowing eyes. Finally he said, "I think we're going to work just great together."

"As long as every time you come back up here, you bring me with you," she said.

"Deal," he said, laughing.

"Deal," she said.

She so wanted to extend her hand and shake his, but she didn't. If she had, she was afraid this might go too far on just the first night together.

They turned and walked slowly back toward camp, talking about some of their various hikes they had done over the years. She loved the fact that he wanted to explore the mountains around them right here. And had been trying to hike these mountains for years.

With luck, they could explore some of them together.

And when they got back to camp, she realized that not one word on the way back had been spoken about the crazy time-travel story.

And for that, she was grateful.

# CHAPTER SIX

*May 23, 2015*

**THE NEXT MORNING** broke beautiful and clear and calm, with the sky the darkest blue that April could remember seeing a sky. April had relaxed some from the craziness of the night before. Ryan's comments about how he had worked for very strange clients before reminded her of a few of her "unusual" past clients as well.

She had worked for one rich woman in her nineties who had insisted that if April made her big mansion parlor look exactly as it had when the woman was young and met her husband in that parlor, she would get "gentlemen callers" again.

Using old pictures, April had done as the woman asked and that project had landed her a number of jobs after that. She had no idea if the woman actually did get any "gentlemen callers."

So designing the interior of an entire lodge in the Idaho Mountains with only supplies that existed in 1900 would land her even more jobs. And if Duster actually kept his word, she might even get a business out of it.

She could put up with a lot of craziness for that kind of payoff.

Ryan also seemed very relaxed and the two of them stayed close to each other through breakfast, something she sure didn't mind at all. He made her laugh easily and his smile seemed infectious.

She wasn't sure how she could be so attracted to one guy so quickly. But she was to him. And when she woke up this morning, lying there under her comfortable quilt in her tent, she figured that the attraction to Ryan wasn't something she was going to let worry her. If something came from it, great.

She sure hoped it would, but she wouldn't push it.

On the other side, she wouldn't hold herself back either.

And then during breakfast, she realized she was really coming to like all four of her bosses. They just all seemed to be very, very nice people.

And they all seemed very mature and relaxed about everything, including her and Ryan not believing their crazy story. They just accepted that and it didn't bother anything.

After breakfast, all six of them climbed all over the ridge area, talking about certain views and where elements of the lodge could be put.

They all agreed that a huge deck and the main dining room should look out over the fantastic view of the Monumental Valley and the mountains of central Idaho.

And April knew of some perfect furniture that was being produced out of Chicago in the late 1890s that would be perfect for the deck and easy to move inside and store during the winter.

That view looked northeast between the two major peaks and over the Salmon River drainage toward Montana. On the other side of the ridge the view would be just as spectacular when pine trees were removed.

At one point up on a ridge, looking west, Ryan pointed down and to the north. "See that giant valley between those steep mountains?"

She could see it clearly and nodded.

"That's the main Salmon River coming in from where we can see it on the other side of the ridge. The river eventually flows into the Snake River. That canyon there is what is called "The River of No Return.""

She just stared at it.

"See the slash in the mountains way off to the west?" Ryan asked, pointing directly out from the ridge.

Again she nodded.

"That's the Snake River in Hell's Canyon, the deepest canyon in the country. If you follow it along to the north, you can see where the Snake River eventually joins the Salmon. Way off in the distance there to the north is where both of them flow into the Columbia."

This ridge really, really was an amazing site to build anything. It seemed to almost be the top of the world, especially on a clear, beautiful day as today. But as Ryan had said, this was all Forest Service land, protected from any construction of any kind.

For the entire morning, not one car had come up the road. So April asked Duster how many people actually came up to this ridge and then on down into the ghost towns in the valley below.

"The people in Yellow Pine say it's less than two hundred people a summer leave Yellow Pine in this direction," Duster said. "I imagine many of them don't make it past Stibnite. So more than likely under a hundred people a summer see this ridge."

"This area is one of the great secrets of the west," Madison said.

April smiled at Dawn. "After that great book of yours, it's less a secret."

Dawn laughed. "Won't change the number of people who dare to make this trip. That's one nasty road up that mountain."

April couldn't argue with that. Very few of her friends even wanted to get out of the Denver area with her for an easy hike, let alone go back into wilderness like this.

The six of them worked for another two hours, seemingly not missing a detail of the ridge. Both Ryan and April were taking notes. Ryan a lot more than April.

Finally Madison called time for lunch. She was getting hungry, even after the large breakfast he had served them all of eggs, sweet ham, hand-made hash browns, and orange juice.

As they turned to go the short distance back to the camp, Duster turned to Ryan. "See a location for a helicopter pad up here somewhere?"

That stopped all of them cold in their tracks.

Bonnie was looking at her husband with a puzzled expression and Madison and Dawn just looked stunned.

Ryan looked surprised as well. But he nodded and pointed back toward camp. "Below the ridgeline rocks on that side of camp, above where the road comes in, there is an area large enough, if cleared and leveled, to bring a helicopter in. And it would be sheltered from what I figure are some pretty intense winds up here at times."

Duster nodded and turned to keep going back toward camp.

"I thought we were building this lodge in 1900?" Bonnie asked, following slightly behind her husband.

"We are," Duster said. "But I figure Ryan is going to build this to last."

Duster glanced back at Ryan. "Right?"

Ryan nodded.

And Duster looked at Madison and Dawn. "I figure you two will keep it maintained so it doesn't crumble to ruin over the century, right?"

They both nodded.

Duster shrugged and turned back toward camp and kept walking. "I sure don't see why one of the main ways for rich guests to get here would be by helicopter flight in from Cascade starting around 1970 or so. Just wanted to know if that was possible."

Madison just shook his head and took Dawn's hand and followed Bonnie and Duster through the trees.

April looked over at Ryan who was standing there just smiling and shaking his head as he watched the other four walk away.

"What's wrong?" April whispered as she moved over close to him.

"My old friend Duster is either the craziest man I have ever met," Ryan said. "Or just maybe he and his wife have invented time travel."

"I just don't believe that," April said. And she didn't and refused at the moment to even buy into the crazy game.

"I don't either," Ryan said. "But you have to admit, the four of them believe it."

He was right. They did.

And that bothered her more than she wanted to admit.

# CHAPTER SEVEN

*May 24, 2015*

RYAN HAD REALLY ENJOYED the company of the five of them for the entire second day on the ridge. But he was mostly coming to enjoy being with April. She was smart and funny and could make him laugh with a sideways look and a raised eyebrow.

And she clearly loved the mountains and camping.

Of course, the way they were camping now, it was more like staying in a hotel, especially with Madison's fantastic cooking. But considering that some of Ryan's old girlfriends would have complained about even this, he liked that April was finding it as wonderful and special as he was finding it.

And he was getting more and more excited about the challenge of building the big lodge with only 1900's technology. That was the most amazing challenge he had ever been offered. The more he thought about it and worked over the building site, the more challenged he got by the project.

That evening, around the campfire, they all tossed ideas around about the lodge, including the very short construction season and the challenges that presented, especially in 1900.

The next morning they had all agreed they would go down into the Monumental Valley and see the old ruins and the Roosevelt town site, now under the small lake called Roosevelt.

In the spring of 1910, a landslide had dammed up the valley and backed water up over the town. Ryan understood from what little reading he had done about the area, the mines were about played out at that point and the destruction of Roosevelt pretty much killed the entire area.

After that, this last major gold rush in the lower forty-eight states was forgotten to time.

After another amazing breakfast, all six of them climbed into Duster's large SUV Cadillac, leaving the camp up. They planned on returning before dark for dinner.

Bonnie and Duster were in the front, Madison and Dawn in the second seat, and Ryan and April in the very back seats.

Even from the back, he and April still had great views. And he really, really liked being so close to her.

"This is going to be interesting to see all this," Madison said as they started down the steep road. Duster was taking it very slowly, since the road was not much wider than the big SUV and there was a thousand-foot-drop on the driver side.

"It will be," Bonnie said, nodding, clearly not happy with the road.

"Haven't you been into the lake before?" April asked a half second before Ryan could.

"I'm the only one that has seen this valley in modern times," Dawn said.

And she left it at that, which Ryan was glad she did.

It took Duster a harrowing twenty minutes to ease the big car about a mile in distance and about a thousand feet down the side of that mountain until they finally reached the valley floor.

Ryan was relieved, as was everyone in the car from what he could tell.

"We are solidly in the Frank Church Primitive Area now," Duster said.

"I thought roads weren't allowed in here," Ryan said, "after the primitive area designation."

"There are patented mining claims still working," Duster said as he took the big car down and through a pretty good stream. "They are allowed to keep and maintain roads into their claims."

That made sense to Ryan.

After another quarter mile, Duster pulled the car over along the edge of a meadow edged with remaining snowdrifts.

Everyone climbed out.

The intense silence of the big mountains towering over them on both sides stunned Ryan. Only the sound of the stream rushing over rocks on the other side of the small meadow broke the silence.

The sun had not climbed up in the sky enough to reach the valley floor. It had been sunny up on the ridge, but down in this deep valley, Ryan doubted if there was more than five or six hours of direct sun a day during the summer.

The air still had a pretty good bite to it, which also surprised him.

"That was some road," April said, stretching as she looked at the road that cut through the side of the hill above them. "Not sure I want to go back up it."

"You can always hike up the old trail," Duster said. "But it might be wiped away by slides in places."

He and Bonnie and Madison and Dawn had all moved over to the other side of the road and were studying the hillside there.

As Ryan and April moved toward them, he could see what they were looking at. Like a slice moving up through the rock-covered slopes, a trail cut steadily upward back toward the ridge where they were camped.

"Is that the old trail in here?" April asked.

"One of three," Dawn said. "No wagons could get in here, only pack animals. Everything in this valley was either built here or hauled in over trails like that one."

"I thought there were pianos in the Roosevelt saloons?" April asked, staring at the trail. "I remember that from your book."

"There were," Dawn said, nodding. "Many of them."

"Playing night and day," Madison said. "You couldn't escape them even if you wanted to, since the saloons left their doors open in the summer."

"And everything echoes in this tight valley," Dawn said. "All the pianos came in pieces over that trail or trails like it."

Ryan was just flat stunned.

He looked up at the tall valley walls and the high peaks a couple thousand feet above him. He was now getting even more excited about this crazy project.

And at the chance of exploring a part of forgotten western history.

# CHAPTER EIGHT

*May 24, 2015*

**APRIL HADN'T MUCH LIKED** the scary ride down into the valley, but now that she was firmly on the valley floor, she was getting more and more excited about exploring.

After stopping to see where the old trail reached the valley floor, they all piled back into the big SUV and Duster took them slowly down the road, working carefully through where streams had washed parts of the road away.

The valley in places wasn't much wider than a six-lane freeway, but then in other areas, it widened out between the steep hills to the size of a large mall parking lot.

The valley floor was covered in pine trees and Monumental Creek looked like it was running pretty high from snowmelt.

At one point, they came around a corner in the forest and Madison said, "You're kidding me."

He pointed at piles and piles of cut lumber sitting among the trees. The piles were about five feet high and each cut piece was two feet or so long.

It instantly gave April a creepy feeling as the piles went on and on and on.

As far as she could see across the valley through the trees, the snakes of cut and piled lumber wound.

"I thought this was strange-looking when all the trees were cut down and the lumber just stacked," Duster said, shaking his head as he drove slowly, staring at all the piles of wood. "But with the trees grown back, this is downright weird."

"What caused this?" Ryan asked as he leaned over April to look out her window at the stacked lumber that just seemed to go on and on and on through the trees. Some trees were growing out of the stacked lumber and the top layer of every stack looked like it had rotted mostly away.

"That," Duster said, as they rounded another corner.

On the other side of the road was a large ruin tucked fairly close to one of the steep rocky slopes. One wall of the ruin stuck up into the air at least two stories and was leaning badly. April doubted it would last more than a few more hard winters.

"Oh, my," Bonnie said, shaking her head and staring at the ruin.

"That was supposed to be a gold mill," Madison said. "All this wood was cut for the boilers to run the mill, but the mine on the other side of the valley played out before the mill got going. The mill equipment was never even hauled in."

April just felt shocked more than anything else. She loved hiking, but in Colorado, she seldom had destinations to hike to. It was clear that in Idaho, history was very much a destination that could be the focus of her hikes.

She loved that idea. Flat loved it. It was one thing to take a trail that thousands had taken to a summit of a small peak, but it was another thing to visit a forgotten part of history that few people ever saw.

She had a lot of research and exploring to do, and that just exited her more than she wanted to admit.

And from the way Ryan was reacting, he might want to join her on a few of those hikes.

And she liked that idea more than she wanted to let herself think about. She was completely falling for this architect she was going to have to work with.

Duster kept driving and they passed a few old log cabins, most just ruins, one with the stream running under and through part of it. None of them had doors or windows.

All four of the people in front of her mostly just shook their heads and stayed silent, as if they were in a very sacred place.

Finally, Duster pulled the car off to one side and shut it off. The road crossed the big stream on a bridge and headed up a narrow side valley.

"We walk from here," Duster said.

"About a mile to the lake," Dawn said.

April looked at Ryan after they had climbed out into the still cool air. The sun was almost to the valley floor here at this wide area. He looked excited about all this.

In fact, she and Ryan were the two most excited people in the group. The rest alternated between stoic silence and mumbled comments as they shook their heads.

"Everyone grab a bottle of water," Dawn said as they climbed out. "And a few power bars and such." She looked at Ryan and April. "I know you are both experienced hikers, but this is over seven thousand feet, so stay hydrated and move slowly."

Both Ryan and April nodded. Their four hosts continued to be subdued, but she felt so excited at the idea of a hike in this magical valley, she almost wanted to jump up and down.

As they started off along the left side of the valley on a trail cut into the rocks,

Madison glanced around with a puzzled look on his face.

"There should be a lot of ruins here," he said. "This doesn't look right."

Dawn stopped and pointed out across the valley floor to where the road went up a side canyon. "This was the high water mark of the lake. Monumental Creek has filled in this area with silt almost ten feet deep over the last hundred plus years. Everything that was left is covered or washed away."

"Oh," Madison said, shaking his head.

April could tell he was very, very sad about this, and Bonnie and Duster had gone stone silent.

Dawn led the way along the trail with Madison following, then April and Ryan, followed by Bonnie and Duster.

After a short quarter mile, the valley floor below them turned to a sort of marsh.

April felt like she might get whiplash in her neck, she was moving it so much to watch where she stepped while at the same time trying not to miss anything around her.

"The lake was almost fifteen feet deep up here," Madison said. "Now nothing more than a meadow."

"All of this area will be a meadow in another hundred years," Duster said, his voice low and very sad.

Then, before April realized what had happened, they came around a small point in the trail and there, spread out from side-to-side in the valley, was a blue-water lake, the color so intense it seemed to have a light of its own.

Monumental Creek poured dirty brown water into one side of it, but that dirt remained a cloud around the mouth of the stream only.

"Oh, God," Duster said.

Bonnie gave a sort of sobbing choke and said nothing.

April wanted to turn around and look at their faces, but decided she had better not.

The trail split, one branch leading on along the lake on the left, the other led down onto what looked like a wide sandy area on the top end of the lake.

A ridgeline covered in trees came in across the valley below, blocking the lake.

April couldn't see the mudslide until Ryan, beside her, said, "See the mudslide with a hundred years growth of trees on it?"

And he pointed to the ridgeline.

"That slide was over a hundred and fifty feet tall when it came in across the valley," Madison said.

"It took almost three days to back the water up over the town," Dawn said.

April just couldn't believe she was standing looking at a disaster that had destroyed an entire town and was then just forgotten by history.

"How many people lived in Roosevelt?" Ryan asked.

"During the prime years in the summer," Dawn said, "there were over seven thousand people in this town and lower valley."

April was again shocked. "Seven thousand in this narrow valley?"

Both Dawn and Madison nodded.

"It was a pretty wild place. And noisy," Madison said. "The music from the pianos seemed to echo everywhere."

"In early May," Dawn said, "when the town was destroyed, less than two hundred actually lived here. Most of the residents had left for the winter and had not gotten back in over the passes yet."

"And most of the mines were played out," Madison said. "So very few people

bothered to came back without Roosevelt here to draw them."

Dawn pointed down into the clear water in front of April. "Main Street was there running down the valley, and those building foundations you can see there were a general store. A very special general store."

April was amazed. She could still see ruins of buildings and foundations and the outline of a street down through the crystal clear water.

All she could do was stare.

# CHAPTER NINE

*May 24, 2015*

**FOR THE NEXT TWO HOURS** they explored the area around the lake. The entire place was amazing. Ryan had a very hard time imaging a town of seven thousand tucked in this tight, steep-walled valley.

And Dawn and Madison gave such vivid descriptions of what the place was like, he was starting to understand why they were such acclaimed historians.

After only a half hour, both Bonnie and Duster said they were going back to the car. Dawn said they would be another two hours and Duster had said to not worry about it.

It was clear to Ryan that the lake and the entire setting really bothered Duster and Bonnie for some reason.

So without Bonnie and Duster, the four of them went along the trail above the lake on the left side. The trail dead-ended into what looked like a huge logjam where the lake flowed over and around the ridge that had been the huge mudslide. But as

Ryan got close to it, he realized the logs weren't just trees jammed in there. They were the logs from buildings, from when the town's buildings broke apart.

Every log looked like a giant Tinker Toy stacked like that. Every notch in every log was clearly hand-cut and a few of the logs still had lines of chinking along them.

And the logjam went down a good fifty feet into the crystal blue water.

Ryan climbed out onto the logjam and just stood staring down, realizing in a very real way that he was standing on the ruins of an entire town. It was impossible to not feel the power and the history.

And the tragedy.

April stood beside him for a moment on one log, staring down into the water through the pile, shaking her head.

Then silently they moved on.

From there they wandered in through the forest over the ridge that was the top of a slide, finding the remains of one log cabin crushed under rocks on the far side.

"Steven's cabin," Madison said as they passed it. "It used to be almost a hundred feet up on the side of the hill above the town."

"The slide came down this side canyon along Mule Creek," Dawn said, pointing to the canyon on the right of the lake. "It started up the canyon about two miles."

"Just below the Dewey Mine area," Madison said. "It just kept coming and kept piling up and up. It was raining hard those two days it took this to build."

"Wow," was all Ryan could think to say.

Beside him April said nothing. But he could tell from her bright eyes and look that she was as excited as he was to be standing there. She clearly loved the history as much as he did.

From the top of the big mudslide, they went down the main valley.

"If we follow this for about two miles we'll find the ruins of the town Thunder Mountain," Dawn said. "Nothing much left there now. It wasn't very big in its prime because of Roosevelt being so close."

They walked for about a quarter of a mile before the trail passed an old cemetery, roped off and with a metal plaque attached to a large stone.

The rope was old and gray and weathered and looked like it would need to be replaced in another winter or two. There were a number of depressions in the hillside where graves had caved in and only a few weathered pieces of wood to mark a couple of depressions. Trees and brush had been cleared back from the square not much bigger than a small house.

About a hundred feet below the cemetery, Monumental Creek crashed over rocks. Besides that sound, the forest and the valley were deathly silent.

Dawn knelt and dusted off the pine needles from the plaque while Madison stopped a few feet back, indicating that Ryan and April should do the same thing.

The intense silence of the day overwhelmed them there in the trees. To Ryan it felt like a pressure pushing down on them. The history of old western cemeteries was always amazing.

Ryan watched as Dawn stayed in front of the plaque for almost a minute before standing and smiling at Madison and then going and kissing him.

Ryan so wanted to ask what that was all about, but he had no idea how to do that. And April just looked at him with

107

a puzzled frown and didn't say anything either.

Dawn and Madison, hand-in-hand stepped past the small cemetery and stopped about ten steps up the trail, giving room on the trail for Ryan and April to move up beside the stone.

The plaque called the little roped-off area of the hillside the "Roosevelt Cemetery." There were supposed to be thirteen known buried in the small area, and ten of the names were on the plaque. The plaque had been donated by The Pioneers of Thunder Mountain Gold Rush.

April bent down and pointed to one name. There was no first name, but a last name of Rogers. Same as Madison's last name.

"You have a relative buried here?" Ryan asked.

"In a way," Madison said, smiling.

"Tell them the truth," Dawn said. "We said we would do that, remember?"

"They wouldn't believe it," Madison said. "I wouldn't have before all this. I sometimes still don't."

Dawn shook her head and stepped away from Madison toward April and Ryan. "I know you don't believe all of us talking about different timelines."

"We accept that you do," Ryan said, and out of the corner of his eye, he could see April nod.

"Fair enough," Dawn said. "Thank you."

Ryan only nodded.

"One of the main reasons we want to build that hotel on that ridge in 1900 is because we have heard about the grand lodge that was built there," Madison said, moving up beside Dawn on the trail. "But we have never found evidence of it ever being built in all the different timelines we have visited."

Ryan shook his head. "If you are actually in different timelines, how can something that happened in one and not happen in another cross over?"

"Duster and Bonnie, with all their math skills," Dawn said, "have been working on that very question now for three years real time and upwards of a thousand years in their varied lifetimes in different timelines."

Ryan was about to ask about that comment, but Dawn waved him off. "It doesn't matter," she said. "Remember, we told you that we could live fifty or more years in another timeline, but when we jump back here to our original timeline, we only have been gone two minutes and fifteen seconds. Every time, no matter what happens in the other timeline."

"Duster or Bonnie could explain the rules of conservation of time and matter and energy," Madison said. "It makes my head hurt."

Dawn nodded and then turned and pointed at the plaque before Ryan could ask another question. "I fell in love with this magical valley the first time I came up here. And something about that plaque and this cemetery drew me to it."

She then pointed to a depression in the ground right near the rock and just inside the rope. "I buried Madison there in another timeline four months after we met and fell in love. On our first trip to another timeline."

Ryan glanced at the depression, then at Madison who just shrugged. "I don't remember. I got hit by a falling rock, broke a leg, and died before Duster or Bonnie or Dawn could get us back to this timeline. It seems you can die in another timeline and still be alive in this one."

Ryan had no idea what to think of that statement at all.

"The Rogers name on that plaque is a timeline echo," Dawn said. "When we got back after that first trip, both of us spent a lot of time researching that name on that plaque. We could find no evidence at all of anyone in this timeline by the name of Rogers even living in Roosevelt or the surrounding area."

Madison grinned. "That name there has been driving Bonnie and Duster crazy trying to understand the echoes that cross between timelines. Even with all their higher math skills, they can't figure it out and they seem to think it's critically important to figure it out."

Beside Ryan, April was just shaking her head.

Ryan turned to Dawn and Madison. "Were there always rumors of the big lodge up on that ridge?"

"Always," Dawn said and Madison nodded. "We had specialists come up here with equipment and take soundings and search the entire ridgeline. Nothing was ever built up there. And there were never plans in the works by anyone that we could find to do the project."

"So we want to build the lodge to live in," Madison said. "Bonnie and Duster want to build it to try to get some answers on how there can be echoes across timelines."

Ryan just stood there staring at Madison and Dawn and at the grave where Dawn said she buried Madison in another timeline.

"Did you take a sounding of that grave?" he finally asked.

"We did," Madison said, nodding.

"There's no one down there," Dawn said. "The grave and the name on the plaque are timeline echoes. Just as is the lodge we are about to build in another timeline."

# CHAPTER TEN

*May 24, 2015*

**APRIL DIDN'T SAY MUCH** after the conversation near the cemetery. The craziness of the entire conversation had just depressed her and she wasn't sure why.

She just wanted to enjoy the beautiful day hiking in a very interesting place with a guy she was attracted to. Very, very attracted to, actually.

As they went back to the lake, Ryan kept asking all sorts of questions about the valley and eventually the history lessons Dawn and Madison were giving about the old town cheered her right up.

As they reached the sandy area near the top of the lake, Madison said, "Would you two mind going on back to the car on your own? Dawn and I want to sit for a moment where our house is built every time we come in here."

"Sure, no problem," Ryan said and smiled at April. "You want to lead or shall I?"

She almost said that he should so she could stare at his great butt, but managed to just say that he could.

They climbed back up the slight incline to the trail and headed away from the lake.

At the corner, before the lake disappeared behind them, Ryan stopped and turned and looked back.

April followed his gaze to get one more look at the lake that covered the old mining town.

Dawn and Madison had climbed up onto the trail as well and were sitting about a hundred paces up the valley from the edge of the water, holding hands.

"They really love this place," Ryan said.

"And each other," April said.

She looked up at Ryan and held his intense gaze for a few moments. She hadn't realized just how wonderful his hazel eyes were. In this bright mountain sunlight they almost seemed an intense green. And he was fantastically handsome.

And smart. There was a real brain behind that handsome face.

Finally he smiled at her and said, "Come on. Let's give them some privacy."

He turned and started ahead of her along the narrow trail.

"This is really some valley, isn't it?" he asked after about a hundred paces.

"This entire central Idaho area is spectacular," she said, looking up at the tall mountains towering over them. Below them, Monumental Creek was winding its way through the marshland, continuing to fill in more and more of the lake.

"I think," she said, "I could spend my entire life hiking it and never see it all or grow tired."

"As could I," Ryan said, glancing back and smiling at her.

Damn she was really, really falling for this brilliant architect. How was that even possible? Especially with all the weirdness going on around them.

They didn't talk much more until they reached the big white Cadillac. Duster had moved it over into the shade under some trees and just off the road.

Bonnie and Duster had pulled out folding chairs from the back of the car and set them up in the middle of the wooden bridge over the fast-moving water of Monumental Creek, staring up the valley and back at the ridgeline where they wanted to build the lodge. Duster

still had on his standard oilcloth coat and cowboy hat, but Bonnie was down to a light white blouse and jeans.

April liked them both, and they seemed to be in a much better mood now.

"Dawn and Madison are spending a little private time," Ryan said as they approached the bridge.

"As they should," Duster said, continuing to stare up the valley at the ridge.

"That's the first time they have been together in this valley in the present," Bonnie said, smiling at the two of them.

"I like it a lot more here when the town is alive and booming and the valley is full of noise and piano music," Duster said, his voice almost angry.

"So do I," Bonnie said, patting his arm.

April had no doubt that these people really had their time-travel delusion set solidly. Yet they did not seem at all crazy except on that one subject. She liked them all, and her little voice was telling her that they were totally safe people to be around.

But that crazy idea they could travel in time sure seemed to be a reality to them. As Ryan said, she had accepted that they believed it.

Bonnie climbed to her feet and indicated Ryan should take the chair next to Duster. Then she looked at April. "Mind helping me unpack that lunch Madison made for us?"

April suddenly realized she was really hungry. She glanced at her watch. It had been over four hours since breakfast.

"With pleasure," April said, and followed Bonnie to the back of the Cadillac.

"What did you think of the valley?" Bonnie asked as they pulled out a folding table and a couple more chairs and then opened the two big coolers.

"This is a strange place," April said. "I love the ridgeline and the views from up there a great deal. And I am in love with all of Central Idaho and these mountains. I want to hike them all."

"Duster is the same way," Bonnie said, nodding. "He knows more secrets about these mountains and their history than anyone alive. I, on the other hand, enjoy my days spent in the wilderness, but prefer my better days to be spent in luxury in San Francisco."

"I wouldn't mind that either," April said, laughing.

"I figured as much," Bonnie said, smiling. "And how are you and Ryan getting along?"

"We're going to work wonderfully together on this project," she said, smiling at Bonnie.

"Only work?" Bonnie asked, grinning.

"If I have my say about it," April said, "there will be more. Just not sure when."

"With someone that good looking," Bonnie said, "I can't imagine how you could do anything else."

April glanced over at where Ryan sat on the bridge beside Duster. "He really is good looking, isn't he?"

Bonnie just laughed. "And smart. A scary combination."

April couldn't argue at all with that.

# CHAPTER ELEVEN

*May 24, 2015*

**RYAN SAT BESIDE DUSTER** on the bridge, staring back up at the ridgeline at the end of the valley. Under them

Monumental Creek flowed quickly, its water slightly brown from all the dirt it was carrying downhill in the spring melt.

Besides the sound of the running water, the valley was silent. Not even a wind stirred the tops of the pine trees. And the sun was warm, making Ryan wonder how Duster could just sit there in that long oilcloth coat and cowboy hat.

Sometimes it seemed he never took them off.

They talked for a few minutes about the construction on the lodge.

Finally Duster chuckled. "You and April think the four of us have gone not only around the bend, but bought the crazy part of the bend on the way past."

Ryan laughed. "April still does, but I'm starting to wonder."

Duster looked at him from under his dark cowboy hat, his eyes intense. "Well, that's a start."

"How many lifetimes have you lived in other timelines?" Ryan asked, deciding to just get to some of the questions he had. "You seem like a far more mature and relaxed version of Duster than I knew just a couple of years ago. In fact, you don't seem to be the same nerd math-guy at all."

Duster sort of laughed and shook his head.

"Madison said you had lived something like a thousand years in the past in other timelines. Is that true?"

Duster laughed again. "I honestly don't know. Bonnie figured it out last year when we were trying to convince Dawn and Madison to go with us. At that point it was around a thousand years. Considering how much I have gone back over the last year real time, it's a bunch more than that now."

Ryan rocked back in his chair.

"You're serious, aren't you?"

Duster nodded. "Remember, a lifetime in another timeline only takes just over two minutes here."

"You and Bonnie always stick together?"

This time Duster really laughed and looked over at where April and Bonnie were working on setting up lunch. "I love that woman. She's my partner. Always will be. But after a few hundred years here and there, we both like to go our own directions. I love living in the Old West, she loves the old cities. In the here and now we stick together."

With that Ryan decided he had better just change the subject. "So you can't figure out why timelines leak from one to another?"

Duster sat up and turned and looked squarely at Ryan.

Ryan smiled. "Madison and Dawn tried to explain it to us at the cemetery. Why Madison's name was on the plaque and his grave there but empty."

"Oh," Duster said, shaking his head and turning back to stare at the ridgeline.

"So can't figure it out, huh?" Ryan asked again.

Duster shook his head. "Bonnie and I have three major supercomputers crunching numbers for us as we speak on the problem. But for some reason I just sit here and expect that big lodge we are designing to suddenly just appear on that ridge up there."

"Sort of a leak somehow?" Ryan asked. He really wanted to keep Duster going on this before April and Bonnie got finished setting up for lunch over by the car. He knew he wouldn't understand the higher math, but if his old friend Duster really had invented a time-travel device that shifted people to other timelines,

Ryan had decided he wanted to be a part of it and sort of understand it. He really liked the idea of being able to live and explore these mountains for a very long time.

"I don't know how," Duster said. "Each timeline is contained in a crystal that grows and changes as events in the timeline shift. Each crystal is distinct from one another."

"There's a place big enough to hold that many crystals to represent all timelines?" Ryan asked, trying to even imagine that.

"Well, not really," Duster said. "But we found a tiny part of it. Bonnie and I both think the crystals go off into other dimensions. But the crystals that represent a few billion timelines close to this timeline all exist in one place."

"In one large space?" Ryan asked, having a hunch that he might give Duster an idea as to his problem. It was a common contamination problem in architecture.

"Sort of," Duster said, still staring up at the ridgeline. "It's a big cavern."

"It's the air," Ryan said.

"The air?" Duster said, turning and staring at Ryan.

"Sure," Ryan said. "A contamination problem from room to room and area to area is common in architecture construction of certain types of facilities. Have you tested the air in the room that all the crystals are in? If they are all existing in the same air, that's what they have in common, as well as the material they are connected to. That material might be the cause of a connection as well."

Duster just stared at Ryan for the longest moment. Ryan wondered after a second if he had actually insulted his friend or something. But he kept going with his wild idea.

"And if you are going back, then there are hundreds of thousands, maybe millions of alternates of you going back with each decision, right? So that much dust in a room that connects you all would be a pretty solid contamination."

Then Duster suddenly stood, almost knocking his chair over backwards and off the bridge. "Son-of-a-bitch!"

He turned and headed for Bonnie at almost a run, his long coat flapping behind him.

Ryan left the chairs and followed, worried that he had said something wrong.

"Bonnie!" Duster said. "Ryan figured it out!"

Both Bonnie and April looked up from the table where they had food spread out.

"Figured what out," Bonnie asked as Duster got close.

"Why there are echoes between timelines," Duster said.

"He did?" Bonnie asked, very puzzled as she looked at Ryan.

Ryan just shrugged at the strange looks on both women's faces.

"We tested the rock," Duster said, "We know it's completely inert and not a factor in the echoes. But we never tested the air around the crystals."

Bonnie blinked.

"And with the room being the central place for hundreds of thousands of timelines branching every time we go back, the dust we move from one timeline to another will be substantial. On our shoes, on our clothes, in our lungs."

Bonnie then blinked again, clearly lost in thought.

Duster just stood there staring at his wife, smiling.

April looked at Ryan with a very puzzled look on her face.

Ryan just shrugged.

Air contamination was so common in architecture designs, there were entire fields of study in it. He was surprised that Duster hadn't thought of that.

Then Bonnie said softly, "We're the cause of the echoes."

Duster nodded. "And all of our varied alternate realities as well. We know the crystals never get dusty. The energy in

them pulls in anything that touches them. But we bring back all sorts of dust and contaminations from different timelines and stir up the dirt on the floor in there as well."

Bonnie slowly smiled at her husband. "The dust and the events of the timeline where the dust is from get absorbed by another timeline and thus create echoes of events, but no actual events."

"Exactly," Duster said, nodding and smiling like a little kid. "We'll need to change the focus and run the numbers, but I am pretty convinced that will be the answer."

Suddenly Ryan got worried that he had just cost him and April a job.

"Are we still building the lodge, then?" he asked.

Duster and Bonnie both laughed.

"Of course we are going to build a lodge up there," Duster said. "Dawn and Madison want a place to live and raise kids. And no matter what happens over the next two months, you two are getting your bonuses. I will guarantee that and put it in writing."

April looked at Ryan and smiled. "What did you do?"

"Just pretending to be an architect," Ryan said, smiling and shrugging. "It's what I do."

# PART TWO

# CHAPTER TWELVE

*July 19, 2015*

THE JULY SUN was starting to really warm up the Boise streets outside as April stepped into the air-conditioned two-story office building Duster had bought her and Ryan for the lodge project. She had on a linen blouse and jeans with tennis shoes. Her long brown hair was pulled up and held with an antique comb. And she had on no make-up. In fact, since starting this project, she had not worn make-up at all, and didn't miss it.

A nice young college student with blonde hair and big green eyes named Cindy manned the front reception area and smiled at April as she came in, handing her a dozen messages over the big wood counter.

Since they were building a log lodge, she and Ryan had decided to decorate their office building with black and white photos of the Old West and comfortable log-style furniture.

The building was full of light and warm colors and lots of plants. It was the most comfortable office April had ever had by far.

She couldn't believe she was half-owner of it with Ryan. This was far, far beyond her dreams and she almost hated to go back to her apartment at night.

Ryan and his architecture crew had the right side of the building as people came inside. April and her interior crew had the left. The center of the building was common meeting rooms and supplies and other equipment.

Duster had given April the Denver interior design business as he had promised right after they got back from that first trip to the summit. April had brought in three of the best people from there to work on this project with her. She left the former owner in charge in Denver to run the rest of the business. It didn't interest her at all at this point.

She wasn't sure it ever would again. She would deal with it all later.

Ryan had brought in two other architects to help him, a computer geek for the computer work, and an engineer for all the problems with the weight of the logs and wind problems. Ryan and the engineer had spent a couple weeks just working on the snow loads of the roof they were designing.

In the building and around employees, she and Ryan had made it a rule to never talk about anything to do with the crazy idea of time travel. April still thought the entire thing crazy and didn't think it was possible, but at least now she was used to the idea of having clients who believed in it like it was something common, like food and water.

Bonnie and Duster had almost vanished from the project over the last two months while Madison and Dawn often met April and Ryan for dinner meetings away from the office.

As far as the office crew was concerned, this was an exercise in wasting money for a major client, but a fun one. And everyone seemed to really enjoy the challenge of it.

After getting back from the summit that first trip, both Ryan and April admitted to each other that they were attracted to each other. Seriously attracted, actually, but if they were going to focus on this huge project and get it done in less than two months, they didn't dare act on that attraction until this was all over.

That had caused them both to relax. She now considered Ryan one of her best friends. They talked about everything and flirted all the time and they made a perfect design team for the lodge.

She really liked the flirting.

Plus, she had come to really like the Boise area. The people were friendly, the mountains really close, the cost of living very moderate. Plus just outside their office were the Boise River and the fantastic paths along its tree-lined shores. And there were three major large parks an easy walk down the river from their office. For a woman like her who loved her job, but also loved being outside, this didn't get any better.

Her office actually looked out over the river.

And she had found a perfect historical house to dream about out on Warm Springs Avenue. It looked out over the river as well on a large estate. It had been built in 1901 and she loved the look of it from the outside. She had never had the courage to stop and ask to go inside.

Ryan loved it as well and they often took the long walk together to the old mansion and back on nice evenings, which seemed in Boise to be just about every evening in the summer.

She and Ryan had also taken two day-trips back up to the summit. And they had done two hikes together around the Boise foothills as a break. She also walked the River Walk every day at lunch. It had been a fantastic two months.

And if April had her way about it, the months would continue on and on.

But today was the day.

She and Ryan were going to present the lodge and the plans to Bonnie and Duster and Dawn and Madison.

She could feel her nerves tied up in her stomach and she had had a difficult time even choking down a breakfast bar this morning.

She gave Cindy at the front desk instructions to show the two couples to the big conference room on the second floor when they arrived. There were computer sketches and interior renderings of every room in the big lodge posted on the walls in there.

But that was only a tiny part of the presentation she and Ryan had ready.

She dropped the messages and her purse off in her office and headed to the conference room. She found Ryan there, sitting with his feet up on the big table, staring out the window at the Boise River.

To her, he had only become more attractive as the two months had gone by and they had worked closely on the lodge. This was almost over and now maybe that agreement they had made could end and they could take what was between them to the next level.

Finally.

She moved over to him and stood behind him, messaging his solid shoulders as she stared out at the beautiful summer morning.

He sighed and put a hand up on the top of hers. "Have I ever told you how much I enjoy your touch?"

"You have," she said, smiling. "And I enjoy yours."

He put his feet down and stood and turned to face her, holding her hand.

As normal, his eyes sent a shock through her and she just stood there, smiling at him and looking into those wonderful eyes that seemed to change color slightly with his mood. Today they were a light green with yellow flecks.

His hand gently squeezed hers.

"This is for luck," he said.

He pulled her close and kissed her.

He felt better against her than she had imagined he would, and she had imagined a great deal, especially alone, late at night.

She just lost herself in his kiss, wrapping her arms around his neck and pulling him close.

And kissing back hard.

No way she wanted this to end.

He tasted wonderful, like a fresh scent of morning forest on a summer day.

Finally, he pushed her back, smiling. He was slightly flushed and she could feel her face red and hot as well.

"Now that's going to be some damned fine luck," he said.

"Don't you think we need more?" she asked, smiling at him, her arms still around his neck.

"I believe we could use more," he said smiling back.

But before she could pull him in close, the sounds of voices outside the door sent them apart like two high school kids caught kissing in the hallways.

He smiled at her as she went to her side of the big conference table.

"We'll continue that later," he said, his smile bigger than she had remembered seeing it.

"Depend on it," she said, smiling at him as the door opened.

And suddenly the presentation they were about to do just seemed a lot less important. What she really wanted was to be in Ryan's arms again.

Waiting and getting to know each other while they worked together had been a good idea. She knew that.

But it was time for that waiting to come to a very sudden, and she hoped, intense end.

# CHAPTER THIRTEEN

*July 19, 2015*

**THE PRESENTATION** to Bonnie and Duster and Dawn and Madison went off without a hitch.

It was the holographic three-dimensional image of the lodge on the ridgeline that really did it. Ryan had to admit, his computer people and graphics guys had done a fantastic job taking the plans and photos of the area and topographic maps and converting it all so that the ridgeline and the plans for the lodge were rendered in three dimensions over the big conference table.

The ridge looked exactly as it had looked when they camped there.

In the old days, they would have used carefully built models. But for this presentation, there would be no need. A three-dimensional hologram projected on the top of the big conference table would be much, much better.

All four of their guests had gasped when he brought up the image at first. The ridgeline seemed to come up out of the surface of the table.

The ridgeline stayed there, covered in trees, until slowly a big wooden lodge spread over the ridgeline, its steep shake roof and dormers and wide decks dominating everything.

The ridge and the lodge filled the entire center of the big conference table, as long as the four of them sitting along one side of the table.

Ryan found it interesting that he sat where one mountain peak would be and April sat where the Thunder Mountain peak would be in the relationship to the lodge.

"That's just flat stunning," Dawn had said as the lodge appeared.

Madison just sat there staring at it, his mouth open.

Duster shook his head and pushed back his brown hat. "I knew I had found the best people for this."

To Ryan, that compliment from his old friend felt fantastic.

From there, he and April took the four of them on a virtual tour of the lodge, first around the outside, letting the lodge rotate, then taking them in the front door.

Ryan would describe the architecture and locations of things. Then April would take over talking about the furnishings and where they could be found in 1900.

Making a perfect tag team, he and April took their four guests through the great room with the huge stone fireplace and views in both directions off the ridgeline into the dining area that could hold thirty, with its large stone fireplace and expansive windows and furnishings.

They showed them the parlor and card room and the kitchen and then down the hall on the main floor to the twenty standard guest rooms on the main floor.

Then in the virtual tour, he and April walked the four of them up the huge grand staircase that dominated one side of the big main room and to the wide hallway and the four suites upstairs.

Upstairs, the huge log rafters seemed to dominate in their shining, golden color.

Each suite had a master bedroom, a huge living room, and a bathroom. The four suites had high ceilings and double-sided stone fireplaces and dormers that looked out over the valleys with seating areas in both. One suite would be reserved only for Bonnie and Duster and one for Dawn and Madison. The other two would be open for guests.

April worked them through the light fixtures in each room and public areas and how in time they could be converted to electrical easily without a problem. Ryan showed them hidden utility rooms in the basement for future generators and how the building could be retrofitted easily for electrical at some point without damaging anything.

117

And he explained how interior plumbing would be set up with a water tank above one part of the building kept warm by the fireplaces from below and gravity fed to the bathrooms and kitchens.

The guests downstairs would share two bathrooms. There would be another off the kitchen. Each suite upstairs would have a bathroom of its own.

Then he pulled the presentation back to show only the outside of the lodge. With the image of the big lodge dominating the table, he and April both talked about the time it would take to build.

Ryan told them that if they got started in the middle of May with all the supplies ready to be brought in and had a large and good crew, it could be built in two summers.

April worked them through how the different pieces of art, furnishings, carpeting, and so on could be bought, mostly in San Francisco. She said it would also take two years to accumulate everything and have it up on the ridge by the end of the second summer. She said it would take two people shopping and having everything shipped to Boise to hold for the pack trips into the lodge.

Then Ryan let the image shrink down in size and pull back as the mountain face grew under it until it looked like a person was sitting on the bridge where he and Duster had sat that day two months before, looking up at the ridgeline.

The lodge was now clear and dominating Monumental Valley below it.

"You told me you wanted the lodge to just appear there that day when we sat on that bridge," Ryan said, smiling at his old friend. "Here you go."

It looked so real, Ryan could have sworn he was back on that bridge looking up the hill at the lodge.

The silence in the room was so intense, Ryan almost felt afraid to breathe.

On the other side of the table, April was beaming at him.

Dawn had tears in her eyes and Madison had his mouth open staring up at the lodge.

Finally Duster pushed back from the table and looked first at Ryan, then at April.

Then he looked at Bonnie who was just sitting there with the largest smile Ryan could imagine her smiling.

"We didn't pay them enough," Duster said. "We got to fix that."

Everyone laughed.

"It's perfect," Dawn said. "So much more than I had ever hoped."

"It is perfect," Madison said, nodding. He looked first at April, then at Ryan. "Thank you both."

"There is one more thing instead of payment that you could give us," Ryan said. He looked at April and mouthed the words, "Trust me."

"What's that?" Duster said, continuing to stare up at the image of the big lodge sitting in the distance on the ridgeline. "Name it."

"If we sign agreements to never disclose, could you show us how you go back? Show us the crystal room you four have mentioned?"

A slight look of panic came over April's face, but then she nodded.

Bonnie and Duster both laughed, then Duster took out a ten dollar gold piece that looked like it was from the last century and handed it to her.

"I bet you would want to see the mine," she said, smiling as she tucked the gold piece into her blouse pocket.

"You will put no pressure for us to go back at all if what you have been telling us is true?" Ryan asked.

"Not a bit," Bonnie said.

"We were hoping to show that crystal room to you," Dawn said. "It is something really special. But it means another trip into the mountains."

"I like the sound of another trip into the mountains," April said.

Ryan was glad she wasn't too angry. He had hoped she wouldn't be. Both of them had come to really trust the four people they were working for.

Then Ryan turned to Duster. "You bet against me?"

Duster laughed and shook his head. "Never again."

# CHAPTER FOURTEEN

*July 19, 2015*

**AFTER THE PRESENTATION** went perfectly, April was stunned that Ryan had asked to see the time-travel crystals the others had been talking about for months.

But she understood the request and was actually relieved he had made it. She had grown to really like Bonnie and Duster and Dawn and Madison, especially Bonnie. So once past the first reaction to Ryan's question, she liked the idea.

One way or another, it would clear the air.

And she really, really liked the idea of another trip into the mountains. Even a quick one.

When Bonnie was in town over the last two months, the two of them had talked a lot, often about decorations and their love for mountains as well as big cities.

And Bonnie had kept April level about the friendship months with Ryan. Bonnie

had agreed it was a good idea to hold off and not complicate anything while they were working so tightly together.

But Bonnie had said at one point, "After the project is over, jump him and don't come up for air for days."

April had said she liked that plan, and now this morning Ryan had started that part of things rolling nicely.

April had also spent a lot of time with Dawn in her office at the University, since it was only a mile down the river path from the office, often going out for lunch with her when she was in town. She really liked the historian and her solid, down-to-earth thinking and passion for the people of the west.

And her passion for Madison.

April had grown to know both of these women. She needed to get this delusion of time travel cleared up or answered, because over two months now of talking with them, a tiny part of her was actually starting to believe time travel was possible, even though she would never really admit that.

Ryan clicked off the last holographic image of the big lodge and smiled at her down the length of the long table.

Damn he was getting better looking by the minute if that was possible. She really wanted to kiss him again.

And soon.

His smile just kept glowing. He was as happy as she had seen him since meeting him.

Duster stood and shook Ryan's hand, then went down and hugged her.

She then got a hug from the other three as everyone stood around smiling like a bunch of kids who had just completed a school play. She had been in a lot of client meetings after presentations and none of them had ever turned out this well.

"So you ready to go?" Duster asked after a moment.

Ryan looked puzzled.

April felt puzzled and just a little panicked.

"Go where?" Ryan asked.

Madison laughed.

"It is only ten in the morning. We can be in the mine in four hours," Duster said. "And back here by ten tonight if we want. Or easily tomorrow morning. Lunch on the way is on me."

Duster shook his head and waved his hand over the table where the lodge images had been. "Hell, after that, I owe you two a lot more than lunch."

"We'll grab some fresh produce and steaks along the way and I'll cook dinner in the mine," Ryan said.

"Perfect," Dawn said, kissing him.

A drive with Ryan up into the mountains sounded really good to her at this point.

No matter what they might find on the other side.

## CHAPTER FIFTEEN

*July 19, 2015*

**APRIL SAT IN THE BACK SEAT** of Duster's big Cadillac SUV and held Ryan's hand as they headed west out of Boise on the freeway in the direction of Nampa and Caldwell.

As he had climbed into the back seat, he had kissed her again and whispered, "Great job!"

She took his hand as they got settled and squeezed it. "You too."

And they just stayed like that, holding hands in the backseat of a car like two school kids riding with parents.

It was interesting to April that she often thought of Bonnie and Duster as much, much older, almost like parents, even though they were only a year or so older than she was. They just seemed far, far older.

And so did Dawn and Madison in their own ways.

For a time, the four in front of them talked excitedly about the lodge, asking Ryan or April questions on certain points.

Then when they got off the freeway just on the other side of Nampa and headed out on the highway toward the Snake River and Nevada beyond, Ryan finally asked, "Where are we heading?"

"Oh, sorry," Duster said from up front. "Silver City."

"The old ghost town?" Ryan asked.

April had never heard of it. There was a lot about Idaho she didn't know. But she wanted to learn. In two months, she felt like Boise was becoming a second home, and if she wasn't careful, it might become her only home.

And that thought didn't bother her at all. As long as it was close to Ryan.

"You been up there?" Madison asked, turning around a little so he could see Ryan and April's faces.

"Never have," Ryan said.

"Never heard of it," April said.

From the driver's seat, Duster laughed and Madison smiled. "Then you two are in for a real treat. Silver City and the area around it was one of the largest gold and silver rushes of the Old West."

Tell them the history of the place," Duster said.

For the next half hour or so, as fantastically beautiful farmland flashed past the two-lane highway, Madison told them the history of the Silver City area, how it started up in the 1860s and had booms and busts for fifty or more years after that.

"There are still a lot of ruins up there," Madison said, "and the town itself has become a tourist attraction in the summer."

"And a few of the mines are still running," Duster said, and Madison nodded.

At that point they had been on the two-lane highway for about forty-five minutes. There didn't seem to be any mountains in site as far as April could see.

Duster pulled the big car into the parking lot of what looked like a very questionable diner. The few buildings along the highway here were no more than a wide spot.

The sign over the building said nothing more than "Café" and was so weathered, even that could barely be seen.

She didn't really want to let go of Ryan's hand, but she did as they climbed out into the summer heat.

"No talk about the mine or what we are doing while in here," Duster said.

"We own a cattle and horse ranch up the Snake River from here," Bonnie said to Ryan and April. "We stop here all the time for lunch or breakfast or dinner and the people who run this place think it's because we're going to the ranch."

"Got it," Ryan said.

The smell of the hamburgers and fries hit her as Duster opened the door to the café. Thick, greasy fries, the best kind.

April suddenly realized just how hungry she really was. She had been enjoying the ride and the history lesson and holding Ryan's hand so much, she hadn't even realized she was hungry until now. That one breakfast bar she had choked down hours ago was long since gone.

"I'm starved. I could eat a horse," Duster said as he started inside.

Bonnie shushed him. "Don't say that, they may serve it to you here."

April glanced at Ryan and then laughed. Damn she liked these people. She just hoped that in a few hours they weren't going to prove themselves to be total crazy nut-balls.

But it was either that or time travel really did exist. She wasn't sure which outcome she hoped for the most.

The café was a combination of large Formica tables and booths, old tile that had the color mopped right off it, and photos from farms and pioneers, many framed and slightly grease-covered.

Each table had a big pile of napkins on it and a partially-empty bottle of ketchup and a bottle of mustard. Nothing else.

The lunch was fantastic. She had never tasted a hamburger so juicy and a bun so perfectly soft. It was if the guy in the back had made it on a grill in the backyard.

For all she knew, he had. And she didn't care.

And the fries were heavenly. Salt-covered, grease-covered potatoes that just tasted like she had bitten into the most expensive meal in Denver.

It had all been served by a heavy waitress with a front tooth missing named Connie who wore an apron with washed-out stains from years past, April was sure. She welcomed the four of them and nodded to April and Madison. And seldom spoke after that.

But the décor or the waitress didn't matter. The food was amazing. It was no wonder Bonnie and Duster stopped here. Under that weathered old sign was the best food April could remember tasting.

They were the only six customers in the place the entire time and Duster tipped big, even though Connie didn't seem friendly and didn't seem to much care.

Then they all piled back into the Cadillac and turned off the main road and headed east. Once she and Ryan were settled, she reached over and put her hand on his.

He smiled at her and whispered, "Nice."

She had to agree with that completely.

In about ten miles, they turned off the paved road onto a wide gravel road that was wide enough for two cars. April had been on a lot of mountain roads, but never one this smooth and wide.

"Silver City sits in a valley between two large mountains," Duster said. "War Eagle Mountain on one side, Florida Mountain on the other. My great-great-grandfather bought a mine on Florida Mountain called The Trade Dollar."

"It officially played out in 1871," Madison said.

Duster nodded, keeping the big car climbing up the smooth gravel road. The hills above and below the road were covered only in sagebrush and scrub brush. April could see trees up higher, where they were going, but here everything outside the car looked hot and barren.

"My great-great-grandfather boarded the mine up and gave up on it. My great-grandfather went back up a few years later and tried to get it going again, mostly doing the work himself. He's the one that broke into the crystal room."

April looked at Ryan when Duster said that and Ryan just smiled and nodded.

"When he did that," Duster said, going on with the story, "he didn't tell anyone. He just closed the mine up again. Many years later he showed it to his son, who then showed it to my dad. Bonnie and I had been married for two years when my dad took us up there and showed us the crystal room."

"So this mine has been in your family for the entire time?" April asked, amazed at the story.

"Did they know what it was?" Ryan asked.

"They had no idea. And the mine was almost played out when my great-great-grandfather bought it. It was a family joke from what I understand for decades."

Duster went on as they neared the top of the steep climb up the side of the hill on the wide, gravel road. "Bonnie and I started to get an idea of what the vast cavern of crystals might be and we worked on it for almost five years during the summers, doing tests of various sorts."

"I still can't imagine what it was like that first time back," Madison said, shaking his head.

"Scary," Bonnie said. "Flat scared us both to death."

Duster nodded. "We didn't try it again for another year and a lot of tests and higher math calculations."

For some reason, it felt good to April to know that Bonnie and Duster could be scared of something. It made them seem more human.

"How long ago was that second trip?" Ryan asked.

"Three summers ago," Duster said as he turned the big Cadillac off the wide road and onto what looked like nothing more than a single-lane wagon track that wound through some scrub trees.

"We're up on War Eagle now," Madison said.

Duster slowed way down and the road got very rough.

April held on to Ryan's hand and steadied herself against the side of the car with her other as the car pitched back and forth. On Ryan's side there had to be a drop of a good thousand feet.

Ryan glanced at it only once and never looked in that direction again.

The talking stopped for a moment as Duster wound them around the edge of the mountain and then started down toward the valley below.

"Someone say something," April said, "so I don't have to think about this road."

Everyone laughed.

"How many trips have you taken into alternate pasts since that second one?" Ryan asked.

Bonnie glanced back at them and smiled. "Four or five hundred. I've lost count."

Then she turned back to watch the road and brace herself.

"When did you two go through the first time?" Ryan asked Madison.

"Last summer," Madison said. "We've gone through thirty-eight times since."

"Forty counting those two false starts that first trip," Dawn said.

"Oh, yeah," he said, smiling at her.

April had to know, but she was almost afraid to ask. But she asked anyway.

"How many years have you spent in other timelines?"

Madison looked back at her with a surprised look and Ryan squeezed her hand.

"About seven hundred years," Dawn said matter-of-factly, not turning around.

"And you spent all of that time together?" April asked, and again Ryan squeezed her hand.

"Almost all of it," Madison said, nodding.

April glanced over at the handsome man sitting beside her holding her hand as they bounced down the rough road off the mountain. Could she spend seven hundred years with him?

Or with any person for that matter?

She honestly didn't know the answer to that question.

But with Ryan, she sure wouldn't mind trying a year first.

Maybe two.

Maybe ten.

And then going from there.

# CHAPTER SIXTEEN

*July 19, 2015*

**RYAN WAS SURPRISED** at how April was asking direct questions about the belief of going into an alternate timeline. He wasn't convinced he believed it really at any level, but at least after two months, April wasn't as actively against the entire notion as she had been.

And he really liked kissing her and holding her hand. He had been attracted to her from the first moment and they had worked wonderfully as a team designing the lodge over the last two months. He hoped they would do a lot more together now.

If he had anything to say about it, they sure would.

Duster finally banged them over a wooden bridge at the bottom of the valley and started up a very, very steep slope on a road that really didn't look like a road at all. More like two ruts washed by rain out of the side of the hill.

Madison said, "Silver City is in that direction about a mile." He pointed to the left up a decent road. "Hang on now."

"Oh, great," April muttered and Ryan smiled and squeezed her hand.

The big Cadillac didn't seem to have trouble with climbing the slope, even with six people inside, but the people inside were bouncing around like the car was trying to blend them all into a milkshake. Only the seat belts and strong grips held them in place.

April and Ryan both braced against each other and held on to the handles above their seats.

Finally, after what seemed like an eternity to Ryan, but was actually only sixty seconds or so, Duster turned the big Cadillac onto a trail going across the hill. If Ryan hadn't been belted in, he would have slid over on top of April. Not that he would have minded, actually.

Then after another forever sixty seconds, Duster turned the big car up into a stand of trees and stopped, the back end of the car down the hill.

Beside them a white Jeep was parked.

"Oh, good," Bonnie said, "Janice and Steve are here."

"Oh, shit, what day is it?" Dawn asked, a slight touch of panic in her voice.

"July 19th," Madison said.

Dawn looked at her watch and visibly relaxed. She had clearly just realized something. And it had to do with another couple here somewhere on this mountain.

Madison looked at her with a puzzled look as Duster turned off the car and turned around and looked down at his passengers. "Everyone all right?"

"If you had the last three minutes as an amusement ride at a fair," April said, "no one would ride it."

"Agreed," Bonnie said, and everyone laughed.

Ryan climbed out, stepping down on dried grass and dirt, and then turned and helped April climb up and out behind him on the passenger side.

The heat and the silence of the high mountains hit him. And the smell of sagebrush and warm pine, two smells he loved more than anything.

The view over the mountains and the valley beyond was amazing. He could make out the hills along the Boise Range and some of the Central Idaho Mountains beyond them.

"Wow," April said, standing beside him and staring at the same view.

He really, really loved the idea that he had met someone who loved the mountains and appreciated them as much as he did.

Duster, his hat and long coat now back on, said, "Follow me."

He turned and strode off through the trees and out into the open.

Bonnie followed him, then Ryan and April and then Madison and Dawn behind them.

The hot air swirled around them. At some point Ryan was going to have to ask Duster why he always wore that hat and coat, no matter how warm it was.

There wasn't much of a path, more like a cattle trail, that cut across a steep slope.

Far below them on the left were the ruins of an old town.

"Silver City?" Ryan asked.

"What's left of it," Madison said from behind him.

Ryan could see maybe ten buildings scattered around the valley and some cars parked in front of one.

They went across the hill to a flat area that looked to be the top of an old mine tailings. There was a weathered old shack about the size of a shed sitting on the flat area. It had no windows or doors, and old, rusted mining car tracks led from it to the edge of the tailings pile.

From the size of the pile, it was clear a lot of dirt had been taken from this hillside at one point in the past.

Ryan looked around. This top area was twenty-paces across and just about as deep. The mine itself was boarded over and had caved in behind the boards.

Sagebrush grew out of the area where the mine had caved in and the mountain went up steeply above the old mine.

From what Ryan could tell, this was where the delusion was going to end.

April looked at the old shack and then at Ryan with a look of worry on her face.

Duster turned and smiled at them both as the six of them stood on the flat top of that old mine tailings pile in the silence and heat. Not even a slight breeze disturbed the air.

"We didn't have you sign anything," Duster said, looking cool under his wide-brimmed hat and long coat, "because to be honest, the four of us have come to trust you. And besides, who would believe you if you told anyone, which we hope you never do."

"About what?" April asked. "That joyride over a thousand ruts?"

Again everyone laughed.

"About what we are about to show you," Duster said.

"Whatever it is, you got my word to not mention it to anyone," Ryan said.

"Mine as well," April said.

Duster looked at Bonnie who nodded.

"Clear," Madison said as he scanned the surrounding hills. "No one above us."

Duster then took what looked like an antique skeleton key out of his pocket and a moment later a big rock beside the old mine sort of slid to one side revealing a large vault door that slid open as the rock moved to one side.

Now Ryan was impressed. Not only did that take some real engineering, but some real power as well. There had been no sign at all that rock could move.

---

Or any source of power.

He had no idea where the power came from way up here on the hill.

"Okay," April said softly. "Now that's interesting."

Duster moved over and went inside, followed by Bonnie and Dawn.

"Entry is too small for six," Madison said as the rock slid closed again.

Ryan had never seen anything like it. There was no sign at all that that rock could move or ever had moved. And it made no noise at all moving. None.

"That's just flat amazing," he said.

Madison laughed. "You haven't seen the half of it yet."

The rock slid back and Madison indicated that Ryan and April should step inside.

Ryan reached over and took April's hand to show her they were in this together, whatever "this" happened to be. Then they stepped into the area behind the steel door and rock.

Madison joined them and the rock slid closed and the big door shut, leaving them for a moment in the dark.

"Just in case we have to open that at night," Madison said, explaining the second of darkness before an interior light came on and an interior door opened onto an old mine tunnel lit with yellow bulbs hanging on what looked to be old electrical cords.

That moment of darkness made complete sense to Ryan once Madison said it. He squeezed April's hand and she gripped his hand back as they took a couple steps into the old mine.

The wooden timbers were a good foot across and the mine itself was more than tall enough for all of them to walk down the middle of it without ducking for anything. The lights gave the mine a golden tint and everything smelled of dry earth.

The ore car rails ran along the floor and dust seemed to cover everything, giving the mine a look of very old age.

Duster and Bonnie and Dawn were waiting for them a few steps down the mine tunnel.

"Welcome to the Trade Dollar Mine," Duster said, his voice echoing.

Ryan studied the old timbers holding up the ton of rock over their heads. They looked old, but he could tell they had been completely reinforced and yet decorated to remain older-looking.

"Is this safe?" April asked, looking around.

"Completely," Ryan said, nodding.

"Trust an architect to see the details," Duster said, laughing as he turned and headed deeper into the mine.

About forty steps in, the mine tunnel turned to the right along with the string of lights, but Duster didn't turn. He just walked right through the wall.

April gasped and squeezed his hand.

"Hologram," Madison said as Bonnie and then Dawn vanished through the wall. "Just like the hologram of the lodge this morning you had done on that table. Just shut your eyes and walk and you'll be fine.

Keeping hold of April's hand behind him, he walked right through where the wall should be.

April followed and then they both looked back.

"Security," Duster said. "Plus I have alarms all the way along this tunnel that unless turned off right, lock the place down and alert me anywhere in the world."

"We'll show you how to shut those off," Bonnie said, smiling.

Duster turned and kept walking toward what looked like the end of the mine, hidden slightly in the dark. And again he walked through the wall.

Ryan flat didn't know what to think at this point. He was starting to feel numb and only April's hand in his gave him any reassurance.

They followed through yet another hologram and into a well-lit natural cavern.

Tables with a massive amount of supplies lined a couple of the walls and there were shelves in the middle of the cavern as well. Clothes of every sort and size and era hung on racks in two different places, as well as a rack of guns and hats hanging on one cavern wall.

From one corner of the cavern on the left, Ryan heard two voices chorus, "Welcome!"

The couple that must have owned the Jeep stood and started toward them. They were both wearing clothing from what looked to be the late 1800s and both had bottles of water in their hands.

The two new arrivals walked across the smooth floor of the cavern, smiling. The guy was as tall as Duster with a slightly balding head and was dressed like a shopkeeper would dress in the late 1800s, with a short coat and vest and dark slacks.

The woman wore riding clothes appropriate for a woman of the late 1800s and had a bonnet pulled back off her dark brown hair.

The guy said, "I see they decided to join the craziness."

"They haven't seen it all yet," Bonnie said.

Then Bonnie turned and did introductions. "Ryan Knott, April Buckley, this is Professor Janice Franks of Stanford and her husband, Professor Steven Conklin of Berkley."

Ryan shook both their hands, stunned at the two newcomers. "I read your book, Professor Conklin, about the construction methods of the Old West. It helped me get through some of what we were going to need to do to build the lodge."

"And Professor Franks," April said. "I am honored beyond words. Your two books on the household furnishings and supplies of Western America have helped me more this last year than I want to admit."

"It's Janice and Steven," Janice said, smiling. "And we're really glad you decided to join this little crazy crew. We have both admired your incredible work as well. It's an honor if our work influenced you in any way."

Ryan instantly had a feeling he would like them, just as he liked the other four with them.

"So you two haven't seen any of this yet?" Steven asked.

Ryan shook his head.

Steven glanced over at Duster and said, "We're ready to head back again, just finished a little lunch. You want us to knock their socks off for a few minutes first?"

Duster laughed. "Might as well."

Steven turned to Ryan and April. "I know how impossible this all seems right now to you both. But trust these four, they know what they are doing."

Then before Ryan could even nod, Steven turned to his wife. "Ready to go again?"

"With pleasure, dear husband," she said.

"We'll see you all in a few minutes," Steven said and the two of them picked up saddlebags and headed for a door on the far side of the big cavern.

"Follow them," Duster said, smiling.

Ryan again took April's hand and they did as they were told, heading for the mouth of a mine tunnel he wasn't sure he wanted to enter.

# CHAPTER SEVENTEEN

*July 19, 2015*

**APRIL WAS STUNNED** that two more of the countries most famous historians were in the old mine far, far up in the Idaho Mountains. She had grown used to being around Dawn and Madison and had loved, over the last few months, when they talked about a new book they were researching.

But now in a big cave at the end of a hidden mine, she had met Professor Janice Franks, the woman who in the last six months had published two major books on the decorations and designs of Western United States furniture and fixtures from 1880 through 1920. And both books had almost instantly become the gold standard for all restoration designers.

It was that era that most of April's customers wanted her to decorate for. And she had used Janice's book in helping her with some of the furnishings for the lodge.

And now the two of them were here. In this cavern, dressed as if they were actually going to the 1890s.

As they walked off and Duster told her and Ryan to follow, Ryan once again took her hand and they did as told, although she wasn't sure how she was getting one foot to move in front of the other. She just felt stunned, right down to her very core.

They went through a tunnel, past a big, open steel door, and out into a cavern so vast her mind couldn't begin to grasp it.

The two of them took about five steps into the cavern and just stopped. She could not move another step.

Beside her Ryan didn't seem to want to move either.

The floor was flat and dirt, a wooden table with some device sat in the middle of the floor near this end of the cavern, and every inch of every wall and ceiling of the vast cavern was covered in what looked like rose quartz crystals of various sizes and shapes.

Every crystal seemed to glow with a power and beauty all its own.

It was the most spectacularly beautiful place she could ever imagine.

And it seemed to go on into the mountain as far as she could see.

The crystal cavern the four of them had talked about for two months was real.

That meant going to alternate universes was real.

She could feel her mind spinning and she forced herself to take a few deep breaths.

She took hold of Ryan's arm with her free hand to steady herself. She wasn't sure if her legs would hold her. And she couldn't imagine being in here without him at her side.

She just kept taking deep breaths and staring at the fantastic beauty around her.

It was impossible.

Just impossible.

"Oh, my," Ryan whispered beside her.

"It's really something, isn't it?" Madison asked. "Makes me gasp every time I walk in here."

"Me too," Dawn said.

As far as April was concerned, nothing would ever describe this cavern of crystals. She just kept staring around her, trying to grasp the incredible beauty of millions and millions and millions of crystals seeming to shine with a light and power all their own. Some of them were about the size of a tiny bump, others were huge and fairly long and seeming thousands of other smaller crystals spread out around the larger ones.

"Where and when are you two headed this time?" Duster asked, moving over beside Steven and Janice.

"1895," Steven said. "Trying to hit May so we aren't snowed in up here for too long."

"We're going to run a general store again," Janice said. "A great way to get to know people."

"Got enough money and all that?" Duster asked like a dad asking a kid if he was all right before going out on a date.

"More than enough," Steven said, patting the saddlebag over his shoulder and the pocket of his suit coat. "We'll make more while there."

Duster nodded. "See you in a few minutes."

Steven did something to the blocky-looking machine on the wooden table.

Then Steven glanced over at April and Ryan. "Just keep breathing. What you are about to see is very real. Honest. I didn't believe it either the first time I saw it."

"I damned near fainted," Janice said, laughing.

Then smiling, both he and Janice put one hand on the machine and Steven connected another wire to the back of the machine and they both vanished from the room without a sound.

One moment they were there, the next they just weren't there.

The machine sat there on the wooden table.

Duster and Bonnie and Dawn and Madison were all looking at her and Ryan.

"I've got to sit down," April said.

"Me too," Ryan said.

Both she and Ryan sank to the dirt floor and held each other's hand and sort of leaned against each other.

"What exactly just happened?" Ryan asked as Bonnie walked over and handed April a bottle of water.

April managed to nod thank you, but at the moment that was all she could do.

She took a drink as Duster explained.

"Each crystal you see in this cavern, and off into infinity, is a physical representation of an alternate reality. Every time someone makes a decision, another crystal is formed."

"The math is almost impossible to calculate," Madison said, "as to how many alternate realities there are in just this area of humanity we can see from here."

He pointed down the huge cavern where it seemed to go off into the distance.

"When you two decided to come with us up here today," Bonnie said, indicating that April should take another drink, "you made that decision in millions of realities. And in millions and millions of other realities, you didn't come up here. Or only one of you did."

"See the wires leading from this machine over to this crystal?" Duster said, pointing to a crystal on the wall about head high that had two wires attached to it.

April nodded and took another drink and then handed the bottle to Ryan who took a drink as well.

April was slowly feeling better. Her mind was starting to process the room and the disappearance of Janice and Steven. It could have just been a trick, and part of her wanted to hang onto that theory. But she couldn't.

This was real.

Not any real she could have ever imagined before this moment. But it was real.

"Janice and Steven have gone back into that alternate reality," Duster said. He again pointed at the crystal on the wall. "If you look closely you'll see all kinds of side crystals growing around the one they attached to as they make decisions that influence that timeline while they are there in the past."

April felt good enough to stand and she and Ryan stood up and moved over toward the wall, still holding hands. She felt stronger with him touching her.

She could see crystals forming, some growing, some absorbing into the larger crystal.

"Never touch a crystal with your bare hands," Duster said. "The energy flowing through them is really amazing."

"How long will they be back there?" April asked, her voice sounding a little dry.

Duster shrugged. "As long as they want. If they unplug the wire from the machine in the year they are in, they will return here. If they die in that timeline, they will return here alive and well."

"In just two minutes?" Ryan asked.

"Two minutes and fifteen seconds," Dawn said. "Which means they will be back in just under one minute and there's something that I need to tell you all."

Now Duster and Bonnie and Madison all turned to Dawn, clearly puzzled.

Dawn looked at her watch again, then smiled. "In just over forty seconds Janice and Steven will return."

All three of them nodded. April had no idea what was happening. She just stood there with Ryan watching.

"For the last year," Dawn said, "I've been keeping one of the hardest secrets I've ever kept."

"You are starting to worry me," Madison said.

Dawn just patted his shoulder. "You won't remember. You were dead."

April had about a thousand questions from that one statement alone, but she kept silent.

Dawn turned to Bonnie. "Remember I was with the two shopkeepers from Roosevelt when we visited you in the hospital in Caldwell when I was on the way back here on that first trip Madison and I took?"

Bonnie sort of nodded, slowly. Then April could see the realization come over her eyes and the shock and disbelief. April had no idea what was about to happen, but it had stunned one of the great math brains on the planet.

"Someone want to tell me what's going on?" Duster asked, clearly not liking being out of the loop.

Dawn glanced at her watch and then turned to the table as Steven and Janice just sort of appeared.

Both April and Ryan took a step back and April was afraid she was going to break Ryan's hand she was gripping it so hard.

Steven took the wire off the machine and then both of them stepped back from the machine and turned to Dawn with huge grins on their faces.

Dawn ran to them and gave them the biggest hug April had ever seen anyone give another person, as if she hadn't just seen them two minutes before.

Then she turned to everyone.

"I'll be go to hell," Bonnie said, shaking her head.

"Madison, Duster, Bonnie," Dawn said, the grin on her face as wide as anything April had ever seen. "I'm sure you remember Craig and Susan from the Roosevelt General Store."

April suddenly remembered that Dawn had said the general store foundations that they could see under the water at the lake was a very special general store.

"That's not possible," Duster said, looking at the wall and then the machine.

"I'll be go to hell," Bonnie said once again.

Madison just stood there staring at them, his mouth open.

Then Dawn turned to Janice and Steven and said simply, "I've been wanting to thank you personally for over a year, for making that winter possible for me to survive with my sanity. Now that we are all on the same page, in the same time, finally, I can. So thank you."

The three of them hugged again and April glanced at Ryan, who looked just as confused as she felt.

April could only hope that maybe someone would explain what had just happened.

And why Duster was pacing back and forth between the wall and the machine, swearing to himself.

# CHAPTER EIGHTEEN

*July 19, 2015*

**RYAN HAD NO PLAN** of letting go of April's hand any time soon. Something totally strange had just happened that actually had Duster upset and Bonnie swearing lightly under her breath.

Finally, Steven turned and said to Duster. "I'll explain it all after Janice and I have a shower to get the trail dust off."

"How long were you back there?" April asked.

"Early summer of 1885 to early summer of 1903," Janice said. "So only eight years. We cut it short to help Dawn."

Again Dawn just smiled and hugged her.

"Sorry," Dawn said. "I've been wanting to do that for a year now."

Ryan was so confused, he just shook his head. He had no idea, none, what had just happened.

"We'll explain it all after showers," Steven said. "But you two really should take a little jump to see Silver City in its prime."

Duster stopped his pacing and stared at Steven and Janice. "Full explanation on what you did? And how you did it?"

"Promise," Steven said.

"Go," Duster said.

Steven and Janice and Dawn all headed out of the room together, smiling and laughing.

Then Duster turned to Ryan and April. "Even if you never decide to go to another alternate reality again, let me show you what one is like."

"Safe?" April asked.

"It is," Duster said and Bonnie nodded.

"The principles of the conservation of energy and matter and time are what caused this room in the first place," Bonnie said. "No matter what happens to you in another timeline, you end up back as you left in this timeline, two minutes and fifteen seconds later."

"It's physics," Duster said. "Can't be any other way. We can explain it all in a lot more depth later if you want."

Ryan wanted to ask why the odd time, but decided he could do that later as well.

Duster put on gloves and walked over to the wall. He unhooked from the crystal there, seeming to make a note of where it was at, then moved about ten paces away with the long cord and hooked it up to a crystal there.

Then he came back to the machine and set it for May 1887.

"Why 1887?" Ryan asked.

"We did all this construction and protections on this place in 1881," Duster said. "We go back to 1887 because it's a good time and this mine has been closed down for years at that point and forgotten by the local residents of the area."

Ryan flat didn't understand. Some of the thousand questions he could ask later.

"If you are touching the machine, you will remember the trip. And you have to touch it to have the machine send you."

Duster put one hand on the machine indicated that Ryan and April should touch the machine in the open area beside his.

April hesitated.

"You'll understand a lot more about what we are talking about if you spend the next two minutes doing this," Bonnie said.

"I trust them," Ryan said, looking at April. "And I would rather have you beside me, holding my hand on this."

He looked into her worried eyes and finally saw her nod.

"Together," she said, trying to smile.

"Together," he said, nodding and squeezing her hand.

"Want to come along?" Duster asked Madison and Bonnie.

"I will," Bonnie said, coming over and putting her hand beside Ryan's and Duster's and April's on the machine. "April will need help with a dress."

"Oh, yeah, good point," Duster said.

"I'll start digging out stuff for dinner," Madison said. "This dinner could really be interesting. Hope everyone likes steaks."

Madison smiled and said, "Have fun." Then he turned around to head toward the door and just vanished.

Duster and Bonnie stepped back from the machine and a moment later Ryan and April did the same. Ryan had no idea why or what had gone wrong.

"Where did he go?" April asked a half second before Ryan could.

"He didn't go anywhere," Bonnie said. "We did."

"Welcome to 1887," Duster said, smiling.

# CHAPTER NINETEEN

*May 1887*

**APRIL FOLLOWED DUSTER** to the big door leading out of the cavern. It was now closed and he had to open it.

As they went into the natural cave on the other side, the lights came up automatically.

April was about to ask where everyone had gone, then realized that if Duster and Bonnie were telling the truth, the other four were in this cavern in another timeline in 2015.

Her mind wouldn't let herself believe any of this was possible, even though every detail was being proven to her.

One detail at a time.

Bonnie helped her into a 1800s-style dress over her jeans and blouse. They seemed to have racks and racks of clothing stocked in the big cavern. Duster helped Ryan into a jacket and cowboy hat.

"No need to button this up," Bonnie said as she also pulled on a dress and put a bonnet on her head. "We're only going out on to the mine tailings."

"So this is in case someone sees us?" April asked.

"It is," Bonnie nodded. "We'll just look like two couples out for a walk."

They headed back down the mine tunnel, with Duster showing them some of the alarm systems.

At the big metal door at the entrance, Duster showed them a view port that allowed them to look in all directions around the mine, including above it, for anyone outside.

From what April could tell, the coast was clear.

She took Ryan's hand and he squeezed hers. There was no way in the world she could have gone through this without him at her side.

Duster showed them the big open button for the door and hit it.

The small chamber around them went dark, then the big door slid open.

They were hit with a blast of cold air that took April's breath away.

It was light, but barely and light snow was blowing on the wind and the ground was covered in a dusting of snow.

They stepped out onto the mine tailings.

The old mining cabin still had a door and windows and a drift of snow was piled up against one side of it.

"Cars will be over there in the future in another timeline," Duster said.

He pointed across an open hillside. There were no trees now and no cars. Just snow.

"We really are in the past," Ryan said, his voice soft and almost whipped away by the blowing snow.

"The past of another timeline, but one so similar to our own as to be indistinguishable," Duster said. "Maybe in this one the only difference is that someone took a job and in ours they didn't."

"Take a look," Bonnie said and eased April and Ryan over to the edge of the mine tailings.

Below, through the light blowing snow, she could see a town with hundreds and hundreds of buildings and smoke coming from the fireplaces of about half the buildings in town.

"Silver City after its first gold and silver rush boom was starting to fade," Duster said. "It had a few more boom periods before it finally became what you saw earlier."

"We are really in 1887?" Ryan asked, his grip on her hand firm and hard.

"Looks like early May," Duster said, nodding.

"Now, can we go back inside before I freeze?" Bonnie asked.

April wasn't sure that she was ready to go back in yet, even though she was freezing as well.

She needed a few minutes for this to sink in.

"Another minute," Ryan said before she could.

"Tell you what," Duster said to Bonnie, "Go on in and unplug us in about ten minutes."

"Will do," Bonnie said and went back inside, letting the big rock slide closed over the fake mine entrance.

"Sit down," Duster said.

He sat down on one side of April and Ryan on the other, staring out over the impossible site of Silver City, Idaho in 1887.

"So, now you see why we wanted plans for that lodge?" Duster asked.

"You're going to build it, aren't you?" Ryan asked.

Duster nodded. "A number of times in a bunch of timelines. Your theory about the dust was spot on. There are millions and millions of us in different timelines who have decided to go back and build the lodge. And we all bring

in dust from each timeline. That's how the echo rumors of the lodge got into so many timelines."

"Because you go back and build it?" April asked.

"Because we do," Duster said, nodding. "In a million timelines at the same time. And all four of us hope you two would come back and help us build and furnish it."

"I'm still trying to grasp that," Ryan said, pointing down at the city just waking up to a snowy morning in May.

"Me too," April said.

But now something had finally snapped over in her mind and she really, really believed this. That's how the four historians inside could write such fantastic books. They had years of time and firsthand research.

They had all the time in all the alternate realities to do so.

"So," April said, "We could live in that city from now, 1887 now that is, for how long?"

"Until you die of old age," Duster said. "And you end up right back where you started inside there, two minutes and fifteen seconds later."

"How many times have you died in another timeline?" Ryan asked.

"Too damn many," Duster said. "Dying in the past is never a pleasant experience and I would try to avoid it at all costs, even though you end up back here just fine."

"Is that what happened to Madison on their first trip?" April asked.

Duster laughed. "I have a hunch I'm going to hear that full story at the same time you do."

Suddenly April found herself standing beside Ryan and Duster and Bonnie in the crystal room.

Bonnie smiled at her and Ryan. "I came in and simply unplugged the machine from the crystal and that brought you all inside."

"We were in that other timeline for about thirty minutes total," Ryan said.

"And only two minutes and fifteen seconds passed here."

April just shook her head and shivered. She still felt cold. Very cold.

"Come on," Duster said, using a glove to take the wires off the crystal on the wall. "Let's go hear a story."

With that, the man in the cowboy hat and duster headed for the exit to the crystal cavern.

"Let's get out of these clothes first," Bonnie said, smiling, indicating the dress she had slipped over her blouse and jeans.

"And something warm to drink?" April asked, rubbing her hands together and staring around at the beauty of the big cavern of crystals.

Some were huge, some tiny. Millions and millions and millions of them. All created by a single decision someone made.

"One question," April said before Bonnie could turn away. "If I had decided to not come up here with you today, where would those crystals be?"

Bonnie smiled. "Our best guess, and it is only a guess, is about a hundred miles in that direction." She pointed down the vast cavern.

"It goes that far?" April asked, trying to grasp that.

"It's infinite," Bonnie said. "More than likely this also exists in other dimensions and in other timelines. Every crystal you can see here and off into the distance is so close to our history as to be indistinguishable."

"Oh," April said, looking at the millions and millions of glowing crystals around and above her and stretching off into the distance. "So in every one of these Ryan and I came with you today."

"You did," Bonnie said, nodding.

"Hard to grasp," Ryan said.

"Even for a mathematician," Bonnie said, "almost impossible."

# CHAPTER TWENTY

*July 19, 2015*

**RYAN WAS AMAZED** that April seemed to now be accepting all this a lot quicker than he was. At least she was asking some really great questions, things his shocked brain couldn't seem to even think about.

They held hands again and went back into the large cavern. After they got out of the period clothing, they followed Bonnie back to an area of the cave that surprised Ryan.

Tucked in what seemed like a side cavern was a completely modern kitchen. Ryan was working on something at the counter and Duster was sitting at the head of a large dining table in the middle of the area, his hat and coat off.

The appliances in the kitchen were the most modern possible, the countertops marble, and a soft tile covered the false floor built in over the cave dirt floor. A living room area, carpeted in a soft brown carpet sat off to one side of the kitchen. Three large couches filled that area with a couple of reading lights and a bookcase against one wall full of books.

Dawn was sitting beside Duster, smiling. Neither of them were saying anything.

"Wow, who built all this?" Ryan asked.

Duster pointed to Madison and Bonnie. "They didn't like the hotplate and icebox I had back here for some reason."

"Restrooms back there," Bonnie said, pointing to the back as she moved over and sat on the other side of her husband, facing Dawn. "Men's on the right, women's on the left. Showers and lockers where Steven and Janice are in the middle."

April nodded and headed that way and Ryan decided he might as well wash up before dinner as well. But he wasn't certain he was going to be hungry for a while.

Five minutes later, both he and April were back out at the table sitting with a few chairs between them and Bonnie and Duster. Madison had brought them both a bottle of water and was getting April a cup of hot tea as well.

Duster was clearly waiting for Steven and Janice to join them, so Ryan figured he had time for a few questions, since what had just happened wasn't really sinking in.

"Can I ask how many people you have shown this place to?"

Bonnie laughed. "The six of us and Janice and Steven. Everyone is here at once."

That actually surprised him and he sat back. "So the lodge is why we are part of this?"

Duster laughed and Bonnie patted his arm and answered. "Actually, no, it's because you both have a keen interest in the mountains and history of the West. And both of you specialize in historical reconstruction and are the best in the country in what you do. We figured that if you had actual access to the past, it would help your work."

"Like it helps our books," Dawn said, and Madison nodded.

"The lodge idea was only a bonus," Duster laughed, "and we figured it was a way to test you both."

"That lodge design is just fantastic," Dawn said.

"It is," Duster said.

"More than I had hoped for," Bonnie said, smiling.

"Thank you," Ryan said.

"Yes, thank you," April said. "And thanks for trusting us enough to show us this."

Ryan nodded. "And giving us a chance to work together."

He put his hand on April's and she smiled at him. When she did that, most logical thoughts went right out of his head. He was really, really falling hard for April, more every moment now that they had broken the ice on going to the next step.

Bonnie and Dawn smiled, and Duster just shook his head and dug into his pocket and handed Bonnie another ten dollar gold coin.

"You bet against me again?" Ryan asked, smiling at Duster.

"No, I bet April would have too much class to fall for an architect."

With that everyone laughed, and April leaned over and kissed Ryan. Then she looked right at Duster. "No one has ever said I had class."

And again everyone laughed.

Ryan could not believe how much he really, really liked these people. All of them were fantastically smart and talented. And here they were in a completely modern kitchen inside a big cavern talking and laughing.

How had he gotten so lucky to have them find him?

And he find April, the beautiful woman who was smart and fun and beautiful and liked camping as much as he did.

At that moment, Janice and Steven came out of the back. Both of them were dressed in comfortable shirts and jeans. Both had wet hair and were drinking from bottles of water.

They sat at the table, one on each side, clearly very comfortable in this space.

Then Janice looked at Ryan. "Any way you can figure out how to put hot showers in that lodge on the pass?"

Ryan shrugged. "Sure, most of it could be done in 1900s technology. I sort of had that planned to be honest."

"Perfect," Janice said. "That's what I miss the most when I'm in the past."

"Okay," Duster said, looking at the two of them. "What did you do?"

Ryan squeezed April's hand and the two of them sat back to just listen.

"We noticed you had a movement pattern on the crystals on the wall," Steven said. "And after hearing Dawn talk about her winter in Roosevelt on their first trip back, we wondered if we could hit the same alternate reality."

"We figured the Roosevelt area was a choke point as well in time," Janice said. "Since there were only seven thousand people in there. We figured there would be a vast number of timelines where Dawn and Madison experienced that horrid first trip. So we tried to hit a timeline that they might be in in Roosevelt that winter, the same one you hooked up to when you four went back, and after almost a dozen trips back, we did."

"We couldn't say anything to you in Roosevelt," Steven said, "because you hadn't met us yet in this timeline and given us a chance to go back."

"We only told Dawn because we knew she could keep it secret for the year and she needed the support after Madison died and you and Bonnie both left, leaving her alone."

"Keeping that secret was the hardest damn thing I ever had to do," Dawn said, shaking her head. "Because it was more than a year. We've traveled for about seven hundred years since last time I saw you. And then I almost forgot about it today."

"We knew you hadn't," Steven said, smiling, "but we didn't tell you that."

"You've aged well in seven hundred years," Janice said, smiling at Dawn and everyone but Duster laughed.

Ryan squeezed April's hand and she squeezed back. He wasn't completely understanding everything they were talking about, but it seemed important enough to not interrupt with stupid questions.

"So when Dawn told you her story of that winter," Duster said, "did she mention you two at all before you went back?"

"None. All she said was that some nice people rode with her from Roosevelt to Silver City," Janice said. "That was it. We didn't realize that was us until after all the events happened in Roosevelt that winter."

Bonnie now leaned forward, a frown on her face. "So when you three got here in 1903, you all unplugged the wire together. Right? Dawn returned a year ago, you two just returned. Right?"

Janice and Dawn and Steven nodded.

Madison stood with a salad bowl in his hand, listening and frowning.

"Damn, I didn't think that was possible," Duster said.

"We talked about it," Bonnie said. "The combined trips formed another crystal under the connection. Remember how time used to spit us out in our first trips until we loosened the connectors and made them expandable on the crystals?"

"Spit you out?" Madison and Steven asked at the same time.

Ryan just had no idea how time could spit them out. He was beyond lost and clearly both Madison and Steven didn't understand it either.

Duster nodded. "When we first started exploring alternate historical realities, we put a tight band connector on the crystal to hold the connection in place. The connector would not let the crystal expand and grow as it should with our changes in the past, which caused all sorts of strange things to happen back in time."

"One timeline the Titanic didn't sink," Bonnie said, shaking her head.

"We finally realized it wasn't our presence that caused the strange events in one timeline, but the clamps constraining the crystals. Once we changed those clamps to let the crystal grow and change as it wants with events in the past, nothing strange has happened and we've been able to stay as long in each timeline as we wanted."

Ryan just shook his head. He had a hunch there was a very long story behind that. Another question he would ask later.

"So I'm confused," Madison said.

"Oh, thank God it's not just me," April said, and again everyone laughed. She was showing the sense of humor that Ryan had come to love over the last two months.

"What happens if you just left the band attached to that one crystal and we all went back and met ourselves in that timeline in Roosevelt?"

"It wouldn't be the same timeline," Duster said, shaking his head.

Bonnie nodded. "The moment we tried that, we would be shifted to a timeline and crystal where we were not there. Again, conservation of mass and energy and time rules. They are very firm."

"In other words," Janice asked, "we can only be alive in one timeline at a time?"

"That's correct," Duster said. "That's why we've never had any worry about moving the cable very far along the wall. Time and physics won't allow us to duplicate up in any timeline."

Something dinged Ryan at that point, and he made a note to figure out what it was later.

"And that's why we can't just jump back ten years in another timeline," Steven said. "It would switch us to a timeline where we didn't exist."

"We actually once tried to stay beyond my birth in a timeline," Duster said. "The moment I was born I found myself standing back here."

Ryan actually nodded at that. There was no way that time would let them go back and meet themselves. As far as he was concerned, that was a very good thing.

But what about the lodge? What happens if they went back and built the lodge? Did buildings have different rules than humans? Again he decided to not ask that question just yet.

"But it seems," Bonnie said, staring at her husband, "that we can all go back at different times into the same timeline. Sort of like we do when you go ahead of us a year or so."

Duster nodded, clearly deep in thought. "That's a good thing to know."

Ryan had no idea why it was a good thing to know, but he was trusting one of the math brains in the room to explain it to him.

At some point.

# CHAPTER TWENTY-ONE

*July 19, 2015*

**APRIL JUST FELT SORT OF NUMB** as the conversation went on for a few more minutes. Then Duster and Bonnie went off to work on some math in yet another side room off the cave that April hadn't noticed.

Madison said dinner would be in forty minutes, so Dawn and Janice and Steven headed off to sit outside in the sun for a while and talk.

That left April and Ryan and Madison in the kitchen area of the big cave.

"Anything I can do to help?" April asked.

Madison shook his head. "Baked potatoes are in, salad is done and chilling in the fridge. I'll put the steaks on just before time to eat."

He took a bottle of water and sat down at the table facing them. "I remember I had about a thousand questions when I was where you two are sitting, so fire away."

"You've really been in the past for seven hundred years?" Ryan asked before April could even think of anything to say.

Madison nodded. "Dawn keeps track of all that, but yes, that sounds about right. We tend to go back around 1887 and stay for thirty or forty years. Once we managed fifty before Dawn got sick and I came back and pulled the plug."

"So that's not that many trips back, really," Ryan said. "How long do you stay here between trips?"

"At first we just turned around and went right back," Madison said. "But Bonnie warned us about doing that too much, so now we try to take some breaks and remember modern society. You know, remember how to drive."

April just shook her head at that comment.

Madison went on. "And we don't try to come up here in the winter. We teach those months and do all the book stuff that is required of publishing books."

April just couldn't seem to wrap her mind around what she was hearing.

"You are talking about lifetimes in the past," she said. "Right?"

"Yup," Madison said, nodding. "The shortest trip we have taken after our first quick ones like you just did with Bonnie and Duster was the one I died in. The one they were talking about."

"You must really love it back in the old West," Ryan said.

"We do," he said. "It's our passion. And we both love that Thunder Mountain area. You two really think that fantastic lodge you designed can be built on that pass?"

"Up until today," April said, "we both thought it only an exercise in futility and a daydream of a very rich couple and their crazy friends, no offense meant."

"None taken," Madison said, smiling.

"But I think it can be built," Ryan said, nodding.

"You two want to help build it?" Madison asked.

April looked at Ryan, who smiled.

"We'll have to talk about that," April said, smiling. She wasn't sure how exactly she felt, but now that the lodge was possible, she wasn't sure how she could turn the chance down.

"So what exactly happened on that first trip back for you and Dawn?" Ryan asked.

Madison shook his head. "I only know the good parts. We had a wonderful trip from here to Roosevelt, after we got over the stiffness from riding horses for the first time in years. Dawn and I completely fell in love along the way."

"And you still are," April said. That much was clear to her. And one of the things she really liked about the couple.

"We are," Madison said, smiling. "Pretty amazing after seven hundred years, huh?"

"It is," April said and Ryan nodded.

"We spent a wonderful three months in Roosevelt in a huge cabin that Duster had built ahead of time for our trip. He had gone back into the timeline a year earlier to set it all up."

"I thought that's what he said wasn't possible," Ryan asked.

"We were all on the same connection, same trip out," Madison said, shrugging. "I honestly don't understand all the math. Gives me a headache."

"I'm starting to understand that feeling," April said.

"Right about the first week of September, I got hit with a boulder coming off a hill up by the Dewey Mine. Killed my horse, broke my leg really badly. Duster got me off the hill and back to the cabin and that's the last I remember until I ended up standing next to Dawn in the crystal room without pants on. They told me they kept me knocked out with drugs until I died."

"No pants?" Ryan asked, but April understood.

"Common to bury people without pants on," April said, smiling at the man she was falling for, "since only half the casket was able to be opened back then."

"No casket for me," Madison said. "Dawn and Janice and Steven just rolled me into a hole up in that cemetery and filled in the dirt.

"Where were Bonnie and Duster?" Ryan asked.

"When I got hurt," Madison said, "Duster took off to come back up here and unplug the machine and bring all four of us back to the cavern. Instant health care."

April nodded. "Same as we were brought in from outside by Bonnie."

"Exactly," Madison said, nodding. "But he was on a train above Emmitt, Idaho, when it derailed and he died when his car went into the river. He was asleep and didn't even know what hit him until he ended up back here as well."

"And Bonnie?" April asked, almost afraid to know.

"When Duster didn't make it to Silver City, I was still alive but getting worse. Bonnie didn't want Dawn to have to bury me on the first trip back, so she somehow made it over the pass and out. But near Caldwell a snake spooked her horse and bucked her off and she broke her back and ended up spending the winter in the Caldwell Hospital."

"In 1903?" April asked and actually felt herself shudder. She had read about hospitals in that time period out west.

"She said she worked on a lot of math in her head that winter," Madison said. "She would have died in a few more months, but Dawn buried me in the fall and managed to get through the long winter in Roosevelt and get back here and unplug the machine and bring us all back. Duster arrived puzzled, Bonnie in a very smelly hospital gown, and me without pants."

"And Dawn didn't tell you anything about how she made it through that long winter in that mining town?" Ryan asked.

"She said she would rather not talk about it," Madison said, "and until today, it got sort of forgotten in all the other trips back."

"Seven hundred years of living will do that for a person," Ryan said, nodding.

April still couldn't imagine living that long. She was still young and healthy, so she never much thought about death, even dealing with so much of the past as she did every day in her profession.

But she had never once thought about living a long, long time.

And basically being immortal in that past period.

And only having a few minutes here, in her real world, go by.

By the time she and Ryan asked Madison a few more questions and then Madison said it was time for dinner, she was convinced she wanted to try to go back into the past.

She loved everything about the past. And she knew Ryan would want to build that lodge himself.

And she wanted to be the one to furnish it.

And live in it with Ryan, if he would have her.

From the memory of that kiss this morning, she had a hunch he would.

At least for a time.

And it seemed that suddenly, they both had a great deal of time.

As Madison went off in search of Bonnie and Duster, April turned to Ryan and took his hand in hers.

"Want to go build and furnish a big lodge?"

"Are you asking me on a date?" he asked, smiling.

"I am," she said.

"Then the answer is yes," he said, smiling at her. "I want to go build a lodge and I want you to furnish it. I'm not sure I understand half of what has been said here so far, or how most of this works, but I'm willing to learn if you are."

"More than willing," she said, "and scared to death."

"Yeah, me too," he said, squeezing her hand. "So we'll get through it together."

She reached forward and pulled him close and kissed him as hard as he had kissed her this morning before the presentation. She just couldn't believe how much she had come to like this man over the last two months.

After a moment, Madison cleared his throat and walked by them. "Not over the steaks."

April pushed back slightly then, smiling at Ryan, she said, "We don't want to leave out the salad, do we?"

"No, we don't," Ryan said, smiling back with that wonderful grin that she could look at for a very long time.

So she kissed him again.

# PART THREE

# CHAPTER TWENTY-TWO

*July 19, 2015*

**THE DECISION,** after the long and wonderful steak dinner among the eight of them, was for Bonnie and Duster and April and Ryan to head back to Boise, get a few hours of sleep, pack some clothing and come back to the mine early the next day.

Ryan liked that idea. He felt he needed a little time to get grounded and seeing the office and Boise and his apartment again might help that.

The other two couples would stay. Janice and Steven said they had a few more trips to take on research and Dawn and Madison said they'd love to go with them.

Ryan had a hard time imagining that in the time it took him and April to head back to Boise, get a little sleep, and then come back in the morning, those four could spend hundreds and hundreds of years living in the past.

Maybe more.

And maybe die a few times in the past as well.

When he actually let himself believe all this, the amount of knowledge and understanding the four of them would gain in the time it took him to go to Boise and come back made him slightly jealous.

But living that long in that short of time really wasn't something he could grasp just yet, even though the idea excited him more than he wanted to admit. He loved living and he loved learning and this seemed to be the perfect opportunity to do a lot of both.

April sat beside him in the back seat of the big Cadillac and it was dark by the time they got down off the mountains and headed back toward Boise. They were holding hands like kids on a date and it felt right as far as he was concerned.

On the drive, Bonnie turned in her seat so she could see them both in the dashboard light and explained to them what kind of clothes to pack and bring. Mostly socks and underwear, since not much time would pass in this timeline. She and Duster already had a few changes of clothes for him and April in the cavern

that would fit the late 1890's styles and they had ordered specially made shoes and boots for them that would pass in the time period as well, even though they were modern made.

"You thought we would decide to go back?" April asked, clearly as surprised at that as much as Ryan was.

"We hoped is all," Bonnie said. "So better to spend a little and be prepared ahead of time."

"Just make sure you bring those plans," Duster said. "Make a couple of copies that we can fold down and put in saddlebags."

"So what are you thinking for this first trip?" Ryan asked.

"I'm going to go back alone to about 1890," Duster said, "and see if I can get that land secured and a bunch of land around it. Then Dawn and Madison will follow around 1898 into the same timeline, then Bonnie and you two and Janice and Steven about 1900."

"We're going to build the lodge?" April asked, squeezing Ryan's hand.

"For the first time," Duster said.

Bonnie laughed since she could see his face and April's face.

"Remember," she said, "every time we go back, if we want the lodge to exist, we have to build it again."

"Of course, with what Janice and Steven discovered, that might not be the entire story," Duster said, shaking his head. "So we'll see about that."

Ryan sat there, his stomach twisted up in a knot. Again he had understood that idea that people couldn't exist at the same time in the same timeline, but what about the lodge.

Something about the lodge existing in so many timelines bothered him but he couldn't put his finger on it.

"You mean we are going to have to build and furnish the lodge every two minutes and fifteen seconds?" April asked.

Ryan glanced at her. She looked as upset as he felt. And was feeling exactly the same thing. His mind wouldn't let him understand living a long time in another timeline.

Duster laughed and Bonnie just smiled.

"In this timeline, yes," Bonnie said. "Only two minutes and fifteen seconds will go by, but you will remember all the work and time it took to build the lodge."

"We'll make sure we document everything," Duster said, "so the second and third times we can do it quicker. And we'll know who to hire the second and third times and who not to."

"In this timeline," Bonnie said, "we might build and furnish that lodge five or six times tomorrow."

"But in the timelines that we build the lodge," Duster said, "you can live in it for an entire lifetime and your children and grandchildren can live in it and you can die of old age in it."

"Yeah, tomorrow alone," Bonnie said, smiling at both of them, "we all could live four or five hundred years."

Duster was chuckling, but Ryan and April just sat there and Bonnie smiled at them. Ryan was very glad that they were now on open paved highway, because he felt almost dizzy.

"Lifetime?" Ryan finally asked.

"Children?" April asked.

Bonnie nodded. "When you move into the other timeline, you are actually there, living, just as anyone else in the world. When were you both born?"

April said, "July 1982."

"January 1982," Ryan said.

"We were both born in 1980," Bonnie said, nodding. "So you two can live in the past right up to 1982. Then the timeline will spit you out and you'll end up back at the mine. However, to live to 1982, you are going to have to live to about 112 years of age or so if we go back in 1890."

"And when you die," Duster said, "no matter when, either young or of old age after seventy years of living, you end up back at the mine as Madison and I did in that first trip with Dawn and Madison."

"Children?" April asked.

Bonnie shrugged. "Again, you are alive in that timeline completely. If you have kids there, they keep on and have kids and so on."

"Will they vanish when we come back?" April asked.

"Oh, heaven's no," Duster said, laughing. "They are part of the timeline, even if you step back to this one. They are there and part of that timeline."

"Think of it this way," Bonnie said. "If you had a child here, now, would that kid suddenly vanish because you went to another timeline for a while?"

Ryan so wanted to ask if Duster and Bonnie had had children, but he wasn't sure if that was beyond the bounds of what was allowed.

April glanced at him and also said nothing.

"Wow, you two really have some restraint," Bonnie said, smiling.

Duster laughed and got them onto the freeway headed toward Boise. "Madison and Dawn damn near climbed all over us when they heard kids were possible in other timelines."

"Have you?" April asked, looking at Bonnie.

Bonnie smiled. "Let's just say that there is more than one timeline where we have left families when we died and returned here. We take back modern drugs with us, but childbirth in the past is not something you want to do lightly."

"Do you miss your children?" April asked.

Bonnie nodded. "Of course, but by this point in time, only great-great-grandkids would still be alive. The kids would not. And living hundreds and hundreds of years sort of dulls the memory of some things you would rather not remember."

"Time can give you a real headache, can't it?" Ryan asked, doing his best to grasp what they were telling him.

"Parts of it can," Duster said, nodding.

"Most of it is just living," Bonnie said. "When we go back in another timeline tomorrow, we're going to try to build and furnish that lodge you two designed. It's going to take years of living and work and fun."

"And I plan on spending some time in the lodge after we build it," Duster said. "My feet up on that deck staring out at that fantastic view and drinking good wine and whisky."

He then glanced over his shoulder. "So which suite did you two design for me and Bonnie?"

"The big one at the end of the hall on the Monumental Creek side," Ryan said.

"Good one," Bonnie said. "I had my eye on that one."

"And for Dawn and Madison?"

"The one on the same side closest to big room," April said.

"So Steven and Janice can have one of the other two across the hall with the view in the other direction," Duster said, "and you two can have the other suite."

Ryan glanced at April and she was looking at Duster sort of stunned.

It might have been just a touch early for them to think about living together.

But honestly, Ryan liked the idea. He liked it a lot.

He just hoped April would as well.

# CHAPTER TWENTY-THREE

*July 20, 2015*

**APRIL FELT NUMB** when Bonnie and Duster dropped her and Ryan off at their office. It was after midnight, but it felt a lot later. Lifetimes later, but that would come tomorrow if what she had seen was right.

And Duster said he would pick them up right here at eight in the morning.

His last words as they climbed out of the Cadillac: "We've got a lodge to build tomorrow and some lifetimes to live."

They both stood there and watched the big white car drive off until the silence of the warm evening finally just seemed far too loud to stand. The air hadn't cooled off completely from the warm day and there was no wind in the trees.

After being in the cavern and then in the climate-controlled Cadillac, she had forgotten the day had been a warm summer day.

In the distance, there were sounds of some college kids laughing. On the other side of their office she could hear the echoed conversation of a couple strolling along the River Walk.

"Oh, my," she said softly.

"I feel like I've been run over by a truck," Ryan said.

"It's not possible to grasp everything they threw at us today," April said, shaking her head. "Just not possible. They can't expect us to, can they?"

He took her hand and turned her toward the sidewalk. "Come on, I'll walk you home."

They had both walked to work that morning, since they lived close to the office. They both had cars, but she seldom used hers, and never to drive the four blocks to work.

He lived about two blocks away in a slightly different direction. About a half-block from his place was an all-night restaurant. They had eaten many great evening meals in there talking. She suddenly realized it had almost been five hours since that dinner and she needed some food and conversation with Ryan right now.

"Something to eat?" she asked.

"Good idea." They went in a slightly different direction through their building's parking lot and down the hill, both walking in silence. She just needed to walk with him and think and try to get some sort of perspective. Around them the warm summer night of Boise was going on.

That helped a little.

Within ten minutes they were in the noisy, but comfortable, restaurant and tucked in the back facing each other across a brown fake-wood tabletop. It was one of their regular booths and that felt good as well.

She sat there silently until the waitress left with their drink order. Then she looked up at the man she had worked with for two months and was falling for. His hair was mussed slightly and his shirt was open and his wonderful eyes troubled. Yet he was the most handsome man she had ever seen.

And one of the smartest and most gentle men she knew.

All she wanted to do was spend time with him and the fact that he was in this with her made most of this seem all right, even though it was completely impossible.

"So," she said, reaching across the table and taking his hands in hers. "You want to live with me in a giant lodge in the Idaho Mountains about a hundred and fifteen years in the past?"

"Honestly," he said, nodding and holding her gaze, "yes, I do. But we have to build it first."

"Details," she said, shrugging and smiling at him.

It took him a moment, but then he laughed and she could feel some of the tension draining from her shoulders and back.

"So what part of all this don't you believe?" she asked.

"If it were anyone but four of the top western historians in the world and Duster and Bonnie," Ryan said, "I wouldn't believe a word of any of it."

"Even after they showed us Silver City in 1887? And transported us back into that fantastic cavern? And people seemed to appear out of nowhere?"

"Yes, even after that," he said, nodding. "That all could have been faked, but there is no reason they would go to such lengths to fool us."

"And give us all the money and the business," she said. "Just to plan a lodge that would be impossible to build at this point."

"So even though it's all impossible," he said, "Every bit of it, I am trying to believe it all."

"So you believe we could live three or four or five hundred years, build that lodge a dozen times, and be back here tomorrow night eating dinner again?"

He opened his mouth and then closed it and just shook his head.

"I want to believe it's possible, don't you?" she said, squeezing his hands and letting go as their water and Diet Cokes arrived.

After the waitress had taken their order for bacon and eggs and toast, he looked at her.

"I want to believe it more than anything."

"So do I," she said, nodding.

"So we go get some underwear and supplies and meet them in the morning," Ryan said, "and see if all this is real. I really want to build that lodge on that ridge."

"What happens if we can't get along for decades?" she asked, suddenly very worried.

"We've been friends now since this project started," he said. "We're always going to be friends, I promise you that."

She looked at the man she was falling for faster than she had ever fallen for anyone. "You don't think sex might spoil the friendship?"

"Who said anything about sex?" he asked, smiling at her.

"I did," she said, smiling back. "As soon as we're out of here and you are packed and we are back at my place."

He raised his arm in the air and said, "Check."

And they were both so tired, they laughed at the old joke.

And that felt great.


## CHAPTER TWENTY-FOUR

*July 20, 2015*

**BY THE TIME** they finished with their late meal, it was almost one in the morning.

As they left the restaurant, April took Ryan's hand and they walked slowly along the sidewalk on the summer night that now had a slight chill to the air. She had really come to love Boise and the weather here during the summer. Dry and warm during the day, yet it cooled down in the evenings. Right now the air almost felt too cold.

Perfect and refreshing after the day they had had.

Even though they didn't have many hours, they walked slowly, enjoying the moment and not really talking. It must have taken them a good fifteen minutes to make the short walk.

She had been inside Ryan's apartment a few times and it felt like him, with a wall of books on varied topics and an old-fashioned draft table against one wall. A large computer with three screens filled one side of the main room of the apartment. The computer looked like an exact match for the one he had in his office at work.

She knew he had done a lot of designing in the evenings here on the lodge.

The furniture was newer and in brown tones and all cloth. She thought about dropping into one of the more comfortable-looking chairs and then decided not to since she was afraid she was so tired at this point, she might not get out of it.

It only took Ryan a few minutes to load a backpack with a change of clothes and a bunch of underwear. He had changed into a different shirt with a light sweatshirt over that and clean jeans. He also brought modern gloves and some heavy socks.

He showed them to her and said, "If we're going to be up there for a while on that mountain while we are building the lodge, it's going to get really cold."

"Very good thinking," she said. "I wouldn't have thought to bring any of that now in the summer."

She could feel herself growing more tired by the moment, clearly letting down from the very long day. She had been so afraid their presentation wouldn't go well this morning, she hadn't slept well at all last night. And then with everything up in Silver City this afternoon and evening, she felt like her mind was shutting down.

Ryan put the backpack over one shoulder and locked up as they went out.

"Strange," he said. "It feels as if I'm going to be gone a long time, yet more than likely, if Bonnie and Duster are telling us the truth, I'll be back here tonight, or in a day at most."

Her tired mind just couldn't hold that idea.

She put her arm though his and they walked the four blocks to her place, again not talking.

Ryan tossed his pack on her kitchen table as she headed for the bedroom. The clock on her microwave said it was almost two in the morning. They had to be back at the office in six hours.

"Change clothes and pack," he said. "We're both going to be so tired when we have to go, you don't want to trust anything to the morning."

She could feel the disappointment at his words, and her relief. She really wanted to make love to him, but right now she wagered neither one of them would stay awake for very long if they tried.

She stopped in the door to her bedroom and looked back at him standing beside her kitchen table.

He smiled at her. "When you are ready and your stuff is here on the table, we'll sleep until our alarms go off."

"Rain check on my suggestion at the restaurant?"

"I have a hunch we're going to have years and years to work on that rain check."

She smiled. "That sounds wonderful."

He smiled back. "It does, doesn't it?"

It took her longer than it normally would to pack underwear and change clothes into what she would wear in a few hours.

Then she decided she didn't want to sleep in her clothes. She wanted to sleep beside Ryan in her bed. If something happened, so be it.

So she took off her clothes and put them on her pack and then walked out into the living room completely nude.

Ryan was asleep sitting on the couch.

She was standing there nude and the guy she wanted to seduce had fallen asleep on her. If she wasn't so tired herself, she might have taken it a little personally. Now she got to tease him about it later.

She went back into her bedroom, set her alarm, then set the alarm on her phone.

Then she pulled down the covers on her bed went back and rousted him.

He blinked twice, then he clearly woke up and stared at her.

"I'm dreaming and your body is better in this dream than it has been in all the others."

"You dreamed about me being nude?" she asked, helping him to his feet and leading him into the bedroom.

"I take the fifth," he said. "But this is far better."

She worked to help him out of his clothes.

His body was better than she had dreamed as well. Solid and firm.

And he was clearly aroused.

She pushed him back onto the bed and climbed in beside him. "I thought we were going to sleep?"

He kissed her, pressing his body against the full length of her body.

And she kissed him back, pressing back.

He had to be the most handsome man she had ever known. And the most sexy.

She wanted him and she wanted him now. Two months of waiting had been far, far too long.

She pushed him on his back and climbed on him and a moment later he was inside her.

And that felt about a thousand times better than she had ever dreamed it would feel as well.

She never took her gaze from his eyes and he stared right back as if he was seeing into her very soul.

They started slowly, but pretty soon their movements, because they were so tired and had put this off for so long, were hard and quick and intense.

They came together.

After a moment, he pulled her down close, kissed her lightly, and then rolled her over on her side, still inside her, her legs wrapped around his waist.

That felt so natural, she couldn't believe it.

He kissed her long and gently, the most wonderful, passionate kiss she could remember.

Finally she pushed him back slightly and looked into his eyes.

"You still want to live with me in a big lodge in the past?"

"More than ever, now," he said, smiling.

She kissed him long and hard, then said, "Sleep."

They cuddled down together, her legs wrapped around him, his hardness still inside her.

That was the last thing she remembered until her alarm was going off and he was kissing her cheek.

She blinked her eyes open to look into his wonderful gaze.

"You really are the most beautiful woman I have ever met," he said. "Even waking up."

She kissed him and then he rolled away and off the bed.

She watched him walk toward the bathroom. His butt was even better naked than in pants. How was that possible?

The next thing she knew, he was gently rousting her again.

She glanced over at her bed clock. They had twenty minutes to get to the office.

"Take a quick shower," he said. "You have anything in the kitchen we can grab to eat and walk?"

"Pop Tarts," she said, slowly sitting up and trying to rub the sleep from her eyes.

He smiled and stared at her.

"You are so damn good looking, I could look at your body forever."

"Let's go for a hundred years first, shall we?"

He laughed and helped her to her feet, then kissed her. "You have Pop Tarts? Really?"

She managed to nod.

"A woman after my heart," he said, kissing her again and then giving her a gentle push toward the bathroom.

"You chose Pop Tarts over this naked body?" she asked, smiling at him. "Now I see how you are."

They left her apartment fifteen minutes later, Pop Tarts in hand, backpacks over their shoulders.

And as she locked the apartment behind them, she felt as Ryan said he felt last night.

It would be a very long time before she returned here later tonight.

## CHAPTER TWENTY-FIVE

*July 20, 2015*

**RYAN SLEPT** all the way from the edge of Boise to the restaurant along the Snake River they had stopped at for lunch yesterday. As Duster pulled into the parking lot and shut off the car, Ryan noticed that Bonnie and April were both still asleep.

They had a groggy breakfast and in another two hours were bouncing once again through the rough climb and parking beside Janice and Steven's Jeep. By that point Ryan felt almost awake and was both excited and scared to face the day.

At the office before they left, he had put all the plans for the lodge in his backpack and given a set to Duster as well. April had picked up all her plans and lists for the furnishings, keeping one set and giving another to Bonnie. So they were clearly thinking of building the lodge today.

But over a number of years and a long time in the past of another timeline.

Going into the mine again brought up all the fear Ryan had felt yesterday. And April took his hand the moment the big rock slid aside outside the mine entrance and they went inside.

From what Ryan could tell, she was feeling it as well.

When they reached the central cavern, the smell of hamburgers reached them and Madison shouted from the kitchen area. "Welcome back. Lunch is almost ready."

Ryan and April put their backpacks on a table near the period clothing and followed Duster and Bonnie to the kitchen. They sat down at the kitchen table in the same two chairs they had yesterday.

There was no sign of Steven and Janice and Dawn.

"So, how'd it go?" Duster asked Madison.

"Interesting," Madison said, smiling. "Seven trips back for me. Got more than enough material for that book I've wanted to write about the great fire up in Montana and Northern Idaho. It damn near caught me once near Wallace."

"Ten trips for us," Dawn said as she and Janice and Steven came out of the tunnel to the crystal room. All three of them were wearing clothing that Ryan dated from around 1950 or later, which seemed very odd to him.

Dawn came up and wrapped her arms around Madison and kissed him long and hard. "I missed you more than you can imagine."

Ryan glanced at April and she just shook her head.

"First shower," Dawn said, giving Madison one more kiss and heading for the back room.

Janice and Steven finished putting some of their clothing and saddlebags on the tables and came over.

Duster just looked at them and shook his head. Clearly how they were dressed surprised him as well.

"Interesting last three trips," Steven said, dropping down into a chair at the table. "All three trips were into the same timeline."

"How?" Duster asked and Bonnie sat forward, looking intent.

"We went to 1946 first," Steven said "and stayed five years, establishing ourselves in Boise."

"We bought a beautiful home out on the River," Janice said, her voice wistful.

Ryan wanted to ask which one, but kept silent.

"So after five years," Steven said, "I came back up here and brought us back, but didn't disconnect the crystal, only one wire off the machine."

Duster nodded and waited for Steven to go on.

"So we set the return time for three months later and went back," Steven said.

"And?" Duster asked.

"Everyone recognized us," Steven said, "and asked how our trip to Alaska had been, which was our cover story."

"So we stayed another five years," Janice said, "and then repeated it one more time."

"Again," Steven said, "we still owned the home and all our accounts were in place. So we stayed until right after Kennedy was killed and jumped back."

"Our repeated visits didn't seem to change any history that we could see at all," Janice said.

"I'll be go to hell," Duster said, looking at Bonnie.

"We knew," Bonnie said, "since we were all traveling back at varied times, that it might be possible. But that messes up a few math problems we thought we had solved."

Duster nodded, his mind clearly off into another place.

"So," Ryan said, glancing at April first, then looking at Steven, "this means

that if we build the lodge in a timeline, we can keep returning to it?"

The idea that they could enjoy the lodge for a very long time made him feel better.

"Exactly what it means," Steven said, nodding, "as long as Duster and Bonnie tell us the math is clear."

"It seemed to work," Duster said, clearly off in his own head still.

"It did," Steven said and Janice nodded.

"After us going back and finding Dawn and Madison on that first trip," Janice said, "we figured it might be worth the test before you got back."

"That opens up all kinds of possibilities," Madison said as he turned over some wonderful-smelling hamburgers.

"And problems," Janice said and Bonnie nodded. "Not aging on this first experiment got mentioned by a few people around us."

"Cover stories will be more important," Bonnie said. "And pretending we are our own children at times."

"And not trying to go back into a timeline where you are already at," Duster said. "We're going to have to figure out a way to mark crystals and date trips to them."

Ryan again looked at April who hadn't said a word. She was just sitting there beside him looking a little stunned.

He took her hand and smiled at her as the rest got into a conversation on how to keep track of trips and mark crystals without actually putting anything on them.

"Easy to mark the crystals," April said, speaking up and stopping the conversation.

"You hold the wires to the crystal with a flexible rubber clamp of some sort, right? One that can expand?"

Duster nodded.

"Just produce a lot of them with two wire connections on them. Each one is numbered and logged as to the trip and dates and who went where."

Duster nodded. "That would work."

Ryan patted April's leg and then looked at Duster, "You ever done a time-recording in the crystal room of the area around a crystal while someone is in the past? See how many crystals nearby change and how far the influence of someone in the past spreads?"

"Wow," Madison said. "Great idea."

Duster just looked at April and then at Ryan and smiled. "Am I glad you two with common sense have decided to join us."

Bonnie laughed. "Four historians and two mathematicians sometimes just miss the obvious real world things."

"Oh, trust me," April said, indicating the cave around her and smiling. "There is nothing real world about any of this."

Ryan could only agree with that.

# CHAPTER TWENTY-SIX

*July 20, 2015*

**IT TOOK THEM AN HOUR** to eat lunch and then get ready to go. April got more and more nervous as the time went on. She almost decided to just let them go ahead, but then Ryan came over to her while she was standing in the cavern, staring at the saddlebags on one table that she had packed with clothing she wasn't sure she would be able to wear.

She had enough modern feminine products hidden in there to last for a number of months, at least through the first summer. And Duster had hidden enough gold in her saddlebags to make her feel very rich. And she would be in 1900 where they were headed.

"Scared?" Ryan asked, taking her hand.

"Terrified," she said, looking up at his wonderful face and eyes.

"Me too," he said. "But I want more nights like last night. And I want to work with you more like we did these last two months."

"So do I," she said, nodding.

"So we have an adventure," he said, smiling. "The ultimate camping trip."

"Exactly," she said, realizing that she had always been nervous before any trip into the mountains, always nervous before any hike. She would just treat this the same.

Ryan's comments had calmed her some, as much as she figured would be possible in these circumstances.

With Bonnie's help, she stripped down to her underwear and put on the riding clothes of a woman of 1900. A white blouse over her sports bra, a dark cloth jacket, dark riding pants, and modern boots made to look older.

She also had a wool dress-coat that was long and heavy, but had deep pockets.

Bonnie showed her where she had sewn into the lining of the coat some modern medicine and first aid supplies.

Bonnie had on the same type of clothing.

Then Duster asked, "Everyone ready?"

April glanced around. Janice and Dawn were both dressed in a similar fashion to her.

Duster had on his long oilcloth coat and cowboy hat. Steven looked like an old-fashioned shopkeeper with a suit coat and vest. Madison had on a short dress jacket over a plaid shirt, jeans, and a cowboy hat. But it was Ryan who took her breath away.

He wore a long coat like Duster's coat, only dark gray. He had on jeans and a wide belt, dark cowboy boots, and a dark hat. He was the most handsome man she had ever seen. He looked like he was the hero of a western novel.

Her hero.

She moved over and kissed him under the rim of his hat.

"For luck?" he asked, smiling at her.

"You got lucky last night, Mister," she said, smiling at him. "Don't push it."

Beside her both Madison and Dawn laughed and followed Steven and Janice off toward the crystal room.

Again, the crystal room just stunned April in its beauty and size. The moment she thought she had a handle on how high the ceiling was or how far the cavern went, she realized she was wrong.

All eight of them stopped near the machine on the wooden table, all carrying their supplies and saddlebags.

Bonnie explained what was going to happen. They had changed the plan a little from what they told them last night.

Duster would go first in 1894, then Madison and Dawn were going to go through into 1895, then Bonnie would change the date and the rest of them would go through into 1900 in the same timeline.

From what April understood as they had planned this in the kitchen, Madison and Dawn would help Duster buy and set up a house in Boise that they would all use for a base.

And also buy the land for the lodge and test some construction crews as well.

"There are eight of us this time," Duster said. "Anyone comes back here

and pulls the plug, everyone returns. Remember that."

"But only take the wire off the machine," Steven said, "if you have to pull the plug on this trip. Leave it on the crystal. That way we can go back to what we have built or got done."

Duster nodded at that and April just looked at Ryan, the panic back in her stomach.

"Everyone gather around and take a spot with one hand on the machine," Bonnie said.

All eight of them did as she said.

To April, the machine felt like a piece of metal and nothing more, a little cool from being in a cave, but nothing special. It was about the size of a large desktop computer without the screen. There was more than enough room for all of them to touch it.

"When the time comes," Bonnie said, "the five of us need to touch the machine at the same moment." She looked first at April, then at Ryan.

They both nodded.

Bonnie turned and kissed Duster. "Behave yourself until I get there."

He laughed and moved over and then, with gloves on, put the clamps on one crystal about shoulder high on the wall and about twenty feet away from the table.

He made sure the wires to it were secure, then came back.

He set a date on the machine, hooked up one wire, then with a wink at Bonnie, he hooked up the other wire, took off the glove and with a bare hand he touched the machine.

And vanished.

April wanted to sprint for the opening of the cavern, but she stayed close to Ryan and said nothing.

Terrified only began to describe how she was feeling.

Madison, also with a glove on, quickly stepped up to the machine and changed the date. Then he took the glove off and said, "One, two, three."

On the count of three, he and Dawn both touched the machine where Bonnie had told them to with their bare hands.

And vanished.

Bonnie quickly put the glove on and April saw she switched the date to May 1900.

Oh, my, this was really going to happen.

April now knew she was going to go back into the past with Ryan and build a lodge.

She made herself take a deep breath so she wouldn't pass out.

Bonnie took the glove off and looked at everyone.

"On the count of three, touch the machine."

April tried to nod, but she didn't think she did.

"Adventure," Ryan said, looking at her and trying to smile.

At that she managed to nod.

Bonnie had everyone step up close.

"One, two, three," she said.

All five of them touched the machine at the same time.

Nothing exploded.

April felt nothing.

Not a damn thing happened.

# CHAPTER TWENTY-SEVEN

*May 5, 1900*

**BESIDE APRIL,** Bonnie stepped back. So did Janice and Steven.

April and Ryan both slowly took their hands off the machine. Ryan looked as puzzled as she felt.

"Let's go see who's here to meet us," Bonnie said.

April just stood there, trying to breathe normally, looking at Ryan.

He glanced at the machine hooked up to a crystal on the wall, then at April, grinning. "I think we're in 1900."

Even though nothing had really happened when they had gone back to Silver City in 1887, she thought this time would be different. But it hadn't been.

Stepping from timeline to timeline, year to year, seemed to be something that happened without a bang or even a slight feeling of travel. Almost disappointing, especially after feeling as nervous as she had been about it.

They had simply walked into this fantastic crystal cave, touched something, and turned around and left.

April again forced herself to take a deep breath. Then, her hand in Ryan's, they walked toward the tunnel out of the crystal room and into the big cavern.

"Adventure," he said again.

"Adventure," she repeated.

Duster was there, looking slightly older and rougher, and his hair was longer. He was kissing Bonnie when they walked in.

"Where's Madison and Dawn?" Steven asked.

"They stayed in Boise, getting things ready," Duster said.

"What day is it?" Bonnie asked, holding onto her husband's hand. Actually, from what April could tell, he was holding hers.

"May 5th, 1900," Duster said, smiling at April and Ryan. "About noon."

"Pretty close to our target," Bonnie said, nodding. "How long have you been here?"

"Since the twenty-second of April. I have horses and gear in a camp outside."

"Weather?" Steven asked.

April understood exactly where that question was coming from. She had a hunch getting off this hill in a snowstorm was not something any of them wanted to try. She always paid extreme attention to weather when making any hike.

"It's been a warm spring," Duster said. "In fact, we can get out of here without a problem this afternoon and, if we are lucky, we can be up on Monumental Summit by the 20th."

"Did you get the land?" Ryan asked.

Duster smiled and April saw clearly that the smile reached his eyes. He was very excited.

"I got it all," he said. "And acres on the Stibnite side for lumber and out-buildings."

With that Bonnie kissed Duster again. "Wonderful!"

"The trail in?" Steven asked. "Dewey doesn't start building that road up to the summit until next summer."

"A little bit of money convinced him to start a year early," Duster said, laughing. "Madison really knows the man and his weaknesses."

April couldn't believe what she was hearing. It sounded like they were really going to build the lodge.

Beside her Ryan just smiled like a kid staring at the front gate of Disneyland. She liked that look on his face.

His long coat and cowboy hat did amazing things for him. Made him even more attractive to her, if that was possible.

The next thing she knew, they were headed outside.

The air on the top of the mine tailings had a hard bite to it and she put on the heavy coat and her gloves. Then from a hidden pocket in the coat she pulled out a brown stocking cap almost the color of her hair and put that on over her ears. Then she put a 1900s bonnet over that to hide the stocking cap.

If she let her ears get cold, she knew she would be cold all day. And she didn't want that.

The sun was shining and the sky a bright blue. Drifts of snow still filled most areas around the hillside and the old mining shack had a large snowdrift up against it.

She and Ryan spent a minute or so staring down at Silver City below them. Now she didn't need to see that town to know she was in the past.

She knew it.

And slowly, the fear she had been feeling was getting replaced by excitement.

A few minutes later, she was introduced to her horse, a black mare she immediately called "Trusty."

"As in Trusty Steed?" Ryan asked, smiling as she was shown by Duster how to get the 1900 saddle on the horse and secured.

"Exactly," she said, smiling at Ryan.

He and Duster both just laughed and then Ryan got his horse ready to go as well.

She had spent time on horses on different pack trips into the mountains. And she had ridden a lot as a girl. But she didn't plan on riding this horse off this hill, no matter how trusty the horse was. She wasn't good enough by a long ways to ride a horse down a steep slope.

The saddle looked very dated compared to modern ones, yet April knew it would be the top of the line for this time period because that was the way that Duster did things.

Also on the saddle was a rifle in a sling. She knew how to fire a rifle and wasn't afraid of guns, but she was surprised to see it there on her saddle. She had a hunch there were a lot of details like that she hadn't thought through.

She mentioned that to Bonnie and she just shrugged. "This is the West. Duster believes we all should be armed. Especially since we are headed up to a gold rush camp. Be careful with it, though. Knowing Duster, it's loaded."

April could think of nothing more to say to that.

At one point, Duster walked over to her and Ryan. First he handed each of them two antique-looking keys to get into the mine and showed them how to use them and where a key was hidden up on the hill in case they needed to get in and had lost theirs.

"Got a question," he said after that. "It's safer in the West for a couple to travel together. You two all right with one tent?"

April smiled and looked over at Ryan. If they hadn't had last night, she more than likely would have said that two were better.

Ryan looked at her and smiled. "Easier?"

She nodded and smiled at Duster. "One tent."

He just nodded. "Hide those keys well." Then he walked away.

Ryan smiled at April and then kissed her.

"I hope you don't snore," he said.

"Who said we would be sleeping?"

He just laughed and went back to work on getting his horse ready.

When they were all ready and the camp had been broken, Duster looked at everyone. "Janice, you and Steven will ride out ahead with me. We'll

take the long way around with the two packhorses. Bonnie, you and April and Ryan go directly down and over the hill. Take your time and walk a lot of it and we'll meet you at the first camp."

Bonnie nodded. "Dinner?"

"I'll have it on the fire and waiting," Steven said, smiling.

Duster and Janice and Steven headed off the mine tailings, walking their horses along the trail past where, in the future, in another timeline, the Cadillac would be parked.

"Why are we breaking up?" Ryan asked Bonnie right before April could.

"Six people up here like this would cause too much attention," she said. "And besides, they are going to be mostly riding. We're going to do a lot of walking to get you used to riding and the saddles over the next few days."

"Oh, thank you," April said.

"Yes, thanks," Ryan said.

Bonnie laughed. "Don't mention it. I have to do a lot of walking as well on the first trip back every spring."

Five minutes later they started off across the same trail. Bonnie in the lead, April in the center, Ryan behind her.

The adventure had begun.

And April was doing exactly what she loved to do more than anything else. She was hiking in the mountains.

# CHAPTER TWENTY-EIGHT

*May 5, 1900*

**RYAN WAS EXHAUSTED** by the time the three of them reached camp. The sun was barely lighting the sky and the air had warmed a little as they got down out of the Owyhee Mountains and into the Treasure Valley. There was no snow on the ground anymore and trees were starting to gain their leaves and the grass was green. The Snake River was running close by their first night's camp. He could hear it in the background.

This camp in 1900 was a very long ways from waking up naked this morning beside April in her apartment in Boise in 2015.

A very long ways.

Sometimes he understood that, sometimes he found it almost impossible to believe.

By the time they rode into the camp tucked down in a small meadow inside a grove of cottonwood trees, Duster and Janice and Steven already had the tents up and the camp set. A fire was going and a wonderful smell of something beef cooking made Ryan's stomach rumble.

He and Bonnie and April all spent the first half hour brushing down their horses, getting them some food and getting them settled for the night with the other horses. By the time they were done, the sky had gone almost completely dark and only the campfire lit up the meadow with orange flickering light.

They had only ridden in half-hour sections, and then walked for a half hour, but even with that, Ryan felt saddle sore. It was going to take him a few more days to really get used to riding, if not longer.

After finishing with the horses and washing up from a bucket brought up from the river, Steven had served them a seemingly fresh stew that Duster had made and brought with him from the mine. The campfire was crackling and the night air was cooling quickly.

Janice had already gone off to her tent to sleep.

From the looks of it, Duster wasn't going to be far behind in his retirement to a tent.

Ryan loved camping like this and he made a point to sit next to April on a wide log as they ate.

Steven made sure they had enough food, then took the remaining stew off the fire, covered the pot, and attached it to a rope and pulled it up high into a nearby cottonwood tree to cool.

Then he pointed to another bucket of water and two towels and smiled at April and Ryan. "You guys get to wash the dishes."

"Glad to," April said.

After fifteen more minutes, only the two of them remained outside a tent, talking quietly as they washed the dishes.

Then making sure the fire was contained, mostly out, and had no chance of spreading, they headed for their tent.

The tent was large, canvas, and looked like a tent from 1900, with walls and two sides, held up by wooden poles and the top held up by two large poles on either side.

A large mattress about the size of a queen bed filled the center of the tent covered by a quilt. He and April had put their saddlebags in the tent earlier, hers on one side, his on another.

The only light in the tent was from the remains of the fire outside coming through the canvas.

"This would be uncomfortable," she said, starting to peal off her clothes, "if I weren't so tired."

Ryan worked to take off his clothes as well, finally getting down to just his underwear. Then he turned to look at her.

She was struggling with a button on the side of her pants and he came over and helped her undo it.

In a moment she was also down to her underwear.

Then she pulled off her sports bra and then her underwear, putting both on top of her clothes on her saddlebags.

Even in the dim light, her naked body damn near took his breath away.

"We're only cuddling," she whispered, kissing him. "Last thing we need on our first night is to keep the camp awake."

He kissed her back, then slid out of his underwear.

As they sat down on the bed, he was surprised. Inside what was clearly an antique-looking pad was an air mattress.

"Nice," she whispered, "I was expecting to sleep on hard ground. Duster thinks of everything."

"He's been doing this a while," Ryan whispered as he crawled in under the quilt and snuggled up against her wonderful back.

She pushed against him. He knew she could feel his hardness against her.

"I am sensing some thoughts on that tired brain, mister," she whispered. "Feels wonderful."

"So do you," he whispered back.

Then he moved slightly away from her with his crotch and whispered, "Sleep. We have years ahead of us to enjoy that."

"Promise?" she asked softly.

"Promise," he said, his arms around her, holding her.

The next thing he remembered, the sun was up outside, the smell of eggs and bacon filled the tent, and April was standing over him, straddling him, smiling.

And she was completely naked.

"That's a fantastic view to wake up to," he said softly, looking up at her wonderful body.

"So is that," she said, pointing at his hardness.

She stood there for a moment longer letting him stare at her as she stared at him.

Then she laughed and moved to start dressing.

"This just might be the best camping trip ever," he said softly.

She leaned over and kissed him. "It's just starting."

He liked the sound of that a great deal.

# CHAPTER TWENTY-NINE

*May 7, 1900*

**IT TOOK THEM** two more days to get into Boise. The weather had held nice the entire time, letting them ride in comfort, which April felt very lucky about. She had done her share of riding in cold rain and it wasn't much fun.

All along the way the sounds of farming and the smells of cooking kept hitting her. Plus the smells of fresh spring growth in the grass made the trip amazing.

Her horse, Trusty, turned out to be wonderful and very gentle, not fighting her in any way. And by the third day, April felt pretty comfortable riding most of the way.

Janice and Steven had left them as they reached Caldwell on the second day. Since they were going to run the general store again in Roosevelt to help in getting supplies in there for the lodge, they headed directly north toward Central Idaho to buy the land they needed and secure the land to build two nice homes down in Roosevelt as well. One for Janice and Steven and one for the rest of them when they were there for different reasons.

Duster said he would have a crew in there building them as soon as they made the summit.

April understood wanting the houses down in the valley. At times, it was going to just be best to stay in the valley instead of trying to make the distance up to the lodge. It made perfect sense.

The four of them finally reached the main part of the Treasure Valley around three in the afternoon. April was stunned as they rode into the outskirts of the capitol of the state, coming in on a wide road along the Boise River. It felt like she was riding right into books in her profession.

She used a lot of old pictures to find different forms of furnishings and designs from this exact time period, and now it was as if those photos had just come alive around her.

And Ryan was looking at everything as well, his head turning from one side to another.

There were some pretty nice homes tucked back on large estates along the river as they rode in what would end up being State Street and toward the downtown area.

The city had been the state's capitol for only a short time at this point in history. As they neared what seemed to be a downtown area, with the three-story Boise Hotel dominating a large intersection, Ryan moved his horse up beside hers and pointed off toward the foothills to the north.

"Construction on the capitol building about five blocks from here won't even start until 1905," he said in a whisper only loud enough for her to hear. Then he pointed in the other direction down a wide road with a bridge over a river. "See the hill? That's where the Union Pacific Depot will be built in 1925."

All she could do was shake her head. The town looked faintly familiar from the one she had come to know, yet so much was missing and different. Now, where large bank buildings would someday stand, a China Town district covered four blocks.

Where a wonderful old theater would be built, a saloon now sat with the doors open and piano music ringing out over the street, playing a song she did not recognize.

They kept going on through town and along the river out Warm Springs Avenue, now only a wide dirt wagon road cutting through the tall poplar and cottonwood trees.

They rode along in silence for a few minutes, April doing her best to catch any glimpse of furnishings or fixtures. Then Ryan eased his horse again up beside hers.

"Our office will be down there," he whispered.

He pointed toward a field and swampland beside the quickly flowing Boise River.

She knew from there the future university would be on the other banks of the river where a large grove of cottonwoods now grew.

If she had ever doubted she was going into the past, this was impossible to refute now.

They rode for a little longer and April knew exactly where they were.

Up ahead would be a wonderful home that she and Ryan had walked past many times. It was one of the old estate homes built on the bluff overlooking the river. They had talked about how wonderful it would be to buy the old Queen Anne style home some day.

Or if nothing else, just take a tour inside it.

An architect and an interior designer daydreaming together. She had really enjoyed those walks in this neighborhood.

Finally, the wide wagon road was down to only wide enough for one wagon to go by when Duster pointed ahead and turned toward a large house sitting on a bluff overlooking the river.

The home was huge, even from a distance, with tall steep roofs and four towers. A wide covered porch ran all the way around the three front sides of the home and a stone staircase led up to the front porch.

April recognized it as well as the neighboring estate to the one she and Ryan had talked about and admired in the future.

But the house they liked wasn't there yet. It hadn't been built yet.

"This is ours?" Bonnie asked Duster, smiling at her husband. "It looks like the Sandford House in San Francisco."

April instantly realized Bonnie was right. The Sandford House was built into a hill and was tucked tight between other large homes on the street. This home sat on flat ground and was all by itself.

In the future, it would be surrounded by a high hedge and trees and she had never really noticed the resemblance before.

"I know how much you love that home," Duster said. "I also bought the two estates on either side of it."

Duster turned and smiled at her and Ryan, but April had no idea why. She was sure that in the last two months neither she nor Ryan had mentioned their few walks past this neighborhood.

So what was Duster up to? The man never seemed to stop surprising her.

They went past the large two-story plus towers mansion that seemed even larger up close than from the main road, then on down a hill on a wide trail toward a stable building. The Boise River ran past about thirty feet down the hill and on the other side of some cottonwood trees that were now clearly in full spring growth.

The stable building matched the style of the large house and inside it had stalls for all their horses, plus the four that were already there. And clearly there was an upstairs to the building as well. More than likely living quarters for stable hands.

They spent the next half hour taking care of their horses and getting them bedded down and fed and brushed. Then together, carrying their saddlebags and supplies, the four of them headed back up the path toward the back door of the large home.

The sun was still in the clear sky and the air almost warm. April couldn't hear anything but the sounds of the river below and the slight rustling of the leaves on the trees in a light breeze.

It was wonderful, simply wonderful.

Ryan was staring at all the details of the big home as they approached. Finally he asked Duster, "Who built this?"

"Madison and I did," Duster said. "This last year, with the help of a couple local architects and a construction crew of about forty men. We used it to test who we wanted to work for us this summer on the lodge."

"Wow, nice work," Ryan said, shaking his head.

"We thought it turned out all right," Duster said. "Bigger than it looked on the plans, though."

Then as they reached the back door, Duster smiled at April. "Dawn used your list of furnishings for the lodge to help furnish this place. Wait until you see."

Suddenly April was scared to death, more so than traveling in time.

It was one thing to present furnishings in a holographic presentation for a big lodge made out of logs in the wilderness, another to actually buy the real items and get them to work together in a Queen-Anne style mansion.

She was either walking into a disaster, or something amazing.

And she was betting on disaster.

# CHAPTER THIRTY

*May 7, 1900*

**APRIL FOLLOWED** Duster and Bonnie up the stairs and through a back door into a porch with light tiles on the floor. There were hooks to hang coats and wooden benches to sit on to take off boots and shoes. The porch had wide windows along one side that looked out over the back and the stable beyond.

Duster took off his coat and hat and hung it on a hook and April did the same with her coat, tucking her gloves inside a pocket of the coat.

Duster knocked and then went in to a large, high-ceiling kitchen that smelled faintly of bread. Tall, white cabinets covered two walls and a large metal stove sat on one wall and two large iceboxes on another. Oak trim for baseboard and chair-rail trim circled the kitchen and all the cabinet hardware was oak handles and brushed-brass trim.

In the center of the room was a large butcher-block island with pots and pans hanging above it.

On the right of the big stove, an archway with two swinging doors led out into the center of the house. Both doors had small windows about head high on them and the entire thing was framed in wide oak trim boards.

Duster pointed at another plain wooden door on the far left of the room. "That goes down into a storage cellar and the other door beside it goes into private cooks' and servants' quarters. Three small bedrooms and a bathroom are back there, but we have no servants here."

To the direct left of the back door was a huge alcove with tall windows on three sides that looked out over the back yard and river beyond. April was impressed by the huge, oak kitchen table that filled the alcove. Ten people could sit comfortably at that table on the ladder-back oak chairs around it. Each chair had a hand-sewn brown pillow tied to the seat.

It was almost an exact match of the table she had designed for the kitchen area of the lodge. Not the formal dining room, the work kitchen area. The lamp over it was electrical and ornate brass with beautiful imitation oil-lamp glass shades.

Around the walls were actual oil lamps as sconces, more than likely to be used if they lost power. It was just as she and Ryan had designed in the lodge.

Clearly the house had electrical. She hadn't seen any wires leading out here from town as they rode out, so more than likely there was a generator somewhere. But in 1900 electrical to houses was still mostly in the center of the cities or for the rich.

There were four of them in this kitchen and they didn't even begin to crowd part of it. There could be ten people in here and it wouldn't feel crowded.

"Where are Dawn and Madison?" Bonnie asked.

"Horses were out there, so more than likely out for a walk or upstairs," Duster said.

"Amazing," Ryan said, staring around at the detail trim along the ceiling and around the windows.

"You've just begun to see the place," Duster said as he went through the swinging doors and out into the main area of the house.

It was a huge room, also with high ceilings. The room was divided by polished wooden Doric columns, two on each side that framed between them glass display cabinets on both sides. The columns and cabinets came out from each side wall, forming a sort of archway in the center, delineating the difference from the formal dining room and the formal living room.

Through an archway on the other side of the living room between two other wood columns, April could see the main entrance foyer and a guest waiting room on the other side as was standard for this era of homes.

A large river-rock fireplace filled one wall of the living room and a built-in mahogany hutch with mirrors and drawers filled the wall between the dining room and the kitchen.

The formal dining room table had a dark-oak dining table with lion paw carved feet. The table was covered in a beautiful, white-lace table runner. A dozen Brittany carved oak chairs were tucked in around the table giving her an idea of how really large that table was.

This entire home was huge.

As April looked around at detail after detail, she suddenly started to understand just how fantastic the lodge was going to look when finished. She was speechless.

"This is just stunning," Bonnie said, kissing her husband.

"How many bedrooms?" Ryan asked.

"Two regular bedrooms downstairs here besides the servants quarters,"

Duster said, pointing off to a door on the left side of the dining area. "A bathroom between them. "Four suites upstairs, all with their own bathrooms and fireplaces and furnished as April laid out the furnishings for the suites in the lodge."

"And you found a good crew to build this?" Ryan asked, walking over closer to one wall. "The workmanship is topnotch from what I can see."

"A fantastic crew," Duster nodded. "Dependable and good."

Duster then turned to April. "And we found a distant relative of yours to help with all the stonework."

"Of mine?" April asked, surprised.

"Buckley family owns a large part of Boise and the top of that flat mountain just above the town."

"Table Rock?" she asked.

Duster nodded. "They have already lined up the contract with the State of Idaho to quarry on the back side of Table Rock all the sandstone needed to build the new Capitol buildings in the downtown area. And they are going to do a lot of the work as well. But Buckley and his crew have agreed to help us with the stonework on the foundation and fireplaces of the lodge before then."

Ryan went over to the large fireplace that dominated the living room. It was clearly made out of river rock and polished and fitted perfectly together. "They did this as well?"

Duster nodded. "They did, and the foundation of the house and all the fireplaces and chimneys throughout."

"Premium work," Ryan said, nodding.

"This entire place is amazing," April said.

Bonnie hugged her husband.

Duster just smiled. "The lodge is going to work, isn't it?"

"It's going to be amazing," Ryan said.

All April could do was smile and nod.

If how this fantastically beautiful home turned out was an indication, the lodge would be something for the ages.

# PART FOUR

## CHAPTER THIRTY-ONE

*September 21, 1900*

THE LIGHT SNOW blew over the lodge construction site, swirling in and around the foundations and piles of logs cut and ready to be fitted next summer, and then vanishing into the gray sky over Monumental Creek.

The trail from the valley came up to his right and went past the lodge and down into a camp area over the hill they had built for the pack trains going in and out of the valley. This was the first big snowstorm of the winter and he had a hunch no one would be coming up out of the valley until spring after today.

Ryan couldn't remember working so hard physically for over four months. Even back when he worked construction in undergrad, he never worked this hard for seven days a week, every hour there was enough light to work.

From everything he could tell, the construction was on time to finish by the end of next summer if they got a decent jump at it in May.

He and the last of the construction crew were supposed to be heading down this afternoon, off the mountain and back to Boise. He had his camp struck and everything loaded on the mules and packhorses and ready down in the stables just off the summit. Those stables had been the first building they had built and they would replace it later with something larger and more secure.

He so looked forward to getting off the hill and everything wrapped up here because he missed April more than he wanted to think about.

When they first arrived in Boise back in May, they had spent two days in a wonderful suite in that fantastic house Duster had built on Warm Springs, making love at night and talking with Bonnie and Duster and Dawn and Madison about the lodge. As every day went by, he fell harder and harder for April.

And he had come to accept that they were actually in the past. He was still having a hard time believing that only two minutes and fifteen seconds would go by in the cave. That would have to be proven to him he had a hunch.

But then on the third day they had all gone to work.

He and Duster and Madison had all gone with the Buckley stone crew up to the summit while April and Bonnie and Dawn had all headed for San Francisco to start the buying of the furnishings.

And as April said, she really, really wanted to see the Sandford House in its original glory.

She had kissed him goodbye that morning as he went out the back door. "That's got to last you for a month or so."

He promised her it would, then kissed her back, telling her that had to last her. She promised that it would as well.

They had talked about seeing each other before the end of June, but it hadn't worked out that way. He had no time away

from the construction site on the summit and from what Duster told him, she and Bonnie ended up going on to Denver and then Chicago while Dawn had returned to Boise and, with Madison's and Duster's help, set up the warehouse for storage of the interior lodge supplies that would start pouring toward Boise.

So he and April hadn't seen each other for the entire summer. He worked himself into exhaustion every day just to keep from thinking of that fact.

But now, in two days, he would see April again and hold her and tell her everything and she could tell him everything about her shopping. And then they could spend the winter together in Boise, really getting to know each other even better.

As he watched the last two of his crew secure a pile of logs, four horses and riders appeared out of the snow coming up from the valley below. He was amazed. He wouldn't have wanted to try that trail up the side of that mountain in these conditions.

As they got closer, he suddenly recognized one of the riders as she looked up at him.

It was Janice.

But Steven wasn't with her.

Ryan's stomach twisted. Something was very wrong. She shouldn't be here. She and Steven were planning on wintering in the valley.

He had been so busy and tired, he hadn't even taken the time to go down into the small but growing town of Roosevelt. He would next summer.

He went to Janice and helped her down off her horse. She was wearing two or three layers of clothing and had a hat pulled down over her head and layers of gloves on her hands. But her face still looked wind-burned and she was shivering.

She nodded to the man in the lead of the four and said, "Thanks!"

"Take care," the guy said back, his words carried off by the wind and snow.

The guy nodded to her, then to him, and then the three horses continued on over the hill.

Ryan signaled for his two men to finish it up quickly and meet him down in the stable. They needed to get down off this summit pretty soon as well, of that he had no doubt. This storm was growing worse by the hour.

"You all right?" he asked Janice as he led her along the trail and to the stables where they could get in and out of the snow and wind.

"Cold," she said, he voice weak. "But otherwise I'm fine."

There was still a fire burning in the iron stove in the stable, keeping the insides at a decent temperature for the last horses. They got her horse inside and near the heat and he took care of it while Janice went over to the stove and started peeling off some layers of coats and gloves to let the heat in.

Then she sat down on a bench and took off her boots and socks to let them dry near the stove.

"What happened?" he asked after he made sure her horse was all right and ready to travel again.

"Steven took a fall two days ago," she said, shuddering.

Ryan wasn't sure it was from the cold or from Steven's fall.

"He slipped on some ice and went down and shattered his right wrist and I think broke a few ribs."

Ryan shook his head. "He has to be in pain."

"He is," she said, nodding as she rubbed her hands together over the fire. "I have him on pain meds and in bed now. I got the store closed for the season and only those three know I came out alone."

Ryan looked at her, puzzled.

She went on as if he understood. "They think I was coming up here to bring you back. No one knows that Steven is injured or that he hasn't left yet."

"So what do we do?" Ryan asked, very puzzled.

"We head to Boise and then Duster and Madison go pull the plug," Janice said, still warming her hands and feet. "Get Steven out of there and healthy again."

Ryan glanced around at the stable and the wind rattling the boards.

There was no choice, he knew that, but all he could think about was an entire summer's work would just vanish.

And they would do it all again.

# CHAPTER THIRTY-TWO

*September 23, 1900*

**APRIL WAS HAVING TROUBLE** containing her excitement. Ryan was coming off the summit and would be into Boise today. Then they were going to get to spend the winter together. It had been a wonderful summer of traveling all over the country with Bonnie, shopping.

A dream summer.

She had so much to tell him and share with him.

But even with everything, she still missed Ryan almost every minute of every day.

She hoped he felt the same way about her. It had been a long four months.

Too long for them to be apart.

The months working together on designing the lodge had made her come to realize how much she enjoyed just knowing he was there to talk with.

And after a few nights of making love in May, she knew they were made for each other, no matter what year they were in.

She was completely in love with him and the months they had just spent apart made that fact even clearer to her.

Now every minute she waited for him to get back drove her crazy. She had arrived back in Boise almost a week ago and the days had gone very slowly, even though she had spent much of the time getting the arriving furniture protected in the warehouse for the winter.

She was now working on her journal in their bedroom at the mahogany sitting desk. All summer she had done a journal of her travels and what she and Bonnie had found and where. Outside her windows, the day was a gray overcast and the air had a fall bite to it. The leaves hadn't yet started to turn to fall colors, but she knew that wouldn't be far off.

She had a hunch that up on the summit it would be very cold and more than likely snowing.

Suddenly Bonnie shouted from downstairs. "They're here."

April had no idea who "they" were since everyone was here but Ryan. Janice and Steven were going to winter over in Roosevelt. She saw plans of the home they had built in there and it looked fantastic. She hoped to see it next summer.

She made it down the slick, wooden staircase faster than she should have and joined Bonnie and Duster and Dawn and Madison as they went out the back door to greet Ryan.

April was stunned.

There he sat on his horse. If it was possible, he looked even more handsome than before. The outside work had given his face a deep, dark weathered look and his dark hair was four months longer, flowing out of his cowboy hat like he was a model in a fashion magazine.

The sight of him took her breath away.

Then he saw her coming down the back steps as he dismounted and smiled at her.

That was it, she couldn't contain herself.

She just flat ran at him and he barely managed to get his feet under him before she jumped at him and into his arms, giving him the biggest kiss she had ever given anyone at any time for any reason.

And he squeezed her and hugged her back as hard as he could, pushing into the kiss.

When she finally let him come up for air, he eased her to the ground.

"I missed you," she said, breathlessly.

"I missed you." And he smiled at her and she wanted to jump him again, but didn't.

Then she looked at the other person who had dismounted and her stomach went from pure joy to pure panic.

It was Janice.

And she was alone.

And that meant something had happened to Steven.

Dawn had gone to her and was hugging her.

"Tie off the horses," Duster said, indicating a tree branch. "We'll deal with them later."

Then he turned and headed into the house as the rest of them followed.

Janice walked between Dawn and Bonnie.

April kept her arm around Ryan and he didn't let go of her either.

"You look wonderful," she said softly to him as Dawn led Janice inside.

"So do you," he said. "A dream come true."

"Good dreams, I hope," she whispered, smiling up at his handsome, tanned face.

"The best," he whispered back and smiled.

And she went even deeper in love than she had been before, if that was even possible.

# CHAPTER THIRTY-THREE

*September 23, 1900*

**APRIL HELPED RYAN** off with his coat and hat and gloves on the back porch and Madison went to work on hot tea and some apple juice for everyone as Janice got out of her coat and hat as well.

Duster sat down at the big kitchen table and Ryan and April went in on the far side of the table with their back to the window.

"Wow, this is really some place," Janice said, looking around at the big kitchen.

"Tour and a hot bath in a little bit," Bonnie said, getting Janice seated at the table near Duster. "We need to know what happened with Steven."

The kitchen was as silent as April had heard it as everyone waited for the answer.

Janice took a deep breath. "He slipped on some ice coming out of the back of the store. He went down, shattered his right wrist and broke some ribs. He's in far too much pain to ride and I doubt the wrist is going to heal."

"He's in Roosevelt?" Bonnie asked.

"He has drugs," Janice said, nodding, "but he is in a lot of pain. I closed up the store and told people we were leaving for the winter. He's holed up in the back of the house where no one can see him move around, what little he can move around."

"How long ago was this?" Duster asked.

"Four days," Janice said, looking worried.

"Damn," Madison said.

Dawn went almost white. After hearing the story of what happened with Madison that first winter in Roosevelt, April could understand why this bothered Dawn so much.

"We need to get him out of there," Duster said. "Madison, you want to ride with me?"

Duster started to stand, but Bonnie put a hand on his arm. "We need to plan this. Give us five minutes."

Duster looked at her for a moment, then nodded and sat back down.

April knew that resetting the crystal room would bring Steven out easily, just as it had taken her and Ryan and Duster from the front of the mine back into the crystal room. And over the summer, Bonnie had told her a number of stories about how being pulled out had saved one or the other of them who had been injured.

But pulling Steven and Janice out of this timeline would take all of them out as well and make them lose all their work. She looked at Ryan and he squeezed her hand. He didn't seem worried that he was about to lose all his work this summer.

"Ryan and I talked over the campfire last night," Janice said. "You want to tell them what we came up with?"

Madison handed her a cup of hot tea and then the same for Ryan.

April let go of his hand so he could take the cup and sip it.

"I don't know much about this time travel obviously," Ryan said, smiling, "since this is our first trip."

April leaned against him. She liked the sound of "our first trip" more than she wanted to admit.

Ryan went on. "If you can unhook one wire only from the back of the machine, it will pull us all back."

Duster nodded.

Ryan went on. "Since we'll have arrivals coming in of furniture from all over, from all the shopping these two did this summer, we need to come back here almost at once to take care of that."

April nodded this time. "He's right," she said. "Fixtures and furniture will start arriving in about a month and continue through most of the winter."

"So Duster and Bonnie and April and I could come back within a day of when we are pulled back," Ryan said, "to take care of things here this winter."

April loved the sound of that. She more than anything had wanted to spend the winter here with Ryan.

"Can it be cut that close to a previous trip?" Janice asked, looking at Duster and Bonnie.

"Duster and I have been working on the math here all summer," Bonnie said. "Without computers, we can only go so far, but I don't see why not. It won't let us come back while we are here, that's for sure."

Duster nodded, but clearly wasn't that excited about the idea.

"So we get back here before the snow," Ryan said "and stay the winter here in Boise. "You four come through in May and head for Roosevelt. If what Janice tells me is correct, none of our work will be gone."

"Exactly," Dawn said, nodding.

"Is that possible?" April asked, looking first at Bonnie, then at Duster. "I love shopping and all, but I'd love to get the furniture and fixtures into the place first before I have to make that shopping trip again."

"It's possible," Madison said, smiling. "We did it, with more time between, right before this trip."

Janice nodded.

"If nothing else," Duster said, "It's going to be an interesting thing to try. Even if it doesn't work, we have to get Steven out of there. That's the focus. If we can save this summer's work, so much the better."

Everyone nodded to that.

"Duster," Ryan said, "if we boarded your horse and Bonnie's in Silver City, and I rode with you and took along Dawn's horse and we boarded those for a few days as well, we'll have rides coming out. And you can teach me the tricks of going back to the mine."

"And I'll bring everyone else's horses and meet you all in May," Duster said.

He thought for a long few seconds, then nodded and said, "That would work. Bonnie, get someone to watch the horses here for a few weeks and you all have the house shut down by tomorrow evening, lamps off and fires out and the place locked up as if no one is home. We should be ready to pull you all out by just after sunset."

April didn't like the sound of Ryan suddenly leaving again. But she loved the idea of spending the winter with him here.

Duster looked at Ryan and smiled. "Good plan, architect. You ready to ride?"

Ryan nodded. "As soon as we get the three other horses ready. And I spend ten minutes with this wonderful woman."

Bonnie and Madison both stood. "We'll get them ready," Bonnie said. "And Janice, I'll take care of yours as well."

"Thanks," Janice said.

"Ten minutes is all you got," Madison said, smiling at Ryan and heading out the door.

Ryan smiled at April.

She leaned over and kissed Ryan, then said, "What can we do in ten minutes."

"Not a damn thing in this kitchen," Duster said, winking at her as he stood to get his saddlebags and clothes for the trip.

Janice and Dawn both laughed.

"How about we just sit here together," Ryan said.

"I'd like that," she said, smiling up at him and then leaning against his strong shoulders. "I'd like that a lot."

Ten minutes later she stood outside on the back porch beside Bonnie as Ryan and Duster, both wearing long coats and cowboy hats, rode out.

Ryan was the most handsome man she had ever known. And if this worked, she was going to get to spend a wonderful winter with him right here in this house.

If this worked.

## CHAPTER THIRTY-FOUR

*September 24, 1900*

**RYAN WAS STUNNED** how fast and far he and Duster were able to ride with a horse each in tow. Duster clearly knew the direct route from Boise to Silver City in those days and their only delay was waiting for the ferry right at dusk to cross the Snake River.

They camped that night without tents and only some cold sandwiches that Bonnie had made them just before they left. They didn't even start up a fire. Neither one of them could see the reason to bother.

By first light they were on the move again.

The morning was bitterly cold, but the sky looked like it might remain clear, which was a lucky break for them. Ryan felt like his body was taking a pounding, but all the work this summer up on the lodge allowed him to keep up with Duster, who seemed to just flat be driven and have the energy of a teenager. When they first came back, Ryan never would have been able to maintain the pace they were at for even an hour.

They reached Silver City and paid the smith there to board the horses for two weeks. Duster gave the man a little extra with a promise for more if he took good care of them.

There was the sign of the first snow on the ground in the shadows of a few buildings. Nothing at all like what was blowing up on the top of Monumental Summit.

The town of Silver City had clearly seen better days, and this late in the year, there weren't many people out at all. Ryan could hear the faint sound of one piano from a saloon and some picks pounding into rock in the distance and that was it.

Most of the buildings looked empty and they all needed work. Very few of them had any smoke coming from chimneys.

Silver City was already well on its way to being a ghost town.

On the hill above them, Ryan couldn't tell which mine tailings was the one they were headed for. There were so many scattered over the mountains like white scars on tanned skin.

Carrying their saddlebags and April's and Bonnie's saddlebags as well, they climbed up along the main street, moving on the board sidewalks where possible. They left their saddles with the smith to repair where needed and then leather polish.

They checked into the Silver City Hotel, a two-story building that seemed to dominate one corner of the center of town. The outside looked just dirty, like dust had been blowing against the white painted board siding all summer and no one had bothered to take the time to wash it off. From the outside the windows looked clean, but that was about it.

Inside, the hotel also had seen better days. It needed paint badly and the carpet in places was worn and torn. Mostly the entire hotel just looked tired.

The air smelled of wet wood smoke combined with a wonderful odor of cooking meat and bread. Ryan's stomach rumbled at that. There was clearly a kitchen nearby.

The man with white hair behind the counter was happy to see them come in, especially when they booked two rooms for two weeks and Duster paid in cash for the rooms.

Ryan just watched what Duster was doing, making mental notes to ask him some questions later. He understood most of the reasons for doing what he was doing, but he would make sure later.

"Francine still around and cooking tonight?" Duster asked the front desk clerk.

"She is," the man nodded as he handed them keys. "Dinner starts at five."

The old grandfather clock against the wall looked like it was still beating right along and showed that it was a little before five in the afternoon. Wow, had they made good time from the other side of Boise.

Duster nodded thanks to the desk clerk and then Ryan followed him up the stairs.

Duster took the first room on the left and pointed for Ryan to take the next one down the hall.

"Wash up and we'll get some food," he said. "Ten minutes."

Ryan used the old key to get into his room. The high-ceilinged room was as tired as the rest of the hotel. About the size of a large modern closet, a worn and faded quilt covered a regular-sized bed on a metal frame. An old and scarred chest of drawers was against one wall with most of the handles missing. A cracked white-china bowl and water pot and a tinted-brown towel were on a stand next to the bed.

One overstuffed plaid chair filled the remaining corner of the small room and in a number of places the crosshatched wallpaper was coming loose showing boards under them.

Ryan tossed the saddlebags on the bed and his long coat and hat on top of them and poured some of the cold water into the bowl. He then washed off his face and hands and using the towel, wet it and wiped the dirt off the back of his neck and up his arms under his shirt.

Surprisingly, it made him feel a lot better.

He had just put his hat and coat back on when Duster knocked on the door.

Duster wasn't wearing his hat or coat, just the jeans and plaid shirt he had on under that, held up by suspenders. His sleeves on the shirt were rolled up to his elbows.

Ryan nodded and tossed his hat and coat back on the bed, then locked up as they went out.

Dinner was in a small dining room off the hotel lobby that at one point in time had pretended to be formal, but now just felt more like a diner with faded curtains.

The waitress, a heavy-set woman with dark, thin hair and a stained apron, recognized Duster and showed him to a table in the back corner just far enough away from the big metal stove to not overheat them, but keep them comfortable at the same time. Ryan soon found out her name was Francine, the one Duster had asked about, and she was also the cook.

There was no one else in the dining room, but the woman didn't talk much and Duster didn't either, so Ryan just focused on the great food as well.

Venison steak, cooked perfectly, with golden potatoes and some slices of fresh apples and warm bread. After the two days of hard riding he had had from Roosevelt Summit to Boise and then the push to get here, every bite tasted like heaven. This was his first real meal in all that time.

Finally, when Francine asked after serving them both a slice of fresh apple pie, why Duster was in town, he said, "Got some family that want me to take a look at an old mine up on War Eagle. Thought I'd do it before the snow flies."

"Nothing up there worth looking at," she said, shaking her head.

"Told them that myself," Duster said. "But they're paying, so we're looking."

She shrugged and moved off.

Ryan knew exactly what Duster was doing. The mine with the crystal cave was up on Florida Mountain. If anyone went looking for them, they would look on War Eagle now. And if he and Duster vanished and didn't come back for the horses, everyone would assume it was more than likely that a cave-in got them.

Very smart.

"Grab your coat and hat and saddlebags," Duster said as they finished eating and went back upstairs to their rooms.

Outside it was getting dark.

They went out of the hotel through the front door and down the street. About a hundred paces below the edge of town, Duster had them turn up on a trail headed up onto Florida Mountain.

It was getting dark, so Ryan stayed close to Duster, who seemed to know the trail even though he couldn't see most of it.

They climbed for a ways, Ryan wishing now he hadn't eaten so much.

Finally Duster stopped and pointed back down.

"We're down the valley from the town, but this rock formation here marks the level on the hillside that the mine is at."

Ryan nodded and looked at the pile of large boulders.

Duster then started across the hill, going back up the valley.

After a few minutes a shape in the dim light seemed to come into form for Ryan.

"Cars will be here?" Ryan asked.

Duster glanced back. "Yup, right here. Good eye, architect."

They went across the hill and onto the top of the mine tailings. The last part it had almost gotten too dark to see anything, but Ryan knew they also didn't want to light anything up here where anyone happening to be looking up the hillside might question.

"Got your key?" Duster asked.

Ryan slipped his finger into the lining of his coat and pulled out one of the two keys Duster had given him. There had been a couple nights after rough days up on the summit that Ryan had pulled out a key and looked at it to try to remind himself he really was in the past.

"Looks clear," Duster said after checking around the old shack and staring back off the way they had come.

Ryan nodded and twisted the key head to the right.

In the dark he could barely see where the big rock slid back.

He and Duster both slipped inside and Duster pushed the close button. After a moment of total darkness, the inside door opened and the lights came up.

And Ryan was once again in the mine.

He took a deep breath, relieved. "A part of me was starting to doubt this was here."

Duster laughed. "I get that way myself after forty or fifty years in the past."

As they went down the tunnel, Duster showed Ryan how to turn off the alarms.

They went right on through the big cavern as the lights came up to the crystal cave.

Duster walked over first to the wall and studied the connector and Ryan tried to catch his breath from the fantastic beauty of the place.

"Is it all right?" Ryan finally asked.

"Looks very secure," Duster said, nodding. "We'll see in the future how it looks."

Duster then moved over to the machine and put on a glove.

"You ready?"

"I am," Ryan nodded, watching from about ten feet away.

"Let's hope all the women are out of the bath," Duster said, smiling.

Ryan laughed. "Oh, where's the fun in that?"

"Good point," Duster said, smiling.

And then he disconnected one wire.

# CHAPTER THIRTY-FIVE

*July 20, 2015*

**APRIL WAS SITTING** in the dark in the kitchen at the large table with Bonnie and Janice and Dawn and Madison. The Boise house was completely closed up and everything turned off. All the fires had been put out and the entire electrical system disconnected.

The only sound was the slight creaking of the building from a gentle wind outside.

All five of them had been sitting at the big table now for almost an hour, just waiting, since the sun had gone down. Bonnie had told her that Duster wouldn't risk the climb up to the mine until dark.

So they had sat and waited at the table from sunset on.

It felt very weird to April, as if they were waiting for a ride, but they wouldn't know when the ride would suddenly pick them up.

Bonnie had a person coming by in the morning to live on the second floor of the stables and take care of the horses each day. If they didn't end up returning to this timeline, the horses would not starve in there and eventually someone would take over the house.

But for now, from the outside, it looked like the house was empty, the residents off on a trip.

April had been worried about Ryan and was having a difficult time believing that Ryan and Duster could make the ride to Silver City as fast as Bonnie thought they could. But Bonnie had assured her that it was possible, and knowing Duster, she said they would make it in time for dinner before going up to the mine.

Janice was getting more and more worried about Steven by the moment. And April understood that. Steven had been in the house in Roosevelt, injured and by himself, for days.

Then, as Dawn was reassuring Janice that Steven would be fine, April found herself standing with her hand on the machine in the bright crystal cave.

All eight of them were touching the machine and all eight of them stepped back almost at the same time.

It had actually happened.

April just flat couldn't believe it.

She was back in the summer of 2015 and only two minutes and fifteen seconds had gone by. Even though she remembered every detail of her summer travels in 1900.

April hugged Ryan and kissed him hard, not really believing she was with him again.

Beside her, Janice and Steven kissed and hugged each other as well. From what April could tell when she surfaced from the long and heavenly kiss with Ryan, Steven was just fine. He flexed his wrist a few times and then just smiled at Janice.

Bonnie kissed Duster lightly and smiled. "Great job, mister. Florence cooking?"

"Steak and apple pie," Duster said, smiling. "Doesn't get better."

Bonnie glanced at April and just smiled, while April shook her head. Bonnie had been right and Duster and Ryan had stopped in the hotel for dinner before coming up to the mine after dark.

Steven and Madison went over to the wall with Duster and inspected the connection from the machine to the crystal there while April watched, her arm tucked into Ryan's arm. She had spent almost no time with him this summer and she had missed him more than she even wanted to admit to herself.

"Sure looks solid," Madison said.

"It does," Duster said.

April sure hoped that meant they could follow Ryan and Janice's plan and go right back.

Duster than turned around to look at his wife. "Shall we try this crazy idea?"

"I don't see why not?" she said. "If it doesn't work, we just start over on the lodge."

"Sorry about that," Steven said.

Janice kissed him and Duster and Bonnie just waved his comment off.

"Let's take some showers," Duster said, "restock supplies to take with us and get ready to go again."

"Food?" Steven asked, smiling as they headed toward the supply cave. "All I had was water and jerky the last three days."

"I'll get you something now," Madison said, smiling at Steven, "but dinner in two hours after we get ready to go."

"Good idea," Dawn said. "We can get caught up and plan out the rest of this lodge construction and what everyone is doing after that gets done."

"How long until we head back?" Ryan asked.

"Four or five hours," Duster said, going down the tunnel from the crystal cave into the big supply cavern.

April squeezed Ryan's arm. "Excited?"

He just laughed. "Completely."

"Me too," she said as they followed the rest into the big cavern. "Me too."

# CHAPTER THIRTY-SIX

*July 20, 2015*

DUSTER GOT TO the shower first, so April and Ryan headed out of the mine with Bonnie to see for themselves that they really were back in 2015. On the way out, all three of them quickly changed clothes into modern clothes and April found them almost odd-feeling. More comfortable, but still odd.

She had gotten used to the dresses and travel attire of a woman in 1900. How strange that seemed to her.

Outside the summer heat hit them hard. It wrapped around her like a smothering cloth. Ryan moved over to the edge of the mine tailings, sat down, and just stared down at what was left of the ghost town below.

"It's starting to sink in," he said.

"What exactly?" April asked as Bonnie stretched and sat down in the sun, her back against a rock, clearly enjoying the heat of the afternoon.

April sat down next to the man she was falling in love with, looking down over the old ghost town below them.

Ryan pointed down the hill. "In 1900, in another timeline, our horses are down there, waiting for me to come back. I only left them an hour or so ago. I'm still full from the meal I ate in that hotel in 1900."

"It will take more time than one trip to get used to all this," Bonnie said. "Sometimes, when I spend decades in the

past, three or four trips in a row, I can't remember how to even drive when I get back here."

"And modern clothes feel weird?" April asked.

"Very weird," Bonnie said, smiling.

Ryan just shook his head.

"Amazing anyone can grasp this is possible."

April reached over and took his hand. "I wouldn't have met you if this wasn't."

"That's true," Ryan said, smiling and leaning over and kissing her. Then he stood and helped her to her feet. "I need a shower and then we can talk about the plans on the lodge with everyone before heading back."

"Good idea," April said. "Bonnie and I have more shopping to do next summer."

"That was fun, wasn't it?" Bonnie said, pushing herself to her feet.

April could only agree. The summer traveling with Bonnie in 1900 had been far more than fun. It had been amazing. From San Francisco to Denver to Chicago and then back to Boise. She had it all recorded in her journal. Every detail, every stick of furniture and fixtures she saw along the way.

Back inside, after Ryan came out of the shower looking refreshed, but still tired, Duster asked them both to come with him. "Got some things to show you."

He walked them over to a wall of the big supply cavern. Then he said, "You have your key on you?"

Ryan nodded and pulled it out of his pocket. "The other one is in my coat lining."

"Insert it right here," Duster said, pointing to a small natural-looking opening in the rock "and turn to the right."

April watched closely as Ryan did as he was told.

Something made a soft click sound and the wall slid to one side.

The light came up in a very large storage room behind the wall that was carved out of the rock. It was about the size of a large bedroom in a modern home. Heavy metal shelves lined three walls and down the middle, making two wide aisles.

It took a moment for April to understand what she was seeing. Then as Ryan gasped, she saw it.

Every shelf and along the floor was stacked high with coins.

Gold coins.

Millions of them.

"Every time you go back," Duster said, "you take more than enough money with you. All of this is dated, so make sure you get the right dates for the time period you are jumping to."

Ryan shook his head and turned to look at Duster as April just stood staring at the vast amount of money in front of her.

"I don't understand," Ryan said.

"The eight of us are all in this together," Duster said. "This is the working fund, just as the clothes in here and the food is supplies. If you end up in the past for numbers of years and make a lot of money, bring some back and replenish the funds here. But bring it back in gold coins."

April was doing her best to grasp what she was seeing and what Duster was saying, but nothing was going in.

"So I'm a little confused," April said. "How exactly do you end up this rich in the past?"

"Knowing history," Duster said, smiling. "I know what banks are going to fail and when. I know what mines are going to boom and when. I know what companies are going to boom and when. It doesn't take long with that advantage of knowing the future to get more than enough money to be rich in the past."

"So you take money back from here and invest," Ryan said, nodding. "And then cash out and bring more back with you."

Duster nodded and said, "Exactly."

Now April was starting to understand. Duster couldn't go back and buy stock in a modern company because that would be stock from another timeline, but he could invest while there and cash out and bring money back for future trips.

"Remember," Duster said, "every timeline we go into is only very, very slightly different than this timeline. Major history remains the same in all of them."

"And you don't mind us using some of this as we get started?" April asked.

Duster laughed. "Same question they all asked," he said, gesturing toward the kitchen area where the rest were. "But they have all brought more gold back than they have taken out by a long, long ways. This keeps up and we might have to enlarge this storage room."

"I don't know what to say," Ryan said, shaking his head.

April was feeling exactly the same way.

"Just don't leave here to go back again without saddlebags and coats lined in gold coins," Duster said. "Understand? Being poor in the past is almost as bad as dying back there."

April and Ryan both nodded.

"We'll stock up when we get ready to go," Duster said, "and I'll show you how to take what you need, and how much you will need. I'm already pretty rich back there this time around, but just in case this plan doesn't work, we'll take enough to start over again. Now, turn the key back the other direction."

Ryan did as Duster told him to do and the rock wall slid back into place over the fantastic room and any sign of anything being inside the rocks vanished.

Duster turned and walked away toward the kitchen, leaving Ryan and April standing there in silence in the big cavern.

"This really is a gold mine," she said softly, shaking her head and trying her best to grasp what she had just seen. It was no wonder Duster could build them an office in Boise and buy her old company and give it to her and build a lodge in the past and furnish it and build a mansion in Boise.

From now on, she would never have to worry about money at all. After spending an entire summer in the past, the thought of where the money came from to buy all the furniture for the lodge had never crossed her mind. She had just been an employee of a rich client.

But now that she thought about it, she could be as rich as well. And would be given enough time. Which it seemed she now had.

Duster had just given them equal footing with everyone else.

He and Bonnie were really trusting her and Ryan with everything. Amazing.

She was going to make damned sure she lived up to that trust.

She looked up at Ryan's stunned face. Finally he smiled and kissed her.

"What do you say we make it a goal," he said, "to put more back in that room than we take out."

She laughed and kissed him again. "I like the part about us doing it together."

He smiled. "Never occurred to me to do it any other way."

# CHAPTER THIRTY-SEVEN

*September 25, 1900*

**RYAN HAD ENJOYED** the two great hours they had all spent over one of Madison's wonderful dinners to confirm their plans. All eight of them would go back again on the same connection. And they would all stay until the spring of 1910, the year the mudslide damned up Monumental Creek and destroyed the town of Roosevelt.

There were a number of reasons they decided on that time. It would allow them to build the lodge in 1901 and furnish it. Then it would allow them all to use it for a few years as a base in the summer and allow Dawn and Madison see if they enjoyed living there and spending the winters there alone.

Both Dawn and Madison were both sure they would, but staying until 1910 gave it a great test. It would also allow Janice and Steven to stay in Roosevelt and run their store until the town was destroyed. Both of them were working on new books and both of them felt that would give them enough time for the research they wanted to do.

If anyone wanted to go back after 1910 into the same timeline, they could. Assuming this plan worked, of course.

Ryan and April would go back with Duster and Bonnie to the day after they all left in September 1900 to see how close they could actually be on a return trip on the same connection.

The other four would come through in May of 1901. Duster would meet them with horses and supplies and they would all head for Roosevelt.

April and Bonnie would continue their shopping through the winter and next summer to get the lodge furnishings and fixtures. Ryan wasn't sure what he would be doing during the winter, but he honestly didn't care as long as he could spend most of it with April.

As it turned out, they had been in the mine for just over four hours in 2015 before all of them took positions around the machine in the crystal cavern and went back.

Ryan felt nervous and excited and April said the same thing. He still couldn't completely believe that if they all stayed in the past until 1910, only two minutes and fifteen seconds would pass in the mine. He found that was a very, very hard detail to get his mind around.

But when the four of them touched the machine, the other four just vanished from the room, left back in 2015.

April and Ryan and Bonnie and Duster hit right on target, just one day after they had jumped out.

Duster and Bonnie had both been very, very happy at that fact, talking all the way down the hill from the mine to Silver City about the advantages that gave them.

It was about noon and the air had a fall bite to it, but the day was still beautiful.

They got the horses out of the smith, who was surprised they were back so soon, but he had the saddles ready anyway. Duster let him keep all the money for the extra time and gave him more as a bonus.

They then headed for Boise on a much slower pace than Ryan and Duster had ridden getting to Silver City.

Ryan did feel uncomfortable at times with the lining in his saddlebag being full of gold coins. But Duster said that he would show them some hiding places for the coins in the big house when they reached Boise.

And he said he would give them both a history lesson on banks in Boise and businesses to invest in as well. Since Boise was a fast-growing town now that Idaho was a state and the capitol had been moved there, making money at this point in history in Boise would be easy.

As they rode, April just looked wonderful. He could hardly keep his eyes off her. And she kept smiling and enjoying the day and looking at him.

All he really wanted to do was just spend time with her this coming winter.

As much time as possible.

And off into the future for as long as possible. He couldn't believe how much he had fallen for her.

That night they camped next to a hot springs along the Snake River that was only large enough for two at a time.

After Bonnie and Duster came back from the springs, he and April went down the narrow trail to the small pool among rocks over the river. They took turns washing each other's backs, as well as other places. And making love, slow at first, then hard and fast, splashing water everywhere.

Finally, as the sunset was coloring the sky with reds and oranges that matched the fall leaves on the trees around them, they sat together in the flowing hot water, just holding each other.

"This is just perfect," she said, smiling at him and then kissing him again.

"So we're in this together?" he asked, hugging her naked body even closer if that was possible. "An adventure through time."

"Through time," she said, hugging him back.

"Perfect," he said.

And he meant it.

Being with her was perfect.

# PART FIVE

# CHAPTER THIRTY-EIGHT

*September 14, 1910*

**APRIL COULD NOT BELIEVE** the ten years had passed so quickly. And they had been a wonderful ten years with Ryan. The best ten years of her life. They had lived as man and wife for the entire time, and about the second year had joked that when they got back to the present, they might want to actually make that a reality.

But right now all she wanted to do was get back to 2015 and turn right around and come back and continue their life here together. And Ryan completely agreed. In fact, after ten years, she was having some trouble even remembering things from the future.

She had always thought she was born a hundred years too late. Now, after ten years of living in the past, she was sure of it.

Ryan finished making sure the generator was off and all wires were unplugged.

She had walked around the beautiful home one last time, making sure all lamps were out.

Duster and Madison would be getting to the mine about an hour after sundown. And right now the sky outside was growing dark.

"Can you believe we've lived in this fantastic place for almost ten years?" Ryan asked, coming up and hugging her as she reached the kitchen.

She looked around at the huge mansion kitchen they had built on the estate next to Bonnie and Duster's home, a kitchen full of wonderful memories and great dinners. Duster had given them the land after they got back that first winter and they had built the house in just six months, using the same crew that had worked all the first summer on the lodge.

Five bedrooms, two stories, plus a full basement, part of which was hidden. The bedroom suite looked out over the river and had a deck that many a warm evening she had sat on sipping iced tea and enjoying the view of the water.

Even though Boise was growing quickly, they were still a very long ways out into the country and she loved that. And everything about the home.

Everything.

Both she and Ryan had designed their perfect home.

By the end of the second summer, not only had she furnished the huge lodge, but their new home as well.

The lodge had turned out even more fantastic than either of them had imagined when designing it. All eight of them had sat on the huge lodge deck overlooking Monumental Valley in the fall afternoon in 1901. That was a memory to treasure.

Since then, Dawn and Madison had lived in the lodge. They planned on coming back as well and having children to leave the lodge to.

April and Ryan had managed to not have children this first time back, even though at times they both worried about it. They both wanted kids, but they wanted to make sure that returning to the future in 1910 wouldn't be a permanent thing as far as this timeline went. They both wanted to be sure they could return and not strand a child in an orphanage in the past.

April wasn't sure she could live with having that happen.

Plus having a child in the past just scared her something awful. And it seemed to scare Ryan even more. It hadn't slowed down their sex life over the last ten years. Just made them very, very cautious.

"You think we're coming back?" she asked, giving their wonderful mansion one more look as they went out the back and pulled the door closed.

"I think so," Ryan said as he locked up. "We did it before. And if we have to, we'll build this home again. More than likely, if our friends can be believed, we'll build the lodge and this home a number of times."

"That's true," she said. "But I like this first one."

"As long as we're together," Ryan said, "it doesn't matter."

He kissed her and she kissed him back.

They had both aged, but could still pass for young. When they returned, they would again be in their early thirties instead of early forties. Neither of them had gained any weight and they had kept their hair the same. So she hoped that given a little time, no one would notice their younger looks.

"So this ten-year trial run at being together has worked for you?" he asked.

"Let's talk about it after a couple hundred years," she said, looking into those eyes that she never got tired of looking at. She was more in love now with this man than she had been ten years

ago. And she could only imagine that continuing to grow.

"Sounds like a plan," he said, kissing her one more time, then taking her hand.

Without a look back at the beautiful mansion they had built overlooking the Boise River, they walked hand-in-hand across their back lawn and through the hedge toward Bonnie and Madison's home.

As they neared the back door of the other house, she had to stop and laughingly adjust all the gold coins she had on in a vest under her riding clothes. In ten years, they had become fantastically rich. Knowing just a little of the near future could do that for a person. Especially with Duster's help. Now, since they had to go back, they were going to replenish what they had taken out of the gold storage room, plus some.

In the vest under her clothes she also had a journal she wanted to get back to the cave. It had all her notes about finding furniture and where she had found it, as well as some ideas on a few books on historical interior design she wanted to write.

She had almost twenty pounds of gold on her and Ryan gladly helped her adjust it, managing to get frisky in the process. Ryan had over thirty pounds of gold coins on him.

Between the two of them, at 2015 gold prices, not counting the value of the coins themselves, Ryan figured they were carrying well over a million dollars back with them.

They went inside without knocking and sat at the kitchen table. April was impressed that neither of them clanked or jingled like a piggybank when they sat down.

Bonnie had the house dark and shut down and someone was coming in to watch the horses tomorrow. Madison and Duster had April and Ryan's favorite horses and would board them in Silver City, since the four of them were planning on returning quickly.

Steven and Janice were thinking of returning and just living in Bonnie and Duster's big place for a time, writing. Bonnie and Duster had both decided that they might join everyone in twenty years or so, see how things were going.

Of course, in the future, all that would take place in the two minutes and fifteen seconds. April had never, in ten years, been able to wrap her mind around that. And after a year or so, she and Ryan had just stopped talking about it.

Now, very shortly, she was going to see how it all worked.

April was about to say something to Bonnie when suddenly she found herself in the bright crystal cavern standing next to Ryan. All eight of them were touching the machine.

And this time something very different happened.

Very different.

A shimmering went through the cavern, like a heat wave off hot pavement.

And suddenly April had two memories in her mind.

Two very, very clear memories.

One memory was of her being hired by Bonnie and Duster and meeting and falling in love with Ryan and building the lodge and living for ten years in the past.

And the other memory was not being hired and going back to Denver, and going to work in Kansas City on a big old house remodel there.

That memory ended in July of 2015.

And in that memory she had not met Ryan.

She glanced around as everyone sort of staggered back, clearly shocked.

Something different had happened.

Something had gone very, very wrong.

# CHAPTER THIRTY-NINE

*July 20, 2015*

**THE CRYSTAL ROOM** appeared around Ryan as he found himself standing next to April, one hand on the machine.

One moment they were sitting down in a kitchen in 1910, the next moment standing in a cave in 2015. He and April had lived ten years in the past and only two minutes and fifteen seconds had passed here.

Then everything in the big crystal cave seemed to shimmer like a heat wave had crossed over them.

That wasn't normal. Or at least it had never happened before in the few times they had done this.

Then he felt the new memories crowd in with the ones he had.

Now he could clearly remember working the summer on two other major projects, still in his old office in the North End of Boise. He had never been hired by Bonnie and Duster and had not met April.

And yet he remembered clearly the last ten years living in the past, building the lodge, living with April, falling more in love with her than he could have ever imagined being in love with anyone.

And he knew instantly the reason why he had two levels of memories.

The Monumental Summit Lodge now already existed.

In fact, in part of his old memories, when he was a junior in college, he and an old girlfriend had spent a night in the lodge one summer, having dinner on the deck and then making love in a big featherbed in the third room on the main floor. He had loved the place, felt attached to it, but the girlfriend had hated it because it was so far away from anything.

They had broken up a couple of months later as school got started and he got busy.

In the timeline where the lodge didn't exist, he and the old girlfriend had stayed together another two months, almost to Thanksgiving before breaking up, clearly because they hadn't made the trip to the old lodge.

He now remembered both timelines clearly.

How was that possible?

He stepped back from the machine in the big crystal cavern and took April's hand.

She squeezed his, clearly not wanting to let go and he didn't want to let go of her either.

She existed. The ten years they had just spent together existed.

That was all that mattered.

Then he remembered their first trip into Roosevelt Lake and what had bothered him.

Madison's grave had actually been there.

Madison had actually died in this timeline in the past.

But yet Bonnie and Duster said that was impossible. That the grave was nothing more than an echo.

But the grave was there and his name was on the marker.

That had been very real.

Now the lodge was real and there as well.

Ryan nodded to the shocked look on April's face and kissed her quickly, then looked at the others.

Dawn and Madison were holding each other tightly, as if they were afraid to let go. Clearly the lodge existing since 1901 in this timeline really made a lot of differences for them.

Janice and Steven both just looked shocked and were staring at each other.

"What just happened?" Madison finally asked.

"I'm remembering two timelines," Dawn said.

Both Bonnie and Duster nodded.

"We all are," Bonnie said.

"We were touching the machine," Duster said. "So we remember the timeline from before any change. And the one after the change."

"So how did the lodge get built here?" Madison asked. "I didn't think that was ever going to be possible in this timeline."

Neither Duster nor Bonnie said anything.

They all just stood around the machine in the big crystal cave, looking more lost than anything.

"The same way your grave got there," Ryan said, deciding to jump in.

"The lodge is built here, now?" April asked.

She was the only one not from Idaho and wouldn't know about the lodge from before. Ryan nodded to her.

"My grave?" Madison asked, looking puzzled.

"It wasn't an echo," Duster said, softly, as he carefully unplugged one wire from the machine, but left the other wires hooked up to the crystal on the wall.

"Well that answers a bunch of questions," Bonnie said, shaking her head.

"How did the lodge get built?" Janice asked.

"We built it," Duster said, turning toward the tunnel to the big cavern. "I need a shower after that ride."

"How did we build it?" Steven asked.

"We built the lodge in that timeline," Bonnie said, pointing to the crystal on the wall.

Then she waved her arm around at the millions and millions of timelines represented by crystals in just the close vicinity to where they were standing.

"The six of us exist in all those timelines as well," Bonnie said. "And in most of them we built a lodge on this trip back into the past."

"So some group of us built a lodge in this timeline?" Madison asked.

"Exactly," Bonnie nodded. "We built it, actually, because there really is no difference from the six of us a million timelines over than the six of us here. And the lodge is a big enough event in our lives to cause the timeline shift."

They stood there in the big room in silence for a moment.

Around Ryan the vast cavern seemed to go on forever in the distance.

"So now what do we do?" April asked.

Bonnie shrugged. "We have dinner and talk about it."

"Does time travel give anyone else a headache?" April asked.

Everyone nodded.

Madison went over to look at the crystal they had spent ten years inside. "Connection's secure if we want to go back."

"I guess we'll need to let the math brains behind all this figure that out," Steven said, looking at Bonnie.

She nodded. "We'll talk about it."

Steven took Janice's hand and turned toward the exit from the big cavern.

"It's weird having two memories," April said.

"Can't argue with that," Dawn said.

Ryan took April's hand and said, "Come on, let's get in some modern clothes, drop all this gold off, and take a look outside."

She looked around at all the crystals around them. "How many more of you and me are going to do that exact same thing right now?"

"Billions," Madison said.

"Maybe more," Bonnie said.

"It's decided," April said, squeezing Ryan's hand. "Time travel officially gives me a headache."

"But you still like it," Ryan said, smiling at the now much younger woman he had just spent ten years with and was in love with.

"Oh, hell yes," April said, smiling up at him.

Ryan kissed her and then they went to get back into modern clothes as the memories of that other timeline without the lodge mixed with the timeline where the lodge had always existed.

Wouldn't he have been shocked as that junior in college staying that night in the lodge to know he had designed and built that lodge one hundred years before he stayed there.

# CHAPTER FORTY

*July 20, 2015*

**THE DINNER** with the eight of them was very interesting. It seemed that April had been bothered the least by the timeline shift and the existence of the lodge. Except for the two months of not meeting Ryan, the existence of the lodge had changed nothing in her memories.

All the rest of them found it pretty major in one fashion or another.

After changing clothes, she and Ryan had restocked the gold room. Their million-plus in gold they had brought from the past didn't even seem to make a difference in the big room, which shocked her. There was far more millions of dollars in gold in that room than she wanted to think about at modern prices.

Then they had headed out of the mine to stand in the heat for a few minutes. Mostly they just stared at the cars on the hill across from the mine. In Boise in 1910, cars were starting to fill the streets, so that big white Cadillac parked on the hillside was the clearest reminder of when they now were.

They went back inside and April offered to help Bonnie and Dawn with dinner and they thankfully agreed. She really, really needed something to do right now besides sit next to Ryan and hold onto his hand.

They gave her some potatoes to peel and slice up as Bonnie worked on a salad and Dawn breaded some chicken.

None of them talked about what had happened until Madison got out of the shower and everyone was gathered in the kitchen area.

"So," Madison asked, getting the discussion going as he dried his hair with a big brown towel. "Is what just happened unexpected?"

Duster shrugged. "No, the math kept pointing us in that direction. But since we never really saw evidence of it happening, we kept trying to find other mathematical reasons why it wouldn't happen."

Bonnie nodded. "What's he's saying clearly is that yes, we expected it, but never saw it until now. It's why we always touch the machine when traveling."

"Touching the machine," Duster said, "allows a traveler to remember both the old timeline and the shifted timeline. We designed it for this kind of thing to happen."

"So that shimmer," Ryan said, "was unusual?"

"I think the shimmer," Bonnie said, finishing the salad and wiping off her hands, "was the entire room shifting in some form or another."

April flat didn't understand that, so she kept her focus on finishing getting the potatoes ready.

Duster nodded, but said nothing.

"So we can go back and live in the lodge?" Madison asked.

"Oh, sure," Duster said, "in the same timeline we just left. I sure don't see why not."

"I agree," Bonnie said, putting the salad in the middle of the table.

April smiled at Ryan who was smiling at her. So their plans to go back were still on.

"So," Janice asked, "what happens now when we hook up to a new crystal and go back?"

"Nothing different," Duster said. "The lodge won't be there until we build it."

"Even though it's now here?" Steven asked.

"You can't exist in a timeline where you are already there building the lodge," Bonnie said. "So the rules of conservation of mass and energy and time will just shift you to a timeline where the lodge was not yet built."

"So you didn't feel a shimmer when you came back from the trip where Madison died?"

January, 2014

"Nope," Duster said. "We didn't change anything major."

"But I still think we need to take a trip into Boise," Bonnie said, "and see if anything else has changed."

"What about our offices?" April asked as she finished cutting the last of the potatoes. "Since in this timeline we weren't hired to build the lodge, will the offices be there? And our apartments?"

"Good question," Duster said. "They should be. You remember them, don't you?"

Ryan nodded with her.

"Then they are there," Bonnie said. "But after dinner, let's go find out. This was a pretty major timeline shift in a lot of areas."

"And anyone not touching the machine won't remember the shift?" Madison asked.

"Nope," Duster said. "The people who occupied that building in the other timeline will not even realize they were shifted to another place."

"So my old boss won't even realize I kept working for him for two more months before everything shifted?" April asked, trying to grasp that.

"He won't," Bonnie said. "This timeline is now the one and the crystals that were the other timelines merged into the timelines we now are in."

"Thus the heat-wave shift?" Dawn asked.

"That or a dimensional shift," Duster said.

April looked at Ryan and he looked as lost on that comment as she felt. So she just turned and worked to put the potatoes into boiling water as Dawn started work on mixing white gravy for the chicken.

Everyone in the kitchen area of the big cave just remained silent, lost in thought and confused memories.

What was important now to her was that she and Ryan could go back to their beautiful home and live for years to come.

But even if they could never travel in time again, they were still together here and that really was all that mattered.

## CHAPTER FORTY-ONE

*July 20, 2015*

**THE DINNER LASTED TWO HOURS,** mostly full of talk that Ryan only understood parts of. He knew that given enough time, like Madison and Dawn, he and April would understand more and more of the time travel complications. But right now he was just trying to grasp that the ten years had only taken two minutes.

And he was trying to sort out which memories were of this new timeline and which were left over.

After dinner Duster drove them back to Boise, with one bathroom stop along the way.

Ryan and April just sat in the back, holding hands. Madison and Dawn and Duster and Bonnie talked about different aspects of time travel, but mostly Ryan only listened and April said little.

What he liked about listening was that they kept coming back to the conclusion that nothing bad had happened and they all could just keep moving forward as before.

But they also decided that no member of a couple should ever go back without the other. That way they could never do anything to cause a shift in the couple being together.

183

Ryan and April both agreed to that as well.

Janice and Steven were headed back as well in their own car. They had all decided to spend the day tomorrow in Boise making sure that not much had changed. Tomorrow, Bonnie and Duster were going to make a drive to the lodge.

Dawn and Madison had wanted to go along, but Duster overruled them. "We look first."

They would all meet at April and Ryan's office the following day at eight in the morning to decide what to do next. But more than likely, unless they discovered something very strange, they would all head back up to the mine and back into the same timeline as planned.

The idea of that had Ryan very excited.

By the time they got back into Boise, it was a little after nine in the evening and the sun was going down. Bonnie and Duster again dropped them off at the office, which Ryan was very happy to see was there.

And that his key worked just fine.

They had only been gone since that morning, but it seemed like a lifetime.

Actually two lifetimes with the weird shift.

They went inside and turned on lights.

Nothing at all had changed.

They both went to their separate offices and Ryan found the plans for the big lodge on his computer. It didn't matter that it now sat up there on the summit. He had designed it here in this office over the last two months.

April showed up in his doorway a few moments later, shaking her head. "Nothing changed. Now I'm wondering what everyone else on the staff thinks we were doing."

Suddenly the memory of that was back for him. "Just as with the original design, we considered our clients eccentric and didn't allow anyone to talk about it."

April nodded. "I remember that now. That's why nothing has changed here."

"Exactly," Ryan said, feeling very relieved. Designing a lodge for the past or one that already existed. Either way the client was eccentric and not to be talked about. Standard for both architecture and interior design.

They headed out, walking slowly in the warm evening summer air. Ten minutes later they found themselves in their favorite booth with the same waitress as the night before.

Less than twenty-four hours before they had sat here, not knowing what was going to happen the next day. And they had made love for the first time after going to her apartment.

Yet that was ten wonderful years ago.

Ryan was having a horrid time wrapping his mind around all this. It would have been bad enough sitting here after living ten years, but having the other memories mixed in were just making everything damned hard to accept.

And on top of that, he was just tired. And so was April. They had gotten up at sunrise in Boise in 1910, spent an entire day getting things closed up and ready to go in their big home. At sundown, they had been pulled to the cave, which was in the middle of the day again.

So they had been up for going on twenty-one hours their time.

They talked about almost nothing while eating, but to Ryan that felt comfortable. As long as she was beside him, he didn't care.

After eating, they walked slowly to her apartment.

As she unlocked the door, she said, "Wow, you were right, this feels like it was an eternity ago that I locked this, even though it was this morning."

"Just ten wonderful years," he said, smiling at her and kissing her.

They crawled into bed together and unlike the last time in this bed, they fell asleep in each other's arms as they had done for ten years.

# CHAPTER FORTY-TWO

*July 21, 2015*

**APRIL WOKE UP** the next morning in her own bed, in her apartment, alone.

For a moment she thought it all had been a dream. She hadn't really lived in the past for ten years in a wonderful mansion with Ryan.

But then she knew she had. She was in Boise, after all, not Denver or a hotel room in Kansas City where she would have been if Bonnie and Duster hadn't hired her. She had that memory as well, but it was fading.

She crawled out and headed for the bathroom, then naked she walked out into her living room.

"Wow, anyone ever tell you that you're looking good," Ryan said, smiling at her from behind her computer.

"Lost ten years in age overnight," she said, stretching and enjoying the feel of her younger body as the man she loved watched her show off. She hadn't minded growing older, but being in her early thirties again didn't suck.

"What are you doing?" she finally asked.

"Oh, sorry," he said, clicking off her computer. "Not snooping, just wanted to look up a couple of things."

"And what did you find?" she asked.

He got up from her computer and she realized he didn't have anything on either. And he was clearly happy to see her.

"I'll show you later," he said, sweeping her off her feet and carrying her back into the bedroom where they could once again explore their much younger bodies.

An idea she very, very much agreed with.

She was starting to realize that coming back to the present and being young again did have some benefits.

An hour later, both showered and with Pop Tarts in their hands, they left her apartment and headed back toward their office. The morning was a perfect summer day in Boise. The air wasn't hot yet, and there was a cool breeze blowing along the river.

The trees were all full and most of the sidewalk they walked was in shade.

The one thing she did really notice was the noise. She had gotten used to the silence of living in the country in the past. Even going to San Francisco and Denver and Chicago on shopping trips didn't compare to the noise that was normal for a modern city.

That surprised her.

They walked hand-in-hand and never in all her life could she have imagined being so in love with a man. Yet she had just spent ten years with Ryan in the past and loved him more than yesterday here in the present.

More than likely it was the sudden memory of how she might have gone on and never met him.

Or it was just that living together made her love him more. Either way, she didn't want to think about not being with him for as long as possible into the future.

"How about we take a longer walk first?" he asked, smiling at her.

Suddenly her stomach twisted and she got excited. "Our house? If the lodge is here, our house is here. Right?"

"Lets go take a look."

He then just smiled at her and squeezed her hand and kept her from walking even faster.

And he wouldn't say another word. The man was just too damn cute at times.

As they strolled down the wide sidewalk along Warm Springs Avenue, she could see the big home that Bonnie and Duster had built. It was surrounded by huge old trees and had a paved driveway going in past the building to what had been the stable behind it.

Then, through the trees, she saw their home.

She wasn't sure if she could even breathe.

From what she could see through the big trees, it was as beautiful as it had been when they built it. Perfectly maintained.

"Oh, my," she said.

"Wow," he said, clearly just as stunned.

They walked a little farther in silence and were about to pass in front of the two mansions.

"Let's go to the other side of the street so we can get a better view of it," Ryan said.

She nodded and they made it between traffic across the busy boulevard.

From there, he was right, they could see the house they had built in 1901 much, much better.

They went to a cement bus stop bench across the street from the big mansion and sat down holding hands and staring at the beautiful home tucked among large trees that hadn't even been planted in 1910.

She made a mental note where each tree was so that when they went back, she would plant trees there.

"It's wonderful, isn't it?" she said, the memories of the ten years living in that wonderful house flashing through her thoughts. There were so many great memories.

"It is," he said, "because it's our home. Our first home."

"And we're going back tomorrow?" she asked.

"We're going back," he said. "I can promise you that."

Something in his voice sounded odd and she looked at him. "How can you be so sure? How can you promise that?"

He had this wonderful smile on his face, a smile she had come to learn meant so much more than he was saying.

"What did you find on the computer?" April asked.

He pointed across the street as a large SUV was pulling out of the driveway of their home. There was a woman about their age with long brown hair driving. Two children were strapped into car seats in the back.

The woman pulled across the street and looked right at them.

For a moment the woman saw them and frowned.

Then she turned with traffic and was gone.

April felt like she had just looked in the mirror.

Or at a twin sister.

"Who was that?" she asked, turning to face the man she loved more than anything in the world.

He was smiling like she had never seen him smile before.

"Who was that?" April asked. "She looked just like me."

"She did, didn't she," Ryan said, not breaking his smile as he stared into her eyes.

Then he finally just kissed her long and hard.

After a moment he pushed back and looked at her. "That was our great- great-granddaughter driving. Her name is Alicia. She and her husband have taken over the family home. She's an architect. He's an engineer."

April just stared at Ryan and into those wonderful eyes of his. She couldn't believe what he had just said.

Yet she knew it was true.

And she knew what that meant.

"We're going back," she said, breathlessly, turning to look across the street at the beautiful home they had built.

"We're going back," he said. "Together."

"Every time, no matter how many years go by?"

"Together," he said, kissing her. "Every time. For all time."

And she kissed him back, sitting there on the bus stop bench in front of their home.

A home that they would soon make into a family home.

---

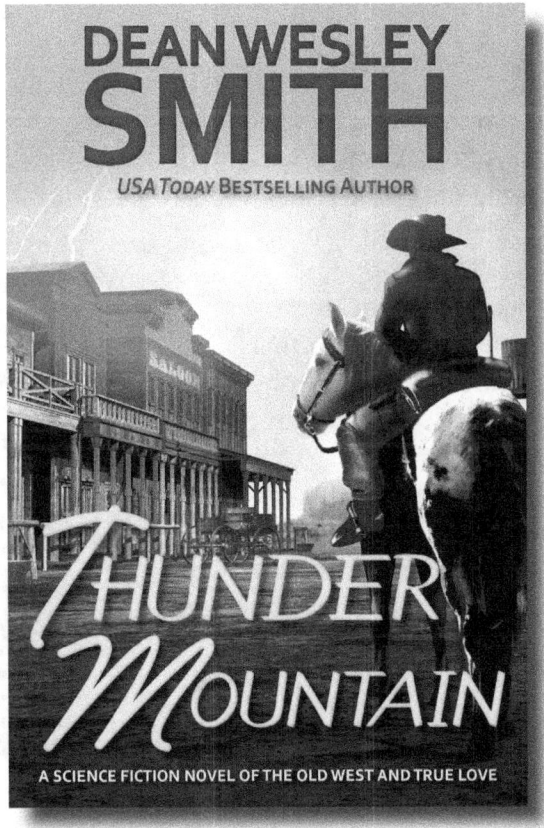
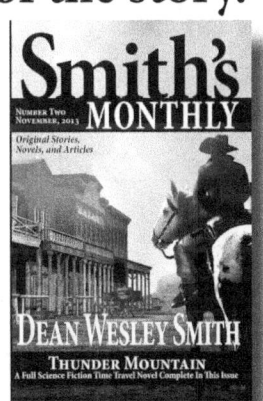

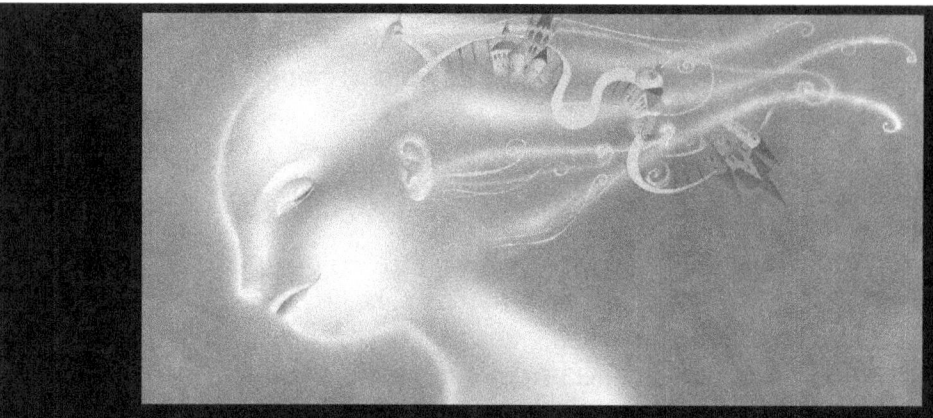

# Poems by DEAN WESLEY SMITH

## Related Holidays

Yesterday was National Bean Day.
I imagined take-beans-to-work programs
spreading all over the country,
proud employees showing off their cans.

I imagined black beans joining with red beans
to protest against the pintos while ignoring bean curds,
with coffee beans staying out of the issue,
having a union and lobbyist of their own.

I imagined beans taking over for rice
in numbers of places, including after weddings,
where guests would throw handfuls of beans at the bride,
giving the word beaned a whole new meaning.

But today is a new day, a new special day, with a new focus.
The beans have been eaten, thrown, and protested over.
I must move on to National Bubblebath Day
as I sit in the tub and fondly remember National Bean Day.